↑↑↑↑↑↑↑↑↑↑↑ Couplings ↑↑↑↑↑↑↑↑↑↑↑

Couplings

Peter Schneider

TRANSLATED BY PHILIP BOEHM

Farrar, Straus & Giroux

New York

Translation copyright © 1996 Philip Boehm
All rights reserved
Originally published in German under the title *Paarungen*, copyright
© 1992 by Rowohlt-Berlin Verlag GmbH, Berlin
Printed in the United States of America
Published simultaneously in Canada by HarperCollins*CanadaLtd*
Designed by Jonathan D. Lippincott
First edition, 1996

Library of Congress Cataloging-in-Publication Data
Schneider, Peter.
[Paarungen. English]
Couplings / Peter Schneider ; translated by Philip Boehm.
p.   cm.
I. Title
PT2680.N37P3313   1996   833'.914—dc20   96-11685   CIP

↑↓↑↓↑↓↑↓↑↓↑↓↑↓↑↓↑↓↑↓↑↓↑↓↑↓↑↓↓ I ↑↓↑↓↑↓↑↓↑↓↑↓↑↓↑↓↑↓↑↓↑↓↑↓↑↓↑↓↑↓

THE MOST IMPORTANT EVENT of the past few years was the change in his sleeping position. For as long as Eduard could remember he had fallen asleep on his stomach. After he had put aside his science fiction novel and switched out the light, he would roll over on his stomach, take the blanket between his legs, and drift off, his face turned toward the earth. This helped him maintain the illusion of floating on his mattress high above some hilly valley, beyond the reach of the everyday commotion. Warnings for overdue bills, news of airplane catastrophes, occasional bouts of impotence, break-ins at the neighboring building, reports of war, raises in rent, acts of terror—Eduard simply turned away from all the unpleasant daily residue to which back-sleepers are helplessly exposed. He enjoyed feeling the mattress press against his stomach and allowing the upcurrent to carry him higher and higher—until the haystacks, the tiled roofs, the onion-domed churches of his childhood gradually disappeared. As soon as he had floated past the alpine wall that separated the valley from the rest of the world, once he had touched down gently in an unknown land beyond the mountains, he fell asleep.

Imperceptibly, this tried and true position had become uncomfortable. Eduard couldn't explain the change, but he knew it was a momentous one. He was convinced that whenever people change their sleeping position they change other habits as well, quite possibly their entire outlook on the world.

People who sleep on their back are a sorry sight. Their lower jaw hangs open, at least in most cases. They seem unprotected, exposed to everything; even in their sleep they look poised for escape. They suggest a man who's being hunted, who keeps his eye glued to the entrance of the café, always on the lookout for the thug with the machine gun. Back-sleepers—now, those were people with problems. In *The Killers* Burt Lancaster lies on his back in a dilapidated hotel room, waiting for his murderers. When Marilyn Monroe, whom Eduard had always considered a stomach-sleeper, failed to wake up, she was discovered lying on her back. Presidents, Mafia bosses, and millionaires all sleep on their back. Among swimmers, it is backstrokers who, as a rule, wind up with protracted cures for damage they have sustained to the spinal column. In Christian parts of the Western world, dead people are laid to rest on their back, while the Aztecs splayed their victims across the sacrificial stone in such a way that the heart faced heaven, before they cut it out. Whatever it might mean that Eduard could no longer sleep in any position but on his back, it was certainly nothing good.

He had just rolled a clean sheet of paper into the typewriter when, for the first time that year, the April sun appeared above the gables of the house next door. The light crashed like surf into the murky courtyard. He glanced out the window; the cement-gray canopy of clouds looked full of cracks. He saw the yellowed remnants of grass, the bare rosebush that never blossomed in any season, the more-than-man-sized wall that enclosed the courtyard. Overnight a sumac branch had strayed through the open window into the room. Eduard clambered onto the window ledge. As he pulled shut the upper window, he noticed the branch scraping against the pane like the tiny bow of a toy violin. The sudden tension in the air infected Eduard, and he began to feel uneasy. He lost all interest in finishing the cost projections for his department's "urgently needed" acquisitions. There was nothing "urgent," especially on Saturday; it had been years since anything deserved to be called "urgent," "pressing," or ultimately "too late." History had at some point secretly stolen away, and apart from an occasional appearance at the newsstand, it kept its distance. All news was read as news from abroad, news which seemed to leave no mark on the lives of the city's inhabitants. Eduard remained completely oblivious to the passage of time, except when he had to see the dentist, or when an acquaintance of his—at last sighting quite childless—stopped to greet him on the street accompanied by a five-year-old daughter, or else when the springtime sun once again made its way into his room.

Eduard walked across the parking lot to The Tent. Whereas just yesterday everything had fit into a small spectrum of color ranging from sand-gray to brick-red, today the same objects stood out in the April sunlight, garish and gaudy, so that the colors on the street no longer matched the blue of the sky. The gray, peeling façades suddenly seemed sad against the dazzling fresh stucco of the renovated buildings; the white was too pristine, the yellow suggested some extraterrestrial lemon, the pink belonged in baby advertisements, the brown was that of shoe polish, and the green called to mind the produce on display at the grocer's. It seemed that all these loud and festive hues had gathered together not in celebration of color but simply as the result of a political program, an ideological reaction to many years of gray: let there be color!

The waiter was just setting up the first tables and chairs in the sunny space outside The Tent. When the shaft of light shifted a little to the right, he moved one of the tables into the newly illuminated spot. But as he was unfolding the white tablecloth, the sunspot managed to travel another couple of yards. Without batting an eye, the waiter obeyed the sun's bidding and shoved the table farther. He did this several times, and refused to give up until the sunlight had completely crossed the street.

Two men wearing coats were sitting by themselves, gazing fixedly at an imaginary horizon. Between them, at another table, a young woman was bent over a book. Her skin was dark, and her tightly braided hair was adorned with small green beads. Eduard first said hello to the waiter and then cast a vague greeting in the direction of the other tables. He was never sure which of the guests he knew. When in doubt it was best to assume he recognized everyone, greet them all at once, and then check their reactions. But he was hardly prepared for the exotic young lady to lift her head out of her book and look him straight in the eye. For a moment he felt the other men expected him to say something, something surprising, unforgettable, something that would implant itself in the ears of the beautiful foreigner. But Eduard couldn't think of a thing; he crossed over to the vending machine and took out his daily ration of cigarettes. In passing he glanced at the open book. In the upper margin of one of the pages he read: *"Die Serapionsbrüder."* A beaded braid cast a shadow like a bookmark across Hoffmann's Romantic classic.

Eduard hadn't been going to The Tent for more than a few months; he didn't imagine he had left a very clear impression among the steady clientele. They would be hard-pressed to describe him, he thought. As far as externals were concerned, he was careful to follow the eclectic ideal: he kept his dirty blond hair brushed back, short on top, long on the neck; he wore a suit jacket with blue jeans, glasses—this was optional, but in any case he looked like the type of guy who might wear glasses. Apart from that: his eyes were a little too close together, of hybrid color, somewhere between gray and green. In fact, the most striking thing about him seemed to be that he was so easily mistaken for someone else. People who had never laid eyes on him were always asking where they had met. Some would even stop him on the street, claiming they had recently seen him standing beneath the vaults of the Moscow State Circus, lying in the sand at Miami Beach, or acting in a road movie by Wim Wenders. His smile was always ready for similar questions, always prepared to render any excuses or pardons unnecessary. He was pleased that the memories he erroneously evoked never seemed to be unpleasant ones. In some far-flung corner of his soul he actually believed himself capable of all the exciting feats which were attributed to him. Some of The Tent's regulars deduced—although he was baffled as to why—that women found him very attractive; he didn't deny it, but he was hard put to explain this riddle.

The fact that he came to The Tent consistently, but without any discernible motive, must have further enhanced his mystique. The hard-core clientele probably considered his appearance there a mistake, a random occurrence—which assured him a status close to that of tourists from West Germany visiting West Berlin. His "relationship" was regarded as stable. He was in the fourth year of an undeclared marriage to Klara, and everyone expected he would soon be celebrating their fourth anniversary, although no one seemed to wish him this completely unbegrudgingly. A person without problems, without visible stress in his relationships, a man who didn't want to talk was, for the patrons of The Tent, a non-person, a bumpkin from the provinces. For his part, Eduard would listen, nod his head, and keep his lips fixed in a smile that steered clear of all conflict, allowing others to search in vain for any sign of mutual recognition.

The mere name of his profession was alienating; hardly anyone seemed able to remember the complete phrase "molecular biologist." The Tentgoers would add and subtract various modifiers and prefixes—"biochemist," "biogeneticist," "microbiologist"—although it was never clear what they imagined these words to mean. Presumably some oddball who counted molecules—instead of, say, beans—under the microscope. However, everyone was in agreement as to the general category of "natural scientist"—that is, a person who steadfastly resists all distraction from work and who has nothing to contribute to the general conversation. Time and again people questioned Eduard as to how he possibly found the time to go out. What's so strange about that, he would parry. Didn't they have to get up the next morning; didn't they, too, have to work? Where did they come up with the peculiar idea that the same temptations which lured everyone else outdoors on a sunny day were alien to natural scientists?

Eduard himself didn't know exactly what it was that had

been drawing him to The Tent. The one thing he did know was that this new habit was connected to the change in his sleeping position, possibly even rooted in the same cause.

"I don't think you're even capable of loving!"

His first reflex had been to dismiss this sentence—which hit him when he was wide awake but lying on his back—as sheer provocation. He considered it a typical example of female prejudice against males in general, and male natural scientists in particular. But when the same sentence, with a very slight change in wording, popped up in a different bed a few weeks later—"I don't think you have the faintest idea . . ."—well, that sparked a certain stubborn curiosity. What if it was true? Where did the fear come from, whence the indignant denial? Why not examine the hypothesis? And if it did prove true, did it apply only to him? How did other examples of the species love, in this city, at this time? And on what basis did the women form their conviction that they alone knew the meaning of love? His methodologically trained brain immediately posed a counterquestion, fashioned after the paradox of the lying Cretan: Is it at all possible for someone who doesn't even know what love is to experience it?

He began to take notes on all the couples in his neighborhood. He titled his notebook "A Concise Treatise on the Average Half-life of Love Relationships." All the data he had thus far collected supported one and only one conclusion, namely, that some strain of separation virus was raging in the walled city. An initial rough estimate suggested that any given relationship had a maximum average life expectancy of three years, one hundred and sixty-seven days, and two hours. Evidently the inclusion of a few outlying districts, which still harbored the vestiges of a working-class milieu, helped boost the mean value to that level. It was further probable that the unusually high number of pensioners and civil servants also exerted a stabilizing influence. However, all the data indicated that the above-mentioned maximum average dropped pronouncedly as the study narrowed its focus to the center of the city, right and left of its magnificent but desolate main avenue. Here it was the high concentration of thirty- and forty-year-olds of both sexes that accounted for the statistical dip. The prognosis looked even worse when Eduard considered that the local population was actually growing, due to a steady stream of immigration. No other city in the world, with the possible exception of New York, contained such a high percentage of the social stratum which subsists on stipends, welfare, illegal labor, and occasional theft. In all probability it was thanks to this powerful "minority" that the median endurance capability of those couples within the range of his study had fallen to the above-mentioned value.

As always, appearances belied the statistical findings. Eyes unbiased by numbers might find abundant evidence to support the hypothesis that the urge to couple continued in the city unchecked. A spring day like this revealed lovers at every corner, standing at their posts in tender embrace. A virtually endless demonstration of people eager for love pushed along the sidewalks, flanked by gently rolling police cars. But anyone who was so rash as to be satisfied with a first impression had no right to expect his further calculations to be any more accurate than those of an amateur astronomer trying to gauge the distance of the heavenly bodies using observations done with the naked eye. Inside each of these love bonds, Eduard could hear the timer ticking away. According to his calculations, out of the 1,265 couples moving past him, one pair would complete a final separation that very day; a dialogue on separation would occur behind 232 windows; one out of 632 people newly fallen in love had that day dissolved a relationship of no longer than 3 years, 167 days, and 2 hours, or else would do so before midnight; approximately one out of a thousand single people roaming the sidewalks had just hired professional movers to carry out a separation of bed and board, or else commissioned a builder to construct a partition within the confines of a recently shared apartment. A considerable fraction of this group would return, alone, to a new or newly divided apartment. Involuntary detachment, that is, abandonment—and this was a corollary of Eduard's observations—seemed to be a sure antidote against any new coupling. On the other hand, those people who had *actively* separated often entered into a new union that very same night, only to dissolve this one, too, in much the same manner as they had the first, after no more than three years, one hundred sixty-seven days, and two hours. The strangest thing about the entire process was that all couples seemed to experience the act of separation—which was perfectly legal and whose date was easily established—as a unique and almost unendurable turning point in their lives. Evidently statistics didn't offer the slightest protection against pain.

AT FIRST he was unable to match a person with the voice, which was distorted by the heavy static. He kept telling the caller to speak up, to please speak more clearly. Once he realized it was his brother, he asked when, how so, why he wasn't told sooner, and where Lothar was at the moment. Phone in hand, Eduard paced up and down the room, in the expectation of some clear feeling. He tried to imagine his father dead, but there was no picture to match the sentence. Apart from in the movies, Eduard had never laid eyes on a corpse.

Some unknown program commanded him to ready himself for a number of quick decisions. But what first? Reserve a plane ticket? Call home? Klara? He *had* to mail the letter to the German Research Society. Cry? Klara wasn't in.

A motion began, without any prompting: no quaking, no whirling, just a slow receding and sinking that had no effect on him, at least not at first, only on the visible objects that surrounded him. It moved the table, the typewriter, the bookcase, back and away, and shrank them to the size of children's playthings. This falling carried in its irresistible wake all further objects, ultimately including the entire visible space, and even spaces only remembered. It was as if the planet of memory, marked with the playgrounds of his life to date, were beginning to wrinkle and crack in slow motion as it spun off into the void. The houses, the cities, the landscapes he had lived in broke apart, capsized, and sank into the deep, toward an invisible center—and Eduard spiraled down after them like a diver sucked below by the ensuing whirlpool. Deep down, at the foot of the funnel, he recognized a narrow, four-storied apartment house. As he came closer, he spotted the iron gate that opened onto the garden, the gravel path that ran between the two ruler-straight flower beds, and suddenly he saw himself, smaller than a child, walking a bicycle across the path. In all the world there is only one door you first pushed open using the weight of your body, one set of stairs where you know which steps creak and which do not, one table you understand so well from underneath.

The puppet-sized being on the gravel path parked his bike in the rack next to the building, alongside the rusty postwar bicycle that belonged to his father. Father was already home. The tiny figure took a key the size of his forearm and unlocked the door. Once inside, he smelled the floor polish used every day to clean the stairwell; he read his father's name on the mailbox and opened the little door that was never latched—Father had taken the mail upstairs. Eduard bounded up the stairs and opened the door to the apartment. He saw his father's poplin jacket hanging on the hook, and on the hat rack above, his black Basque beret. Father never left the house without his beret. Eduard knocked on the door of the study and opened it; he ran through all six rooms, into the bathroom, right up to the toilet. The apartment was empty.

———————

The first thing that struck his eye when he stepped inside his parents' house was his father's Basque beret lying on the billiard table. This had been his father's magical cap; it had kept him invisible during his escape from a POW camp, and he had preserved it as a talisman. Several of Father's coats were hanging on the coatrack; missing was the zippered windbreaker he always wore when riding his bike. Eduard embraced Margot, his father's second wife, and her eyes immediately filled with tears: Eduard didn't know how to respond. When he looked over her shoulder and saw her sister's face nodding with compassion, he felt as if he had been caught red-handed. Go ahead and cry, she told him, cry all you want, but he only answered with an embarrassed smile. He sensed a similar expectation in the eyes of the other mourners, but his struggle for tears was in vain. He closed his eyes, rested his face on Margot's, and felt his own cheek moistened by her tears. At that moment Lothar came into the front hall carrying three overstuffed plastic bags; evidently he had taken upon himself to tend to the guests, who managed to consume an ungodly amount of juice, wine, and all sorts of salty baked goods as they streamed in and out of the house. Why in the world is he doing that, thought Eduard, after all, these are only second- and third-degree relations. Their eyes met, and Eduard felt he owed Lothar a word of explanation. His brother must have had the impression that, within the dichotomy of active and passive mourners, Eduard had immediately allied with the former, who needed to be looked after and consoled by the calmer and more collected. He accepted a handkerchief that was handed him and wiped Margot's tears off his face, then went into the kitchen, took the kettle off the stove, and filled it with water. He was still holding it when Margot's sister came up and put her arms around him. As he pressed against her, he again viewed the scene through the eyes of Lothar, who was packing bottles into the refrigerator: the mourning couple, frozen in embrace while making tea. Eduard was embarrassed when Margot's sister finally took the kettle out of his hand and placed it on the fire, as if he wasn't capable of performing such a simple action just then, as if he shouldn't be capable of doing so. He picked a few potato peels from underneath the brewing kettle and tossed them into the garbage. Then he took the sponge, moistened it, and wiped off the kitchen table. As he bent over for a scrap of food, he suddenly saw his father's well-worn Salamander shoes (round, conservative) on the kitchen floor. It was strange how both shoes fit onto a single tile. Then he saw the cuffs of the blended brown trousers (a little too high) and finally the entire figure, complete with cheap poplin jacket and black Basque beret—all the size of a single kitchen tile. He wanted to ask his father why in the world he had shrunk so much. "To tell you the truth, I had imagined him a whole lot taller, even a little on the violent side, not quite so gentle and fragile"—Klara's remark after meeting his father for the first time had perplexed him. Evidently, through all the years of squabbles and half-reconciliations, he had never stopped seeing his parent through the eyes of a child. Even long after he was grown-up, and taller than his father by half a head, he had continued to lash away at him with the mercilessness so typical of the weaker party, without noticing that his father's body was slowly crumpling closer and closer to the earth. Eduard now recognized the motive for this deliberate blindness. As long as he viewed the man as awe-inspiring, larger than life, his father had offered him protection, he had served as a buffer between Eduard and death. In one short moment of kneeling Eduard had lost this protection. But this was not what brought tears to Eduard's eyes; it was the fact that his tile-sized father had once again forgotten to unclamp the clips on the right leg of his trousers.

That same afternoon a quarrel broke out between Eduard and Lothar concerning the circumstances of their father's death, and the argument soon escalated into a conflict of principle. In the morning a friend of the family had seen Father riding his old bicycle into town. The friend had watched Father pedaling away as a city bus kept honking at him to move aside. Because the cobbled streets in the center of the medieval town were so narrow, a cyclist being pursued like that had only two options: either accelerate or else jump off the bike onto the safer sidewalk. No one who knew Father was surprised that he chose to challenge the bus to a duel. Ever since he had sold his medical practice to devote more and more time to his musical and religious inclinations, Father had developed a biblical wrath against German motorists, against "this daily war of total destruction currently being fought on the streets—you know after 1945 all they did was exchange their tanks and antiaircraft guns for cars." The thought of yielding to several tons of public transportation or especially of abandoning his bike would have struck Father as a second historical failure, or else an admission of his age—and so far the years had treated him quite kindly. Eduard recalled a Sunday walk from a few years before, when his father had performed a straight-backed flip around the horizontal bar for his acrobatically untalented son. He didn't smoke, didn't drink, and was proud of weighing as little at seventy as he had at eighteen. Eduard had never worried about his father's health; he had always expected his father to outlive him.

However fit his father may have kept himself, there was something about his duel with the bus that defied explanation. Given his reluctance to yield to the traffic Nazi, why didn't he just keep on pedaling at the same pace? Why had he—according to eyewitness reports—pushed so hard against his opponent, like a racer in the Tour de France?

He had arrived at the Ludwigskirche overwrought and out of breath. According to several alto and soprano witnesses, he had begun choir practice punctually, exactly as the bell was ringing. With one tap of his baton on the wooden music stand he intoned the A and waited until the choir had attuned itself precisely, whereby tuning forks and pitch pipes were more likely to err than Father with his own perfect pitch. "Page 97, 'Commit Thy Every Grievance.' " At the second phrase Father allegedly cupped his hand over his left ear as if he had heard a terrible mistake and peered out into the chorus with a look of intense horror. Unsure which one of the thirty voices was responsible for the wrong note, the choir members continued to sing. Judging from Father's expression, within two measures the entire chorus had managed to clear itself of any wrongs committed against the score. But all of a sudden Father swung his head back, toward the loft, and flung his arms out wide—just as if he were beginning a dance. Then, without uttering a sound, he sank to his knees and crashed in a wide spiral to the floor.

This image—his breathless entrance into the church, his striking up a Bach chorale, his pirouetting and collapsing— now seemed to Eduard like a formula for his father's entire life, which could be described as a great struggle to avoid any respite, a constant refusal to pause. When had he ever seen his father relaxed or, for that matter, even exhausted? When had his father not pitched in to move a heavy wardrobe, when had he declined to climb a wobbly ladder? There had been two or three times when Eduard had seen him standing by the window, motionless, his eyes filled with terror. He had gripped the window latch tightly, with both arms, as if he were fighting some insidious weakness that had attacked him unawares. When Eduard asked him whether anything was the matter, his father had looked at him with bewilderment that bordered on anger. What's supposed to be the matter with me? Then he released his breath with a heavy snort, like a diver who's been too long underwater. But the silence that preceded this gasp seemed to allow no time for taking stock. It was as if he had strayed into the unlit deep, where every sensory organ was deprived of perception. As if he were simply pushing ahead, with closed eyes, simply waiting for the disturbance to pass.

Evidently he had lived his entire life under a constant pressure from which he could never find relief. But supposing this was true, what was the underlying pain, what unanswered question was asking to be heard in that moment of respite so constantly avoided?

Up to this point in their reconstruction he and Lothar managed to agree. The quarrel broke out over something Lothar said concerning the actual cause of death: he claimed that various unexplained "subconscious burdens" had led their father to his premature death—not some kind of organic suffering.

As far as I know he died of heart failure, said Eduard.

And how do you know that?

It's on the death certificate. And when someone dies at

seventy years of age, it doesn't exactly mean his death was premature.

Lothar looked at him very closely. It's a well-known fact that embolisms don't just happen overnight—their father's sudden death had been building for decades.

Presumably ever since nine months before he was born, Eduard interjected. And there's plenty of reason to suspect that we've both inherited this disposition and so we better prepare ourselves for a similar end.

He knew the "inherited" would get a rise out of his brother, but in his haste he couldn't think of any other word, and he didn't go out of his way to avoid it.

Lothar responded as calmly as possible. It was strange how quickly Eduard contented himself with the medical findings, especially considering the fact there'd been no autopsy. One should never lose one's ability to analyze—even in mourning. He, Lothar, had recently come across certain facts hitherto suppressed from the family history which provided some clues about the dark, unexplained side of their father's life, and which had apparently gnawed away at his spiritual health for decades. He would acquaint Eduard with the details as soon as he had finished his investigation.

Eduard was bewildered, he felt himself under attack. Suddenly, it seemed to him, the subject of conversation was no longer their father's death but rather his, Eduard's, perspective on this event and on the world at large, his general approach, which Lothar constantly criticized as a "preference for biological models." For his part, Eduard suspected that his brother was once again following his own tendency to psychologize events by tracing them to specific social—and therefore alterable—conditions.

Not this again, said Lothar, not right now; Eduard agreed, not right here and now. But that was exactly what they were doing. Before they even knew it, they were locking horns once more as part of their ancient quarrel.

It was the Twin Controversy all over again. Both brothers had published on this subject in their respective professional journals—Eduard as a biologist and Lothar as a sociologist—so that they faced each other as seasoned specialists. The debate began, appropriately enough, in Minneapolis, where Professor Bouchard and his team of researchers had conducted their famous long-term study of identical twins, which many observers believed would finally solve the great "nature vs. nurture" riddle, namely, is human behavior determined primarily by hereditary factors or by environmental influence? In Eduard's eyes all the evidence indicated that the "nurturists," along with their philosophical allies, should simply admit the bankruptcy of their theories. Case studies showed that identical twins separated in infancy and raised in extremely different circumstances displayed characteristics so similar it was ridiculous. Divided by oceans, class, even the Iron Curtain, they followed their inherited program, with which they defended themselves against their environment with an inconceivable heroism. Deprived of all contact with one another, even unaware of each other's existence, they smoked the same brand of cigarette, preferred the same ghastly green suits, divorced buxom blond wives named Linda at the exact same age, and ultimately wound up living only seven miles apart, the white-haired schoolmasters of their respective villages.

All Professor Bouchard's reports generally elicited from Lothar was laughter, although Eduard failed to understand what was so funny. Lothar had the habit of reading the articles out loud to him, while questioning the validity of their claims by referring to background information garnered from remote journals invariably published in Russian, a language Eduard found completely inaccessible. It had been shown, Lothar maintained, that the long-term study had been financed by the CIA. Of course, the Bouchard twins' apparently bewildering preference for cigarettes, suits, women, and cars of the same make had been staged over a number of years. Bouchard's project would end much as the infamous Cyril–Burt scandal over fifty years ago. At that time it came to light that the empirical data of a study of twins, which had ostensibly proven that intelligence was an inherited trait, had in large part been faked.

Eduard always reacted to such objections with a vehemence that could not be explained by the subject matter. He was convinced the true target of Lothar's polemic against the "gene faction" was the "inborn talent" their father had always attributed to Eduard. "Talent" or "genius"—notions which Lothar never uttered without an indulgent smile—did not in Lothar's opinion occur in nature and could at most be defined as social conventions, holdovers from the childhood of science. In Eduard's case the "talent" with which he had been favored could be traced unequivocally to Father's wishful thinking. Because he himself had failed to fulfill his ambitions as a medical scientist, he projected his dreams onto the firstborn, or actually the first-best, to use the language of the social sciences. This projection—and Lothar conceded this much—did in fact give Eduard certain advantages. Father's one-sided, blind faith had in reality called into being the same unquestionable aptitude which he claimed Eduard had received in the cradle. But Lothar went too far in his defense of the nurture theory: oh, without a doubt, had he,

Lothar, grown up in the house of Mozart or Einstein, then he would have been the one to bequeath to the world the same achievements later attributed to the "genius" of these men.

Margot opened the kitchen door and interrupted Eduard in the middle of his reply. Lothar stood up to bring another chair, but she had no intention of sitting down. She chose an apple from the wire basket, took one bite, then put it back and pulled out another. Now for the first time Eduard felt the extent of Margot's grief. She moved as if in a dream, and her face seemed overcome with helplessness. Lothar took her arm as the three of them walked downstairs. Without looking left or right, Margot crossed the street. Her half-bitten apple and absentminded stare forced a rapidly moving car to a halt, and something like shame passed between the two brothers.

The morgue was wintry cool. The white stubble made Father's face look ringed with frost. He had never grown a beard, so no one had noticed that his facial hair had grayed much more quickly than the hair on his head. Eduard examined his father's taut face and thought he read signs of surprise at—but also acceptance of—his sudden end: evidently he had been given only seconds to prepare. Underneath the long gown, his body looked boyish, indifferent. He hardly knew his own body, thought Eduard, neither its horrors nor its joys. Father's idea of happiness was entirely spiritual, a spiritual candor attained only by constant toil.

In fact, Father looked completely alive, and if he hadn't been lying there in a white shirt which Eduard had never seen him wear before, he probably would have greeted his son. There you are, my boy. Only the flowers bowing down to him from all sides declared the man dead.

In one corner of the tiled room Eduard spotted an open plastic bag containing the zippered windbreaker and the Salamander shoes with the round, scraped toes. Suddenly he was bothered by the idea that Father's bike had been standing in the parish bike rack without a "master."

Eduard bent over the dead man's face and instinctively held his ear closer, as if to better understand some whispered word. But the narrow, perfectly slack lips seemed only to repeat the question Eduard already knew, now in silence: What's supposed to be the matter with me?

Eduard felt an arm gently shoving him toward his brother, who was standing behind him. He would have liked—Eduard heard Margot speaking—he always wanted the two of you to make up. At the same time he felt his brother's hand—perhaps guided by Margot's—on his own shoulder. He heard a throat being cleared in agreement; then he turned around and embraced his brother, all the while as alert as a judo wrestler who keeps his opponent's body at just the right distance. For his part, Lothar seemed to regard the embrace as the first move in a shoulder throw; in any case, his grip was a little too hard as he pulled Eduard toward himself. They stood that way for several moments, each resting his head on the shoulder of the other, their two bodies flaring down to form two sides of an acute triangle, each waiting with tensed calves to see who would risk losing the first points. All of a sudden Eduard felt the tension in Lothar's body go slack, and drew him in close.

After all three had resumed their seats in Father's car—Eduard at the steering wheel, of course, Lothar in the back as always—Margot spoiled her attempt at reconciliation with a single sentence. She reminded them of their father's custom whenever he attended funerals: he had always insisted on following the pastor's eulogy with a few words of his own, a personal leave-taking of the departed friend or relative.

Saying this, Margot looked at Eduard as if she had just expressed Father's last wish. Eduard checked the rearview mirror for Lothar's reaction, since Margot's proposal must have struck him as a final slight. He turned around to pass the commission to his brother. But Lothar generously declined.

WHEN HE STEPPED OUTSIDE THE AIRPORT, the tremendous heat nearly knocked him over. The air seemed to boil as it streamed off the asphalt, shaking the street and the walls of the building in a quiet, relentless quiver. Clutching their suitcases, the passengers shuffled about like invalids, dragging their feet in small steps; every movement seemed designed to produce the least amount of sweat. The bus driver sat sleepily at the wheel, his eyes half-closed; he did not look up when Eduard requested a ticket.

As the bus drove into town along the elevated highway, he could see the outskirts of the city. To his left, abandoned warehouses loomed among the weekend garden plots and the asphalt-colored waterways; the brick-red factory buildings on his right looked like blocks of Lego, and behind them he could make out the contours of some workers' housing. There was not a single moving object in sight: Eduard felt as if he were sitting at a drive-in where the film seemed completely static; the only thing that betrayed the presence of a running projector was a thin plume of smoke rising from a chimney.

The first signs of life didn't appear until after the bus had exited into the center of town. Hundreds of naked bodies zoomed into unpleasantly sharp focus as they lay stretched

out on the green grass of a municipal park officially desig-
nated as a "lying area." A few people were strolling up and
down among the bodies like survivors of a war looking for
fallen friends and relatives. Some were plunging into the
muddy water of a tiny lake; others were already standing motionless in the knee-deep broth. Eduard got off the bus at
the next stop. As he walked home through the familiar
streets, the city suddenly seemed foreign; wherever he looked
he found an overabundance of unnecessary walls. He saw a
children's playground enclosed by walls taller than any human being. Street cafés were nestled in the shade of fire
walls so acoustically alive they could amplify the clinking of
a spoon inside a coffee cup into the clanging of a churchbell.
Off the streets, behind the entranceways, yawned courtyards
the size of gymnasiums, secured by barbed wire and dissected
by several walls into solitary cells, each containing a single
maple tree. Nowhere else in the world were there fire walls
like these: five stories of brick masonry, utterly windowless
except for the occasional well-hidden bathroom window,
which lit up every now and again, a mysterious sign of life
within.

At first, when he was new here, he had examined the border wall, whose most notable feature was that it divided the
city down the middle instead of surrounding it. But the view
from any one of the lookout towers built to afford Westerners
a glimpse of life behind the Wall had invariably disappointed
him. In no place did the infamous construction achieve the
height and breadth of his imagining; it looked more like the
cheap realization of an architectonic formula that achieved
its fullest expression in the center of the city. At that time
he developed a mental image of a city expanding evenly from
the edges toward the center, following a program of contin-

uous cell division that seemed exclusively designed for inward expansion. The strangest thing was that the inhabitants appeared not to notice their own Wall complex, for their unceasing separations seemed to trace a pattern that was etched inside their souls.

The sidewalks were empty except for occasional groups of pedestrians wearing nothing but gym shorts, who went trudging by lugging cans of Coca-Cola. It was as if the sun had miscalculated the latitude by several degrees. As Eduard watched it glowing—hugely magnified—in a thin, whitish haze, he recalled a scientific prophecy: If and when the sun's nucleus burns out, the star will undergo a violent expansion and fill half the sky. The seas will evaporate, the planets will leave their orbits and collapse into the former sun. Astrophysicists had described this event in minute detail—the only controversy concerned the date. But there was not the slightest disagreement that no one would be around to witness it.

Outside the door to Klara's apartment Eduard realized he had spoken to her only briefly over the telephone since he left. He felt uncomfortable having to use his father's death to explain himself; he preferred not to talk at all. Klara opened the door like someone just awakened from an afternoon nap. As she stood in the door, her eyelids half-open, unsure what to expect, Eduard saw her the way he had when they first met: her surprised eyes caught in a child's dream she had never given up, her nose with its broadly sculpted, flared nostrils—you have the most beautiful nose I know— her generous mouth, her whole face beautifully aligned, dark, always caught in a soft shadow that did not depend on light.

Klara looked at him questioningly, then gently pushed him away, since he didn't want to let go. Displacement behavior —the zoological term came clearly to mind. The main thing is that she not ask me any questions, not now! Sure, it would be great if we could speak without losing any energy or warmth. When had he ever demonstrated he was capable of unprotected communication, of baring his soul: My heart, my life, I am nothing without you? Sentences never fail to drag other sentences in their wake, there is no bridge between the spoken sentence and lightning flashes of desire.

He tossed his bag on the floor and started going after Klara, in the hallway, with the door half-open; as he was undressing her, his foot got caught in his shoulder bag. Whatever it was that drove him: the heat, the soft luster of Klara's naked shoulders, his father's death, the fear of his own—he smothered every question with a rush of kisses. Klara looked at him in utter disbelief, as if a good friend had just turned into a gorilla. But after a moment her astonishment succumbed to her curiosity.

The bag seemed ridiculously small beside the discarded articles of clothing, like a magic prop that spawned an endless supply of undergarments. All of a sudden everything was very simple, and he perceived what followed as if he had been blinded by flashbulbs, as a series of unfocused black-and-white photographs: Eduard with Klara on the rug in the hallway, Eduard under Klara and both beneath the kitchen table, Eduard behind Klara on the threshold of the study, both below the potted palm tree—how did the soil get on her stomach—Eduard on the revolving chair, Klara on the desk in a position that craved his tongue and all ten fingers. Writhing, squirming, gasping, they conquered the apartment, then finally made their way back to collapse on the kitchen bench, happily exhausted.

The strangest thing was that Eduard felt his father's presence throughout, though this did not disturb him in the least. It was as if his father were watching his son's doings from on high, with a forgiving shrug of the shoulders. Wasn't this, too, a way of taking leave, a way of celebrating life to honor the dead? A sensation of weightlessness entered the room and dispelled all scruples; a strange physical force had catapulted him out of the present calendar, back across a thousand routine days, all the way to the beginning of his relationship with Klara.

It was a courtyard romance: Klara in the front house, Eduard in the back. A romance for which they owed the city's founding fathers, even though they didn't always thank them. The front house was separated from the back by a dark, prison-like, rectangular courtyard, which looked like a cheap imitation of an Italian atrium. Around 1900 the city had passed an ordinance decreeing that all new courtyards should be of sufficient size and shape to enable a contemporary fire engine to turn around. While the building code had long since lapsed, the courtyard remained, and now served to house the trash bins.

For an entire summer Eduard had seen Klara only from his kitchen window, as she emptied her garbage. The first thing he noticed was how carefully she emptied her bags, which she then folded and placed on top of the garbage, in order to protect her hand when she stuffed it inside the bin. As soon as he heard Klara's wooden clogs echoing in the courtyard, he would leave his typewriter and hurry to the kitchen window. There he would watch her as she moved among the garbage bins with the dignity of a princess reviewing a parade. At times she would bend over and absentmindedly pick up a few scraps that had fallen on the ground and cautiously toss them into the bin. As soon as she had closed the lid, she would spin around on the heel of her clog and step back along the cement slabs that led through the garbage bins, straight as an arrow, undeterred by alien can tops, potato peels, and little snippets of paper. For a few seconds Klara's royal gait, untainted by anything remotely related to garbage, seemed to transform the courtyard into the atrium of its dreams.

It took him months to realize that he might empty his garbage bags at the same time as Klara. To do this he had to keep a full bag of trash by his door for days on end, so that he could be ready at a moment's notice to grab the stinking pretext and race downstairs, where he might effect a meeting beside the dumpsters. Strangely, Klara did not discern his crude design. When Eduard looked into her eyes for the very first time, across the open lid of a garbage bin, he had to admit that Klara wasn't seeing him; chances were she hadn't ever even noticed him. She seemed absorbed with other images, her perception focused on the distant past or perhaps the future. In her eyes he saw a picture forming, impossible to blot out or erase—a garden, a house, a few fruit trees, a lake, a child, and finally a man as well, the inevitable father of the child, but on no account a tenant from the back house holding a garbage bag astride a pork chop half consumed by maggots and flies. At the same time he saw the shadow in her face, which may have stemmed from her dark hair draped over her forehead but which Eduard regarded as a shadow cast by Klara's soul. This tall, erect woman was carrying some hurt, well concealed within her vigorous body. Eduard imagined she lived together with a man who was too young, too small, too blind to guess her secret and who had no idea how to awaken her passion.

For half a year Eduard seemed to belong to the world that found no reflection in Klara's eyes. Whenever he ran into her and gazed at her just a little too long, he felt he had been overlooked, or at best registered as livestock bearing some connection to garbage bins. She didn't actually return his glance until he physically blocked her way and forced her to do so, with a manic fury so well planned it had lost all spontaneity. She looked at him as if she'd never seen him before. Eduard realized he couldn't wait for the border guard lurking behind her eyelids to declare him *persona non grata*, so he began to babble away without rhyme or reason.

When both of them later recalled this scene, his memory denied all responsibility for the opening sentence. Even years later, he and Klara were still arguing about its wording. Eduard had intended to utter a daring, ruthlessly honest sentence, one of those sentences with which a man places his life in the balance; he had braced himself for every conceivable reaction, even the most unfavorable one, the silent about-face on the wooden heel; after all, total defeat was more honorable than cowardice in the face of strong desire. But the actual sentence, the one that ostensibly escaped from his mouth, according to Klara's stubborn recollection, caused his cheeks to glow red with shame. Something like: I can think of a better place for a meeting than these garbage bins—how about a café?

The only odd thing was that following this sentence—or some other—they stood facing each other for an eternally long time without any discernible intent of emptying their garbage bags. His mind went blank, all circuits loaded or burned out. After a silence that took him back to the dawn of speech, he finally began to form syllables which took several seconds to reach his ear, delayed as they were by the bouncy acoustics of the courtyard.

In between the echoes he was able to make out half-sentences which revolved around the words "Eduard," "garbage bins," "Klara," and which unquestionably sprang from his lips.

Two days later he rang her doorbell, his head full of new sentence ploys, which shattered to pieces at the threshold. In the dim light of the entry hall behind her, he saw a man who was indeed smaller and younger than Klara. The man's look hinted that Eduard was the protagonist of a story which had afforded them both much laughter: the garbage guy. Klara passed on Eduard's invitation to a party; the man in the hall received it nonchalantly. Where, when, in Eduard's car or Klara's? A modern couple.

The three of them drove to the party, a large bash of the type then popular in coops around the city. Two high-performance stereo speakers ensured that people could not communicate unless they shouted telegrammatic sentences at the top of their lungs. Immediately after their arrival Eduard dragged Klara to the dance area and kept her there until the next slow number. Once he caught her doing a slow turn on the wrong foot and had to hold on to her to prevent her from falling. At some point the pretext began to annoy him and he pulled Klara toward him, tightly. He sensed the same astonishment in her body that he had discovered in her eyes at their first meeting: a hesitation, as if she was waiting for a legible, recognizable signal. Suddenly she seemed decided and began to respond to his touch. They danced on, tightly intertwined, oblivious to the pounding of the Rolling Stones. Then she broke away from Eduard unexpectedly and walked over to her escort. Without a word of explanation she demanded her car keys and asked Eduard to drive her home. Someday she's going to be every bit as abrupt and ruthless when she picks her keys up off the table and walks out on me! But since he was the cause and not the victim of the sudden breakup, Eduard quickly forgot the warning signs.

That night they had made love with a ferocity he was not prepared for. It was as if their lack of speech had freed them from all reserve, but this seemed to surprise only Eduard. Not until Klara sat up after a few moments of wordless fatigue and switched on the light did the absent, even dismissive astonishment return to her eyes. With growing mistrust, actually in blind rage, so it seemed to Eduard, Klara looked around the room. What was she looking for in front of the window, behind the curtain, on the wallpaper, by the light switch, underneath the table? Like the camera in a detective film her gaze zoomed in on tiny details never before noticed. She counted the ribs on the radiator, studied the window lever, scrutinized the painted ceiling, even seemed to read the fingerprints on the doorknob and the windowsill. Patty Hearst—the idea flitted through his head: the look of a hostage released from the closet after weeks of captivity and relieved of her blindfold. In Klara's eyes he read the same judgment Patty Hearst had passed on her kidnappers when she first laid eyes on them: My God, these people are so ordinary!

Without a word of explanation Klara stood up, dressed, and fled the apartment, barefoot.

The next day he and Klara had gone running around a small lake in the west of the city. She hardly seemed to hear what he was saying to her—now for the first time using complete, coherent sentences—about his work at the Institute for Genetic Research. At times she would begin a story—as if she were speaking to herself—but always in the middle, so that there was no beginning or end. That's where she went swimming with an old girl friend from school. That was where she once ate when she was eight years old—scraps of memory from childhood and school, which she apparently formulated just for herself; she wasn't concerned whether they were communicated or not. Nevertheless, he did discover that she held a master's degree in art history and that she worked in a museum, designing exhibits and compiling catalogues. As she was talking he asked whether she was as laconic at work as she was with him. She bounded off in front of him, so erect she was almost stiff, her dark hair hiding her forehead and eyes. Occasionally she stopped to pick up a leaf, which she twirled between her fingers, or else to draw unintelligible signs in the sand. An overpowering silence emanated from her, and Eduard was convinced that while he might sleep with her from time to time, he would never actually speak with her. He reproached himself for not having given her any time to observe him from a safe distance.

It wasn't until weeks later that he discovered why Klara had fled that first night. The intensity, the speechlessness of his desire, her guilty conscience with regard to her former lover from the front apartments—none of that was it, that was all back-building thinking. Had he really forgotten who had stuck the key in the ignition?

What had really caused Klara to panic was the discovery

that her bedroom in the front had the same doorknob, the same window grip, the same radiator, the same painted ceiling as Eduard's room in the back. Finally her sobered eyes had focused on the man in bed and unmasked him as well: Eduard—the rear version of the front bedfellow. Never with the back house!—the maxim was etched among the other graffiti on the elevator wall, but she had apparently overlooked this bit of wisdom when she left his bed in the middle of the night and fled back to her own apartment.

As far as Eduard knew, no one had ever studied the effect of tenements on the love life of the tenants, but there was evidently enough material to formulate a suitable hypothesis. Had Eduard and Klara met in a different architectural setting they might never have seen each other again. The trash bins in the courtyard transformed a chance encounter into the inevitable product of an iron law, the fulfillment of architectonic will, which evolved over the years into a living arrangement that granted both partners visiting rights in both apartments.

But there was one sentence he had been guilty of neglecting for years, one sentence abandoned at the beginning of the story. Before his father's death he had been unable to determine this unknown variable in the equation Eduard = Klara; now, however, he found the solution with the surprisingly simple formula: I want to have a child with you!

4

He didn't see a single familiar face as he and Klara passed through The Tent looking for a place to sit. The early burst of warmth had drawn a number of guests as well as a stream of roving salespeople and solo entertainers. Tamil flower sellers wandered among the tables hawking roses that were dripping wet; on the sidewalk a two-man band from Brazil was beating a samba, while skateboarders flashed by in silver helmets and shining armor.

Eduard and Klara sat down at the only open table, where a black triangular reserved sign stood out against the white tablecloth. Eduard had only recently obtained the privilege of sitting at a table he had not requested but which was nevertheless marked reserved. At The Tent all tables were reserved, from the time it opened to the wee hours—even on Mondays, when the place was glaringly empty. Any random visitor who was turned away would first look at the vacant but reserved tables in utter disbelief, then conclude that the restaurant managed to get by without any customers. He couldn't know that the little black triangles served exclusively to keep people like him away. The waiters invoked unwritten rules to decide whether a reserved table was free or not; occasionally they resorted to eye contact with the owner, Pinka, but only in questionable cases. Nothing was known concerning these rules except for the fact that they were not demo-cratic. The only thing democratic about The Tent was the bar, where all those newly separated or fallen in love could intoxicate themselves without spending a fortune. It was amazing how quickly Pinka's left-leaning clients abandoned their protest against her "elitism." For whatever criteria Pinka used to determine her yes or no, they could not be reduced to a simple profit motive. Data obtained during a control period of one season revealed that her split-second decisions were almost entirely error-free. Pinka's looks and nods seated at her tables a careful mix of people, an extended family, in which the euphorias and depressions of individual members were kept in artful balance, and which enjoyed greater stability than more traditional families behind four walls and closed curtains.

Eduard had no sooner ordered than he felt a hand on his shoulder.

I had one hell of a night, said André.

He looked as if he had just finished the city marathon. Saying hello to Eduard and his friends, he glanced at the neighboring tables as if he expected a whole chorus of greet-ings. Exhausted, he plopped down on the chair next to Klara, simultaneously managing to adjust the chair with his foot so he could see the people strolling by. As far as André was concerned, to sit with his back to the street was to miss out on life. He firmly believed in the promised woman, the dream of his youth, the one and only, who would walk up out of nowhere, just by chance.

Esther? asked Klara.

It's unbelievable! said André. He laughed bitterly and beat his head. Unbelievable but true: we're finished.

Again? asked Eduard.

I have an invitation to your wedding! Klara protested.

For heaven's sake! Who's going to write all the cancellation letters!

It's supposed to be the latest rage, said Eduard: wedding parties without the bridal couple.

It's easy for you to laugh, said André, but he joined in. The inseparable couple. So why don't you two go on and get married?

Because we don't believe in marriage, said Eduard.

Because Eduard's too much of a coward, said Klara.

We were talking about André's wedding, said Eduard. What's going on?

André looked at both of them as if he'd never seen anything more disgusting in his life. It wasn't until he began answering the question that it was clear his loathing was directed against the institution in question.

Something happened to us, something completely banal and ridiculous; let's forget it, it's impossible even to talk about it.

He took a swig from Eduard's glass, shook himself, stood up, and smiled his way over to Pinka. For a moment he seemed to have forgotten everyone else.

André was medium tall, thin as a rake, and irresistible. He had the fine hair of a newborn, a narrow birdlike head perched on a strong neck, steeply sloping shoulders, stiff legs connected to amazingly limber hips—a graceful body despite its middle bulge. But the most striking thing about André was his large, broad mouth, which one of his many admirers had once described as "rhapsodic." The word only made sense if you thought about Chopin at the same time. With his face deadly earnest, André was telling something to Pinka which made the latter break out laughing. Shortly afterward he came back, with Pinka in tow, carrying a glass of champagne, and went on:

Esther and I were recently sitting in a pub, in as good a mood as you are now. No bad thoughts, unless you consider weddings bad, just completely engrossed in the details of the ceremony: when, where, and with whom. A few minor differences; Esther wanted to have a Jewish ceremony at the Jewish community center, I was in favor of a converted S-Bahn station. Esther's father absolutely insisted on inviting their thirty aunts and grandnephews from Russia, my father insisted on flying in the relatives from Los Angeles and New York—the usual wedding diplomacy. Our main problem was really that our fathers refused to realize that it was our wedding and not theirs.

We had just disagreed on the type of champagne when a haggard man walked up to our table. I saw right away he was a love-cripple, one of those internally homeless people who make the streets insecure at night, and since I knew the poor soul from better days, I offered to buy him a drink. He drained his glass—evidently not his first one of the day—in one guzzle, but kept a bitter silence. I myself was still in my wedding mood, and against my better judgment I asked the man how he was doing; naturally I counted on his good manners to produce the usual innocuous reply.

I had no way of knowing that my unsolicited guest was not your ordinary sufferer. It turned out I had invited a walking virus to my table, a wedge-wolf in silk coat and beard, a separation vampire who couldn't wait to sink his teeth into our necks. With an insidious glance he proceeded to warn me about the consequences his answer might entail: There are stories about breakups that inevitably lead to the breakup of those who hear them. You'll have to admit that after an

introduction like that it was impossible for me to feign dis-
interest and ask for the check. Esther tugged at my wrist in
vain. Happy as a clam I just laughed in his face, held on to
Esther with a firm grip, and then, trump in hand, demanded
that this couple-murderer tell his story. One evening—that's
how the wedge-wolf began this indescribably banal story—

André broke off in mid-sentence and looked at Klara and
Eduard as if he had just realized they were there.

No, I'm not even thinking about it, he went on, I refuse
to inflict this damned story on you! Suffice to say its effect
was amazing: just two hours after hearing it I discovered that
the door to our five-room apartment had been bolted from
the inside, while just outside the door I found five of my
favorite shirts, freshly ironed, too, all very neatly scissored
into two dozen ribbons.

André waved to someone in back of Eduard. That was
something Eduard couldn't stand: André's eyes were always
somewhere else; he couldn't even concentrate on his own
catastrophes.

I'm afraid I already know the story, said Theo, pulling up
a chair. May I tell my version?

Only if it's about you and Pauline, said André.

Theo came from the other side of the Wall. Although he
needed an exit visa to visit The Tent, he was a frequent, if
somewhat irregular, guest. He possessed a so-called double
passport, a name as strange as the privilege it indicated. This
passport provided the bearer with a visa valid for several
years, good for exiting as well as re-entering the half-city
across the Wall.

Why exactly Theo should enjoy this special privilege was
the subject of some speculation. After all, he was rumored
to belong to the tiniest terrorist organization in the world:

anarchic poets. He was in conflict with everyone, with the petit bourgeois socialism of the East, with the "peep-show society" in the West, and above all with himself. He considered politicians—regardless of party—his biological enemies and was happy to illustrate this fundamental antipathy with a story about fish. Marine biologists had studied the behavior of herbivorous fish which travel in large schools, searching the shallow waters for food. From the distance, each school looks like a closed V, in which each fish has a fixed place. Closer examination, however, reveals a different picture: The entire school, consisting of thousands of fish, is in permanent, chaotic motion, as the fish on the edge are constantly pushing toward the middle of the school. The explanation is obvious: because the outside fish will be the first to fall victim to any predators the school might encounter, they try to move to the middle, even if that means pushing other fish—who are also swimming toward the center—to the outside. The true picture, then, is of a mass of individuals swimming from the outside toward the center, where only the outlines of the V are fixed and stable.

Researchers next wondered what enabled the pilot fish that led the school to escape this push toward the middle. Because it appears that the leaders of the school never change their position, they seem completely oblivious to the fears which play such a great role in affecting the behavior of the group. They swim on with puzzling tranquillity; evidently other fish have no desire to take their place. An anatomical study revealed that these pilot fish were brain-damaged—their brain is exactly half as large as that of their fellows.

Eduard had never succeeded in finding out where and when this investigation had been carried out and in what journal Theo had found its description. Theo considered Eduard's interest in bibliographical detail petty.

Patrons of The Tent all agreed that Theo made the most out of the Wall. The double passport allowed him to disappear for days or even weeks on the other side—whichever it might be—even if it was only to sleep off a hangover. Over there—again it made no difference which side he meant—he led a life which those he left behind knew only from rumors. Where else in the world could you suddenly become completely invisible, without having to explain yourself. For Theo, the Wall was a cloak of invisibility, enabling him to appear without warning and disappear without a trace. Whenever he wanted to cancel a reading, shirk a responsibility, or postpone quarreling with a lover, Theo invoked his dual existence and disappeared. Where others racked their brains for an excuse, or resorted to illness or family affairs as a screen, Theo could always rely on a ready alibi of unquestionable authority: difficulties crossing the border. In any event, behind all Theo's cancellations as well as his surprise appearances, you could feel the wind of history blowing.

What kind of story was it he told the two of you? asked Klara stubbornly.

Stories like that are a dime a dozen, said Theo. It's just that, thanks to a particularly German craving for innovation in literature, nobody ever writes them anymore. They only live them.

André snorted angrily.

All right, he said, since you insist . . . but I'll give you the abridged version—short and sour. Basically it's about the age-old question whether lovers should tell each other when they've been untrue.

Eduard looked at André, thoroughly disappointed.

And that's all? Not that old song and dance! You're not going to tell me that's what's endangering your wedding.

My exact words, replied André, but unfortunately Esther and I hadn't worked the issue out yet. And when Esther playfully referred the wedge-wolf's question to me, I made one crucial mistake: I tried to answer it.

How? asked Eduard.

How would you answer it? asked Klara.

Just a minute, it's André's turn, said Theo.

That people in this country are too inclined to take principles on faith and that it's best not to make any contracts about things like that.

Eduard nodded, hesitantly. Pinka laughed out loud and exchanged knowing glances with Klara. Theo ran his thumb along the bridge of his nose.

And Esther? asked Klara.

She thought that I was getting off easy with an answer like that. To tell the truth, I'd never really considered the question very much. But since she insisted, I started to improvise an entire philosophy on the matter. I vaguely recalled a line from Simone de Beauvoir, who seemed to me to be beyond suspicion in this matter: Lies are actually more honest than telling the truth. *Voilà!* Esther looked at me as if I'd just delivered a confession. I then launched into an elucidation of Simone de Beauvoir, so enthusiastically that I surprised myself, and developed my own—or really her—concept regarding the proper timing of a confession. Confessions immediately after or even just before an affair generally do little more than relieve the confessor's own guilt and qualify as evidence of emotional cruelty. The honesty fanatics of '68 sparked genuine bloodbaths in the name of this barbaric ideal, all for their nearest and dearest. For the most part, the fleeting enjoyment of an affair is nothing compared to the pain caused by the confession. Thus the silencing of an affair and the resultant bad conscience is far better testimony of consideration and love for the betrayed partner than trumpeting out the truth.

You can't be serious—the words just slipped out of Klara. What did Esther say?

She immediately asked whether she should interpret every lateness of mine as evidence of an affair I was keeping quiet out of consideration for her. Like when my plane ticket from Munich recently showed a departure time of 10:00 p.m., but by some miracle I didn't arrive at its destination until eleven o'clock the next morning.

What was going on in Munich? asked Theo quickly. André ignored the objection and continued:

Esther was beside herself. From now on, she said to me with fluttering eyelids, you can take your own suits to the cleaners! And with those words she stood up and threw a claim check in my face.

Eduard found it hard to believe that of all people André had become the victim of such a trite and trivial story. The wedding preparations had changed him greatly. Since Eduard had known him, he had always thought of André as the happy exception, the champion of chaotic relationships—but without problems. Whenever they met, André would always introduce a new girlfriend, grab Eduard by the wrist so tightly it hurt, drag him aside, and whisper in his ear: How do you like her? Think I ought to marry her?

Strangely enough, despite all the commotion, André had

never made any serious enemies among these women. He even pulled off a date with six different women for the same evening at the same restaurant—"Sheer restlessness," he excused himself, as he wandered from one table to another. How André survived all his mishaps was a riddle to Eduard. After lengthy observation he concluded that André's special gift was his absentmindedness. He staged his outrageous performances with an innocence that was beyond question, so that Eduard asked himself whether guilt in love existed if it was not felt. André's absentmindedness had something existential about it. He rushed around in the morning with his shirt on backward or wrongly buttoned. He had always just lost his checkbook or his coin purse or his passport or his key; his throat hurt and needed massaging, or else he couldn't turn off the faucet; that he managed to flick a light switch now and then was a minor miracle. When André suddenly leaned over to an unknown woman sitting next to him, this gesture was without the usual aggression of love-hungry men, it was more a request to be picked up and petted. He conquered legions of battle-tried women by approaching them not as a man but as a child. And this same André, of all people, wanted to involve himself with the most sinister invention of Christian civilization: the monogamous marriage.

Why do you want to marry Esther, anyway? asked Eduard.

Because I love her!

How do you know you love her?

How do I know? asked André, astonished. Because I say it to her every morning before breakfast and at least once before going to bed. Of course, I say it to her in French. By the way, what is it you have against marriage?

Eduard was just about to launch into an answer, when he noticed the entire table holding its breath. He was glad that Theo interrupted.

It is Eduard's opinion, explained Theo, that this respectable institution has a fundamental flaw in that it declares what is at best a happy but highly improbable exception—lifelong love—to be the norm.

Pinka stood up. Eduard followed her gaze and saw that a spectacle was taking place inside the restaurant. A young, deathly pale woman was screaming in the face of a man who was sitting down, and whose only reaction was to look around in painful embarrassment. This prompted the woman to pick up his wineglass and fling it in his face. However, even then the man did nothing to defend himself, he only shook his head and wiped off the wine and a few drops of blood. He was so passive, in fact, it seemed he felt he deserved to be maltreated. The woman spun around brusquely and stomped out the door, then hesitated at the curb, as if considering something; for a moment it looked as if she couldn't make up her mind whether to cross the street or not. All of a sudden she turned back. In two bounds she was back at the table by the entrance, where she grabbed a steak knife right out of the hand of one of the diners. Eduard had the impression the raging woman was enjoying the terror she caused among the guests. Knife in hand, she stormed across the street and plunged it into each tire of a parked Renault, as if she were finishing off some rabid beast. Then she strode off, head high, without looking back.

Pinka wanted to buy a round of drinks, but Klara stood up abruptly. The next morning she had to get an early start, to attend a planning session for an upcoming Caravaggio exhibit, and besides, she was happy to leave the three men to

their talk. Theo, André, and Eduard outdid one another inventing reasons why Klara couldn't leave just then. While she
seemed to enjoy their competition, she refused to be swayed.
Then she left them, without the slightest note of disapproval;
even so, the mood at the table darkened. Eduard was annoyed at his friends' suspicious stares. Their compliments on
Klara's patience, her easy, laid-back way of dealing with him,
sounded like last warnings. He suppressed every attempt to
project André and Esther's conflict onto himself and Klara.

Theo suddenly started attacking him. Didn't Eduard realize
that Klara's quiet departure could be traced to the exact same
doubt as Esther's angry outburst? And it wasn't the particular
cause that mattered, it was the fundamental fragility of all
relationships, this base instability, the constant red alert, the
readiness for breakup. Instead of focusing on success, people
prepare for separation, for retreat, for moving out at a moment's notice. And you sit back like polite members of an
audience waiting for your stories to end in the worst possible
way. Love without purpose, without craziness, without some
reckless assertion isn't worth a fucking thing!

Eduard recalled André's hypothesis that most of Theo's
sentences pronounced in the second person (singular or, as
in this case, plural) could be translated back into the first
person. Theo conversed with himself by attacking others; but
while he was ripping apart the soul of the person next to
him, he was really searching for his own point of view. He
showered his friends with advice in the hope he might come
across some wisdom for himself. However, this interpretation
didn't change the fact that Theo's attacks hit their mark in
Eduard. One of Theo's many talents was his ability to infect
others with the same insecurities that afflicted him.

Pinka brought some new drinks. When she proposed a

toast to "the good, the bad, and the ugly," not one of them wanted to raise his glass. Theo ordered a cigar.

If it just wasn't all so damned boring, he said. What bothers me about André's story is its interchangeability, its galling capacity to be repeated. If you were to switch on a tape recorder at every table, at this place or somewhere else, the result would be a set of choral responses with astoundingly few variations. New rules for coexistence between the sexes have had about two decades' worth of tests, and an entire generation has served as guinea pig. Your grandchildren will probably be the first ones to name and use the new rituals now being evaluated. But all the guinea pigs learn is that the existing understandings between the sexes no longer work.

What do you mean "you"? asked André.

Theo nodded like someone caught in a bad habit. Naturally my problems differ from your problems as to the circumstances, but otherwise they're exactly the same. There's nothing new about the old rules being disobeyed. In all times and at all places marriages have been broken, women betrayed, men cuckolded. What's new is that these old rules no longer have any authority. The old vows have lost their validity, lying has almost become unnecessary. The institutions of love are in an obvious state of decay, because the underlying social and cultural controls are disappearing—the seventh commandment, the patriarchy, the economic dependency of the woman; you can't even count on the biological drive to reproduce anymore.

So why not simply start with the mutual assumption of disloyalty as a rule, why not finally recognize the inevitability of breaking up, the finite nature of every love? Assuming that everlasting love is nothing more than a touching relic of the distant past, like wisdom teeth or the fear of flying, why should we continue to follow this outmoded program of our feeling mechanism? Why do we constantly lament, why are we always disappointed, why don't we finally declare ourselves in agreement with our experience, that transience is the normal attribute of love?

André first found Theo's exposition tempting, but upon reflection he thought it was merely despicable. A libertine, a Don Giovanni, who acts with impunity, breaking no rules, risking no run-in with the Commendatore, whom nothing is drawing toward the abyss . . .

This objection seemed to touch a nerve with Theo as well; evidently he had just been waiting for the chance to develop his own rebuttal.

It turns out that love, or what we imagine to be love, is the least likely thing on earth, he said. The question is: What basis can we have to satisfy our need for a lasting relationship, now that the necessary external conditions no longer exist? Either we discover new, better reasons and invent new rules or we say goodbye to the whole project forever. As far as I'm concerned, I have no desire to go on suffering like a laboratory mouse with no will of its own. And I refuse to wait for the end of the study. If I can't be the experimenter, then at least I'll be the troublemaker, the one mouse that ruins the entire experiment.

Afterward, Eduard could no longer say what had impressed him and André more, the schnapps that Pinka kept buying them or Theo's strategic attack. For a moment Theo's commanding overview had transformed the unintelligible tumult between the sexes, the vast tangle of individual duels, into great movements clashing on the battlefield of history.

By the gray light of dawn all three decided to declare war on the dragon of separation. Whoever failed to show up in

The Tent one year later to the day, still coupled with his current partner, would have to finance an entire ski vacation for six people in the ski resort of Sils-Maria.

By the last round of schnapps they still hadn't managed to agree on a common approach. Each developed his own plan, which the other two immediately doomed to failure. André wanted to save his wedding to Esther by agreeing to a contract of mutual disloyalty. Eduard announced his intention of fathering six children with Klara. Only Theo came up with a surprise: he determined to spend an entire year without any connubial contact with Pauline, so that their love would blossom once again.

† † † † † † † † † † † † † † † † † 5 † † † † † † † † † † † † † † † † †

Later that evening Eduard uttered a sentence—as if he were conducting a test—which unleashed a quarrel between him and Klara that kept them up all night. It was strange, he said, that despite the number of years they'd been living together, they had yet to produce a child.

A simple statement of fact, nothing more, he later defended himself. But Klara misunderstood exactly what Eduard had meant, and spared no rage in answering him. Who if not he was the champion of prophylactic thinking, the grandmaster of coitus interruptus? The fact that she herself had begun taking precautions in the meantime was simply a reaction to his terrible fear of fatherhood. In her anger Klara invented new curses: You're just one big paternophobe, a complete interruptus!

Both were well rehearsed in this conflict and in the art of settling it by reversing roles. Eduard's "conditional" rejection had not silenced the desire for a child: on the contrary, they each expressed this wish more and more frequently, though not always at the same time. Once Klara had finally gotten it out of her head, Eduard suddenly found a thousand reasons that spoke in favor. When, weeks later, Klara took him at his word, Eduard confessed that while he remembered the impulse, he wasn't feeling it at the moment. The minute he observed that the feeling had suddenly made its reappearance, Klara found the weather report more interesting.

This game of denial may be as old as the battle between the sexes, but it had lost all its innocence due to a technological advance sold under the innocuous name "the pill." This small pink object enabled the creation of a human being hitherto unknown on earth: the planned-and-wished-for dreamchild. Evidently the master design of creation had failed to provide for this unlikely creature, since it required of its progenitors that both possess the urgent and simultaneous desire to have the child and—in the worst of cases—that they maintain this common desire over a number of years.

It gradually became clear that most potential parents were not up to this task. Couples who planned their progeny remained childless for an astoundingly long time, while a study of families with multiple offspring determined that most of the children had arrived unexpectedly and at the worst possible moment. The concept of family planning itself seemed plagued with a congenital defect: it quite often led to a childless marriage. Evidently no people in possession of both the pill and their senses would consciously choose to bring into the world a kicking, screaming being who would spend the first three years robbing both parents of their sleep and the next fifteen thinking about murdering one or the other.

Eduard and Klara had noticed that many of their peers had secretly begun restoring chance to its rightful place. Reports that the pill increased the risk of cancer provided the occasion: indignant women asked why they should be the only ones to risk their health. Only Stone Age specimens of the male genus could ignore this argument, and more and more women had stopped taking the little tablets. But risk of cancer and the unfair allocation of burdens only partly explained the recent aversion. An entire generation wanted to escape the newfound freedom to make love without consequences, and silently retreated into the realm of chance.

One morning Klara stuck out her tongue defiantly, with a pink pill perched on the tip. Since Eduard declined the hormone kiss, she spit the thing out and tossed the rest of the package in the trash. From now on, she was saying, he would be forced to continually choose between his aversion to condoms and his reluctance to have children. Eduard was amazed to find he was somewhat relieved. And so, partly because they wanted to and partly because they had to, they reverted to the prophylactic methods presumably responsible for their own existence. After fifty years of arduous and diligent research, condoms and interruptus were all that remained.

But once summoned, the devil of planning could no longer be dispelled. Despite the fact that they both kept "miscalculating" or "forgetting themselves," the risk of pregnancy balanced out to zero.

Eduard recalled some statistics Klara had computed for him several weeks previously. One Sunday morning, over breakfast in bed, she had used a calculator to quantify his three most obvious vices. Taking cigarettes, alcohol, and sex as the leading indicators, she arrived at the following conclusion: If all the cigarettes consumed by Eduard over twenty years were stretched out end to end, the poisonous thread would run straight from the door of their building, cross the famous Wall, and stop exactly at the entrance to the Pergamon Museum. During the same time period he would have guzzled at least 6,000 liters of white wine, the approximate yearly yield of the vineyards of Colle Urbine. Her final calculation showed that Eduard would have secreted approx. 2.75 liters of the white substance whose exclusive purpose —according to the Vatican—was the procreation of children, without producing a single pregnancy.

This last bit of data disturbed him the most. Why had he always simply assumed he was capable of fathering a child? Until recently he had felt absolutely certain, but this certainty had been based solely on his refusal to become a father. What if he couldn't? Klara quoted findings on chronic infertility according to which in 50 percent of the cases the man was the guilty party. Now, after the death of his father, he wanted to know whether he was capable of having children—in case he did want one.

One Monday morning Eduard got up at seven o'clock. The alarm was an unwelcome reminder that on this particular day he was expected in a laboratory as the subject, and not the director, of an experiment. His doctor had handed him a plastic beaker and a small piece of paper describing the procedure. It did not, however, offer any practical advice as to how to maneuver the sample into the tiny cup. Eduard knew how to remove the most inaccessible sections of tissue from the body of a mouse. But he was baffled as to how he should go about producing a secretion which as far as he knew had never been elicited by fantasizing about light microscopes.

He couldn't wake Klara to ask her to perform this unusual service. He had kept his intentions quiet; he wanted to wait until he had the results. In the search for an appropriately stimulating image he made a disturbing discovery: the scenarios he had tucked away in the museum of his sexual dreams suddenly seemed silly, the pitifully repetitive bunglings of a burned-out imagination. Neither the Sunday idyll which played in a colleague's country villa and which featured the lady of the house, who for some strange reason was standing naked beside the kitchen stove, stirring cherry marmalade, while Eduard kept her in rhythm from behind, nor the more daring picture of a three-way romp in the animal laboratory caused the slightest stir. All of a sudden this consistently gullible oaf, for whom no scenario was too clichéd, no plot too contrived, this quintessential simpleton was now making aesthetic demands, insisting on innovation, calling for art instead of Harlequin romance. But it was also possible that the test subject simply refused to participate in anything that might provide the slightest evidence against him. It wasn't until Eduard evoked a romantic scene from his schooldays—forest, meadows, cherry blossoms—that the examinee consented to a halfhearted cooperation.

Catching the milliliters in the plastic beaker proved difficult. With a bitter smile Eduard recalled the cheap laughter that accompanied Laurel and Hardy whenever Ollie turned the pot on Stan's head.

The doctor had impressed upon him that he had half an hour to convey his semen to the laboratory. He also advised Eduard to maintain it at body temperature, since cold air and drafts could further retard the already limited mobility of the sperm and negatively influence the test. Eduard remembered his ski glove, with its aluminum-reinforced filling—a by-product of NASA research—guaranteed to keep your hand warm even in outer space. He shoved the beaker into one of these wonders of technology, threw on his clothes, and raced out into the May morning, ski glove in hand.

The laboratory lay situated in a residential neighborhood on the outskirts of the city—a strange location for a place which had to be reached in half an hour! Anyone would agree that a fire station constructed twelve kilometers outside of town would constitute an error of urban planning. Concerned though he might be, Eduard was not quite ready to risk his life for the mobility of his sperm and buckled on his seat belt. He shoved the ski glove between his legs, where the sample was as close as it could be to the natural warmth of its origin, turned off the air conditioning, and roared away at breakneck speed. It felt strange to be escorting such atypical freight that morning, among all the drivers hauling wallpaper, drinks, electrical appliances, or simply labor. But honk as they might, Eduard refused to yield: besides, ice-cold Coca-Cola would keep better.

The longer he drove, the more certain he became that the sperm, which might have been happily frolicking about its beaker when he set out, was now beginning to tire. How could the little cells be expected to prove they had enough stamina to climb Fallopian tubes if they first had to be dragged across the entire city? He knew from his readings that at least a hundred thousand sperm per milliliter had to start moving in order for one to reach its goal.

Low houses surrounded by yards and gardens signaled that he had arrived at the neighborhood in question. Still, it seemed unlikely that the house which matched the address on the little piece of paper could be the laboratory, hidden as it was behind a small forest of exotic ornamental trees. Children playing in the yard testified to the fertility of the owners. Eduard got out of the car and crossed over to a wooden annex—the closest thing around to a laboratory. When some horses poked their heads through the open cracks and started sniffing at his ski glove, he realized he must have made a mistake. Evidently the founding fathers had named more than one street after the popular Prussian queen. Checking a city map, he located a second street with the same name, in the district adjacent to his own.

As he drove back he was overcome by a benevolent feeling of indifference. It was all the same to him whether the sperm in the beaker could display any motility at all by the end of the journey. He'd just hand over the beaker with its heap of half-dead cripples and resist all temptation to extract a fresh sample. Of course, it might not make any sense to even go through with the test. But he was eager for a result even if it was bound to be inexact. Maybe his sperm stayed active after thirty-five minutes; who could know?

The laboratory assistant, a woman, received him as if he were a sales representative hawking unwanted wares. She asked when he had produced the ejaculation. When he answered she cast a slightly reproachful glance at the clock: he was exactly four minutes too late. She checked the doctor's referral, inspected the label on the plastic beaker, and arranged his sample neatly in a row with other, identical beakers. Dr. Nastase would inform him of the result. The image of the labeled beakers accompanied Eduard on his ride home. Inside one of those transparent beakers, which looked so much alike they could be easily mistaken, an oracle was waiting to be heard.

6

EDUARD DIDN'T BELIEVE IN THE STARS, but he did think about them from time to time. For him the heavenly bodies were a mixture of gaseous, liquid, and solid matter, and the fact that the human organism was generally constructed from the same material had always been enough to satisfy any need for a connection—until now.

Since he had been sleeping on his back, he suspected he had fallen under the influence of some malevolent star which was beaming unfavorable rays right into his exposed chest. Things were suddenly happening to him he used to think could happen only to others. He recently awoke with a partially dislocated jaw, which he had to open and shut like a nutcracker until the ball of the joint jumped back into its socket. A few days later he fell victim to a rash that enjoyed playing hide-and-seek: scarcely had the little red pimples disappeared from his shoulder than they popped up once again, a yard downstream as the blood flows, on the back of his knee.

His doctor was unable to provide him with any satisfactory information. Instead of prescribing a fast-working ointment or a package of tablets, the holistic healer lectured on the psychic origins of such a condition. Now, in addition to the itch, he acquired the plague of self-doubt. The two maladies exacerbated each other, so that every time he scratched, Eduard had the feeling that his fingernail was digging into his soul.

In the institute a slim student came bounding down the stairs, splaying his legs in such a way he almost scraped Eduard's head with his gym shoes. Laughing, the man jumped up and turned around, with neither excuse nor greeting, as if he expected Eduard to greet him.

Tell me, Dr. Hoffmann, what exactly is it you're working on? he asked in a tone that suggested he already knew the answer.

Good ideas should be kept quiet, as long as they're just ideas, said Eduard.

Rumor has it it's a very tricky project. Are you sure a security level of two is enough? There are people who are genuinely afraid of you.

Eduard didn't remember having seen the man in the institute before, this stair-tripper who wore a star stitched onto his leather jacket. His behavior seemed familiar enough, though, the antiauthoritarian tone, which harmonized well with "Hey, asshole"—a voice for choral shouts, in love with itself and accusatory, easily seduced by every slogan.

All insolence aside, the student's question demonstrated an alarming lack of expertise. The institute was always full of experiments that required sterile conditions. The security measures served more to protect the cell cultures from unwanted environmental influence than to guard the experimenters against murderous bacteria. Every researcher was always struggling to keep foreign germs out of his laboratory, germs that could interfere with the results of his experiment. One might not expect an ecologically minded student of German literature to realize that viral and bacterial cultures also required protection, for example from neophytes who went around blowing their noses inside the lab. But until then he had never encountered such ignorance in an employee of the institute.

No sooner had Eduard opened his office than he was called in to see the director. It was unusual for the secretary to summon him like that. He and Betty often met several times a day; at other times a whole week might pass without their meeting, but until now everything had always happened informally. More often than not, Betty would drop in and engage him in an amusing dialogue on any of three subjects: bacteria, the universe, or sex, the human version of which interested her least of all. She most enjoyed speculating about the love life of bacteria: she owed her advancement to her work on the replication of so-called F-plasmids. Ever since Joshua Lederberg proved that even single-celled microorganisms differ as to gender, the sexual life of bacteria and yeasts had become a serious subject of research. The rules by which such bacteria and yeast cells attracted and repelled each other had been only partially explained, a state of affairs that inspired Betty to bolder and bolder thought experiments. She enjoyed trying out her ideas on Eduard and jumping from the smallest things to the largest within the space of a single sentence. Recently she had astounded him with the assertion that stars were created male and female. Hadn't the ancient Greeks and their Arab pupils imbued the stars with sexually specific characteristics? She recalled the astrophysicist Fred Hoyle's theories of "engendered" material in certain "areas of conception." Eduard believed he remembered that the same Fred Hoyle had ultimately earned a name as a professional grumbler. For years he tortured the entire scientific community with the claim that the famous imprint of the prototypic bird Archaeopteryx in the Solnhofen limestone was really a hoax from the Victorian era.

Eduard liked the brilliant woman, whose face reminded him of an early photo of Rosalind Franklin. Betty abhorred clothes and costumes; she always wore a man's jacket over a dark T-shirt, pants, and pumps. Although she seemed little interested in emitting erotic signals, she did exert a surprising attraction: half the institute was in love with her. Her rejection of stereotypical female fashion-mindedness enabled a different kind of beauty to emerge. Her mobile mouth, which quietly spewed crystal-clear, logical deductions punctuated by long pauses, seemed to harbor a secret which aroused the curiosity of women as well as men.

But this time Betty was sitting behind her desk holding a notebook.

Dr. Hoffmann, what exactly is it you're working on at the moment? Is there an experiment I don't know about?

The formal address, which Betty was using very much against her custom, sounded ironic, but the question didn't seem rhetorical. The papers she was holding contained something which set the tone between them back by several years.

What makes you say that? asked Eduard, annoyed. Is someone suggesting I am?

I never would have suspected that you might have enemies. Betty blinked as she squinted at him. It looks as if somebody's out to get you.

She tossed the notebook on the desk, but didn't seem inclined to hand it to Eduard. Evidently she wanted to find out what he thought someone might be holding against him.

Presumably Eduard remembered that for about six months all kinds of things had been disappearing from the institute. Here a work report, there a diskette. A recent inspection revealed that seven laboratory journals had vanished since that time. It was curious that the missing documents mostly came from his department. Did Eduard have any idea who could be so very interested in what was going on there? Was there anything in the works that would interest a thief?

A thief? asked Eduard, surprised. He would be happy if a robber deemed his petri dishes worth the trouble.

Have you ever played the stock market? asked Betty. When you're buying, it's not the actual share value which is so important; you have to guess what thousands of other potential buyers think of that particular security. Genetic research works along similar lines. It's not enough for the researcher to know his experiment is harmless; unfortunately, he also has to consider how and whether he can convince public opinion that it is. Sensational reports on gene transfer and cloning have already caused trouble for other laboratories, and a rumor campaign targeted at Dr. Eduard Hoffmann and the dangerous experiments being conducted in his lab could have serious consequences.

Betty asked for a protocol on the current status of his projects and, reaching for the telephone, waved him out of the room.

The suspicion upset Eduard. Everyone in the institute knew that a few older lab journals had been mislaid over a long period of time, but no one had paid that much attention. On the contrary, the institute was proud of its reputation as a haven for the creatively untidy. Once it had happened that a very rare and expensive culture had been flushed down the toilet, along with a stamp from Mauritius honoring molecular biologists. On another occasion a student had come very close to smearing his sandwich with a highly infectious agar culture. No one ever discovered who had put the stuff in the common refrigerator for food and drink. The cleanup action that followed uncovered a bar of margarine four years beyond its date.

In this environment no one thought twice about a couple of missing lab journals. A thief hoping to discover sensational findings had obviously poorly researched the matter, since all the journals contained were some fairly pedestrian speculations.

The primary characteristic of Eduard's work was its uselessness. The majority of his projects fell into the category of basic science, and the most important source of inspiration for these experiments was, in Eduard's words, still the same *idée fixe* that had inspired Galileo four hundred years earlier to climb the tower in Pisa and simultaneously drop two objects of different weights: he simply wanted to see how they would fall relative to each other. The motive behind this eccentric performance had since become known as Thirst for Knowledge.

Eduard and his colleagues at the institute were examining the behavior of objects infinitely smaller than Galileo's falling bodies—bacteria, yeasts, chromosomes, molecules. But their motive was the same. The scientists wanted to understand how the tiny bodies behaved in a specific situation, and it made absolutely no difference whether the knowledge gained was of any use or not. In fact, Eduard contended that if you squinted so as to discern the ready application, you automatically narrowed your vision and obstructed your entire thought process.

He considered basic researchers a strange lot, something like a worldwide fraternity of monks. They invested their efforts, their inventive talent, their health, and incidentally significant sums of money in undertakings that promised little

except knowledge, and at best prestige. Because this particular thirst for knowledge was rarely encountered, it tended
to provoke suspicions concerning the scientists' "true" intentions.

Economic and military applications of basic research—
generally the chance by-products of some experiment—were
always being imputed to the scientists, *ex post facto*, as their
goals. According to this logic, Niels Bohr was thinking about
the atom bomb when he developed his model of the atom,
and Watson and Crick were driven by the ambition to create
a "new man" when they deciphered the structure of DNA.
The scientists were declared to be the fathers of those mon-
sters who had come into the world as the unwanted children
of their drive to discover. Among politicians who allocated
the subsidies for research, this misunderstanding in turn led
to scurrilous practices and schemes. They obviously didn't
realize that the money would be best used if thirst for knowledge remained undistracted by hunger for power, the com-
pulsion to save the world, or other influences alien to the
field of study. Cancer research had ground up millions without producing significant results. Meanwhile, the experts realized that new breakthroughs in the etiology of cancer
would occur where people hadn't already looked: in virology
and molecular genetics. Many useful scientific discoveries
had happened unintentionally—lucky numbers on the rou-
lette wheel of knowledge, subject to the play of thought and
curiosity. Eduard believed that nature unlocks her secrets
only to those who approach it without pressing intentions.
And the reward for all the hard work lay somewhere between
an ulcer and the Nobel Prize.

Eduard was conducting a long-term project about cell se-
nescence, which hadn't brought him much of anything ex-

cept gray hairs. But like everyone else at the institute, he was plugging away at two or three more worldly ventures. These he named like horses at a racetrack—"Erika," "Montparnasse," and "Karajan"—and hoped someday to apply for a patent. The utility of these experiments defied all calculation. And just because in principle every experiment could lead either to a footnote in a professional journal or to a revolutionary discovery, the disappearance of a few lab journals could be ascribed to anything from mere slovenliness to intervention by the secret police.

As he was compiling his lab notes on his diverse projects into a readable report, he realized there was one document missing. For a limited time he had been working on an experiment designed to uncover the pathogen responsible for multiple sclerosis. A project with modest chances of success. To begin with, the idea that there was such a pathogen was itself controversial, and even more so was Eduard's presumption that it was a so-called endogenous viral defect. Such pathogenic genes did exist, of course, in mice and chickens, but had not yet been proven to inhabit humans as well.

In keeping with the regulations, he had registered his proposal with the ethics commission and received permission to proceed. But the written notice was gone. Because he kept all documents concerning current experiments stored in his desk, the loss was a puzzling one. He wrote a letter to the ethics commission kindly requesting a copy of the mislaid paper.

7

ALL OF A SUDDEN the weather was up to its old winter tricks; the skies again stiffened into the motionless, cement-gray canopy that always runs up the suicide rate—which is high enough to begin with—between the months of November and May.

The Monday Void reigned in The Tent: a few single men and women perched at the bar seemed engrossed in the assortment of bottles behind the counter, while a Turkish couple in festive dress was sitting among the empty tables. People said that the two came every Monday to celebrate the anniversary of their first meeting. People also made bets as to exactly how soon the inevitable Monday would arrive when only one would be sitting at the table.

Eduard was just about to turn around when he discovered André at the bar, nursing a glass of red wine, alone, surrounded by taciturn singles, without the slightest prospect of a flirt: Eduard had never seen him like that.

Postwar forever, André mocked: exhausted men, dangerous women. Have you seen Theo?

Eduard shook his head.

I don't ever see him, André explained, and I don't want to, either. I think alcohol is gradually eating away the rest of his brain cells, don't you agree? All he can do anymore is stammer. He was recently spouting a lot of unqualified nonsense about my concert for percussion with orchestra.

He is too quick to judge, agreed Eduard.

Too quick? He's talking out of his ear; his judgments are based on complete ignorance. He didn't even go, and I can prove it. The tickets to the opening which I had reserved under his name were never picked up at the box office.

Maybe he went to the second performance, said Eduard.

Don't be ridiculous; he flew to New York for the film festival.

To New York? asked Eduard. The last time I met him he told me he was on his way to the theater festival in Avignon.

He probably flew from the theater festival in Avignon straight to the film festival in New York, said André. Why does he still insist on living behind the Wall, anyway? Sheer coquetry. He travels more than anybody I know in the West.

Probably because he lives on the other side of the Wall, said Eduard.

You're defending him. As far as I'm concerned, his various allures are beginning to wear thin. He's bursting with ambition. Do you know what weighs most on the mind of this great socialist writer? He's already fighting tooth and nail to make sure his name appears in letters as large as my own on the poster for the opera which I'm composing. And he hasn't even written the libretto yet.

It was always like that whenever Eduard met one or the other of them: the first mean word always applied to the missing third party. As the only scientist in the trio, Eduard invariably felt he was the outsider. André and Theo were collaborating on a Don Giovanni project with the working title "The Unchastened Libertine." The concept was in a state of permanent revision because the authors' constantly

changing love lives kept influencing their view of the protagonist. Whenever Eduard heard the two of them arguing
about their ideas, he secretly congratulated himself on having abandoned all desire to become an artist when he was
ten years old. But he had learned to take the occasional "permanent" breaks between the two of them with a shaker of
salt. Despite their constant quarreling they stuck to each
other with a tender malice. Both treated Eduard with the
usual respect artists have for scientists, a respect rooted in
the conviction that the natural sciences are too lofty for ordinary mortals. Whenever the opportunity arose, Eduard
would repeat that genetic research is a jigsaw puzzle for
grown-up children; he was absolutely certain that within
three months he could teach any grade-school dropout all he
needed to know in order to start setting up his own experiments. While Theo and André stuck to their complex with
an almost religious conviction, they also exacted their revenge by declaring Eduard to be a dilettante in the areas of
art and love. For his part, Eduard willingly conceded that the
first aspect of the artists' complex was completely justified:
it was without a doubt easier for a scientist to grasp the
essence of *Don Giovanni* than for a poet to comprehend the
double helix.

André suddenly looked tired. For days the title *Accidental
Death of an Anarchist* had been going around in his head—
had Eduard seen the play? He didn't know it either, but the
title was a pretty accurate indication of what he was feeling
at the moment.

Esther? asked Eduard.

André nodded.

I'm getting married, he said, and a triumphant smile flitted
across his face. At the same time he grabbed Eduard's arms

as tightly as if an abyss had suddenly opened beneath his bar stool, and looking for a place to plant his feet, he stomped on Eduard's own foot so hard that Eduard cried out.

What happened? asked Eduard.

André explained.

The day after their last evening together in The Tent, André had taken the train to Paris for his premiere. He had spent his days there in bed, mostly on the phone with Esther. Although he couldn't get her to have anything to do with a contract of mutual disloyalty, he did manage finally—after substantially enriching the phone company—to persuade her to set a new date for the wedding.

When he returned to their shared five-room apartment, all he could recognize was the address. The entire building looked as if it had been picked up and deposited a thousand miles east: the tall rooms were filled with the smell of vodka, onions, and fish, and he tripped over open suitcases everywhere he turned. Hatboxes and plastic bags crowned swaying towers of unpacked containers, which came crashing down on him at the slightest provocation, much to the delight of the many children milling about. For her part, Esther greeted him as enthusiastically as if he had survived a train catastrophe.

André had seen Esther's parents once before, in a photograph she carried as a keepsake, but that picture had not shown any of the numerous relatives who now greeted him in the hall of their apartment. Before he even had a chance to survey the scene, Esther's father put him in a body-lock embrace and forced him to exchange the kiss of brotherhood. When André looked at the sturdy old man, with his strong calves bulging down from his short pants, he realized that while this new relative was ready to rescue him from any danger, he could not save his son-in-law-to-be from the wild hopes he had brought with him.

How in the world, André asked himself, had Esther been able to keep herself so elfin, so delicate, surrounded by all these overweight relatives? Or would her figure, too, follow her mother's example, a few years down the road?

The family's emigration had come as a surprise; Esther was no more prepared than André for the multiple arrivals. Even so, after a few days she managed to relocate the two aunts, together with their small and large children, in a small pension nearby. The move itself seemed to leave Esther's father, Yuri, feeling orphaned. He kept pacing from room to room, shaking his head and using his heavy legs to measure the length and width, then proclaiming with his rolling *r*: This cannot be, 170 square meters? In Russia we living eight people in single room.

Using Yuri's formula, André made a rough calculation of the number of relatives ripe for emigration who could fit into his apartment, and quickly changed the subject. Yuri turned over the afghan rug for the third time: How much you pay? Thousand mark? I have nose for this, you can to buy twenty for same price.

Esther's mother was able to talk him out of the twenty afghan rugs, but not out of trusting his nose with other purchases. Yuri never left the house without coming back loaded down with plastic bags, three in each hand, all filled to the point of bursting. Within a few weeks he had become the star of the Turkish vegetable and meat markets. Whenever the shopkeepers saw him in the distance, they nodded their heads and greeted him from all directions: Good morning, Yuri Marenkov; how are you, Herr Yuri Marenkov; long life to you, Herr Yuri Marenkov. Yuri would wave to them, wrap his arm around André's shoulder, and declare proudly: Everything my friend. The snippets of German he managed to learn had an unmistakable Turkish accent.

From the bags he toted home each morning, Yuri prepared his favorite dishes: enormous amounts of salt herring and lox, as well as cucumbers, onions, tomatoes. Soon he had found a source for beluga caviar and was shoveling spoonfuls of the substance into the mouth of his son-in-law, who couldn't stand caviar of any kind. Yuri's loving care was impossible to resist. Scarcely had Esther and André cleaned the platter of hors d'oeuvres than Yuri refilled it, interpreting every protest as a discreet request for a second helping.

His trust in his own talents as a buyer inevitably led him from the food stores to the flea markets, where he converted the money he received from the welfare office into a constant stream of wedding presents. On his very first trip he returned with a set of plates adorned with the painted images of Paganini, Lehár, and Johann Strauss, each of whom he considered André's predecessors. André had to work hard to dissuade him from mounting the plates on the walls of his studio. In a short time Yuri's purchases began to fill the apartment: gold- and silver-plated samovars, babushkas in all sizes, fur slippers and fur caps, fake icons, brilliantly colored bathrobes, polar bear and marten furs. Yuri gave out of the fullness of his heart and the emptiness of his pockets; no matter how much money he left the house with, it had vanished completely by the time he came back. Of course, he was convinced each time that he had struck a tremendous bargain; every one of his distinctive purchases had been acquired, after merciless haggling, at rock-bottom prices. The fact that someone might not want to surround himself with all the things that could be bought for half price—this he did not understand.

Only gradually did André realize that Yuri's moving care, his almost superstitious admiration, was not entirely free of expectation. Esther's father firmly believed that his son-in-law was capable of solving virtually all the problems that beset his extended family—visas, welfare petitions, residency permits, insurance—and he repaid André's efforts in his own currency: with a generous heart and lifelong friendship. His attachment to André took on increasingly bizarre forms; he was convinced that his health and happiness depended on André's presence in the city and that as soon as André left town all the misfortunes of the world might come crashing down on him. He looked on in horror whenever André ordered a plane ticket over the phone, and was more urgent than Esther in asking about the exact day and hour of his return. André felt overwhelmed by Yuri's trust and tried desperately to use connections which he first had to create.

During this time he came to know Esther better and appreciate her even more. Only now did he realize how much it must have cost her to tear herself away from her familiar surroundings and become the highly ironic and slightly crazed city creature he had fallen in love with. At times she was a little hard on her parents, so that André was forced to act as a go-between. It went so far that André wound up asking Esther for a little more patience in putting up with certain of Yuri's habits: her father was always going around the apartment wearing nothing but a pair of gym shorts from Yale University—a practice which brought André himself to the verge of despair. Apart from that, Esther did everything she could to relieve André of some of the burden. Over his objection she took on two additional evening classes at her language institute, in order to help with the additional expenses incurred by Yuri's buying sprees. Long before André, Esther had recognized the danger that can threaten love whenever it begins to resemble a welfare office.

While the encounter between East and West in the five-room apartment definitely furthered André's understanding and admiration for Esther, it did not deepen his desire. When they first met he had found her mysterious, he had discerned within her traces of a different culture, he had been drawn to her foreign way of looking at the world. Often he had no idea exactly what she was thinking; she kept him guessing; her perceptions and reactions were unpredictable. But now that the distance between East and West had shrunk to fit within the 170 square meters of his apartment, he longed to return to the earlier state of guessing.

The arrival of Esther's family seemed to render the quarrel over loyalty and candor meaningless. Occasionally, when he was waiting in the lobby of some local bureaucrat, he had the suspicion that Esther would overlook whatever escapade might come his way as long as he could provide her family with room and board. At the same time, Esther began to make him feel uneasy more and more often, although he couldn't tell whether this feeling was more disappointment or jealousy. A strange reversal took place: not Esther, but André felt suddenly neglected, deceived, even cuckolded, except that the cause of his torment was not another man but one of man's best friends.

By far the most irksome part of Esther's potential dowry was her dog, Caesar. At first the only thing André had noticed about him was his eccentric habit of stretching his hind legs out behind him, like a pig, instead of storing them under his belly when he lay down, so that André immediately began to question Caesar's canine credentials. But the beast also displayed talents which would have been at home in the circus; he greeted all his guests with one of two gender-specific rituals. For women he performed a kind of courtly bow which consisted of bending his left front leg and gallantly stretching back his right; men were welcomed by a nod of his woolly head. Esther's mother maintained that Caesar had invented these ritual greetings himself, Yuri referred to an earlier existence at the home of a Polish prince who had been dispossessed by the Communists. Wherever he might have learned his chivalrous manners, it soon became apparent that they had not survived the move to the West completely intact. After a few weeks Caesar could no longer distinguish women from men; suddenly he started nodding affably to Esther and bowing gallantly even to the shirtless, hirsute Yuri. A further symptom of mental confusion soon became evident. As long as he remained inside a room Caesar moved about entirely normally, but once he wanted to move from one room to the other, he seemed to go completely lame. He would lie down on his stomach, stretch out all fours in his own swinish style, droop his ears, whimper to melt your heart, and refuse to budge no matter how hard you implored him.

André was amazed by how much the dog's strange behavior upset Esther. Each time the dog lay whimpering on one of the many thresholds, uncertain which way to turn, Esther would let out a little cry, kneel next to him, and whisper sweet Russian nothings in such a way—so André believed— as to make the animal an addict. Esther just brushed aside such reproaches and wouldn't let André rest until he had accompanied both her and the dog to an animal psychiatrist. At the clinic the patient was officially diagnosed as balophobic: Caesar suffered from the fear of thresholds, he wanted to be carried, possibly for the rest of his life, in any case over every threshold.

Esther insisted on psychotherapy.

The therapist came twice a week. After six hours of individual analysis he actually succeeded in getting Caesar to place first his left and then his right paw on the threshold, although the dog acted as if he were being made to walk on hot coals. The concern with which Esther followed every millimeter of the dog's progress drove André crazy. He never saw her anymore but with the dog on her lap; whenever he sat or lay down next to her, the dog would come and wedge himself between them. It wasn't the beast *per se* that bothered André so much as Esther's willing indulgence of its brazen insolence. Not only did she allow him to slobber all over her; she even returned the affection by scratching his belly, pursing her lips, and showering him with tender phrases André himself had never heard. He had to resort to threats to convince her that the dog had no business in their bedroom. Even so, at night, when André began to make overtures to Esther, Caesar would break in with his howling three thresholds away, so that Esther would rise like a somnambulist, leaving André in a stiff state of despair, not to return until he had fallen back asleep amid thoughts of revenge.

At some point André remembered who was footing the bill: since the canine therapy cost no less than biped analysis—which André himself felt more and more in need of—he broke off Caesar's treatment.

After Esther's mother flew to Chicago to visit a relative, Yuri underwent a change. He made fewer expeditions to the various markets, and in general seemed loath to leave the house. Esther took off every morning at six-thirty to teach her language courses and didn't come back until the evening. So André was left to spend the day alone with Yuri and Caesar. One morning he heard muted three-note violin chords coming out of Yuri's room and steeled himself for some new and deadly acquisition such as a boom box. But then the melody suddenly broke off and was repeated, only a little faster this time, but with perfect phrasing. André opened the door and discovered Yuri whirling barefoot around the room clutching a violin under his chin and playing the schmalzy Yiddish songs which André had listened to as a child on his parents' records. Yuri's technique was sloppy, he lost entire half-tones because he didn't use resin, but he played with the wonderful clarity and forceful flair of a born talent.

When André saw the half-naked old man twirling around with his violin, which Yuri held without any padding, when he heard the unresined bow transform the instrument into an orchestra, he felt that Yuri had come into the world with this very violin which he had grafted onto his body as it grew. Yuri sensed that André was watching him; what he did not realize was that from that day on he had won his son-in-law's heart.

The two men now began to take Caesar out together on his midday walk. Outside, the dog acted as if he had an invisible leash; whenever he dashed ahead of them he would stop after a few meters and wait for his master to call him back; occasionally he would lift his leg by a tree, but forget what he was supposed to do there, and then trot on off. Yuri himself grew more and more sedate; his booming joviality faded into quiet speech, and for the first time André could remember, he began to ask questions.

Recently he had been walking alongside his wife, when all at once her steps had seemed so loud to him, so piercing.

Every step is stab in heart. Inside the café he suddenly embraced André, pointed to their reflection behind the counter, and said: We both still young! Forty years we live still! Why to marry?

André didn't lose a beat in providing him with several answers, but Yuri refused to be satisfied with any.

8

ALTHOUGH HE HADN'T TOLD KLARA about the test, Eduard sensed that she was waiting for the results as impatiently as he was. A kind of unnegotiated cease-fire set in, apparently designed to maintain the status quo, with the result that both parties hoped for some event, some outside push or impetus that would accelerate their feelings. Meanwhile, they wore themselves ragged in domestic squabbling. Klara developed a peculiar animosity for the slightest imprecision or exaggeration on the part of Eduard or his friends. A quarrel ensued if he spooned his spaghetti sauce the wrong way, confused the name of a street, or forgot what hour a store opened—such incidents provoked a firmness of stance he missed elsewhere. While Klara considered it absolutely unforgivable for him to lose or even misplace a key, it was quite forgivable for him to weasel out of answering the question of whether he loved her. For his part, Eduard couldn't bear certain phrases Klara began using, like "It really has been beautiful." But it was mostly her restraint that tried his patience, her insistence on going to bed "punctually," her tendency to declare something over and done with when it was just beginning—Have you ever once in your life decided to spend all day doing just one thing, have you ever said to hell with it all, nothing else matters today? The turtleneck sweater, the long scarf she tied around her neck even when the weather was unseasonably warm, her prophylactic lifestyle.

One time he saw her on the street, sneaked up behind her, and grabbed her arm so that she couldn't know who was touching her. Her lack of reaction amazed him; her only defense was to ignore the provocation, and he wondered whether this was how she would deal with a real danger. Sometimes, when he watched her sitting and listening to his friends with an absentminded gaze, he had the impression that she was pining over an ancient wish she no longer even dared name. But wasn't he himself the cause of all the half-heartedness he was protesting? Hadn't he haggled with her until she lowered all her demands, her hopes? Even when we're no longer together, Klara once told him, I will always stand by you. What if not his own frugality drove her to declare her love the way she did, while simultaneously declaring their impending separation?

Or were both simply experiencing—independently of their own will or behavior—the laws of transience formulated by Theo? They had been together over three years, in a few months they would reach the ominous one hundred sixty-seventh day of the critical fourth year. Until now he had never considered that the average half-life of love relationships, which he had calculated in such detail, might also apply to him and Klara.

The same old hassle with the mailman: he didn't start wheeling his bicycle through his delivery zone until just before noon. Whenever he took his mandatory vacation and was replaced by a substitute, the whole street sighed with relief: everything important or unimportant was in the box by 9 a.m. But the moment the three weeks were up, the official post retarder would again retrace his snail-paced rounds. Eduard generally didn't leave the house between nine and ten, and since he consistently stayed a little longer at the institute, he often didn't retrieve his letters until late in the evening.

Eduard's relationship with the mail was not free from irrational tendencies. He considered an unexpected letter more important than one he was waiting for. Nor did it have to be an invitation to Harvard or a communication from the Nobel committee. Greetings from a forgotten friend, compliments from some colleague on one of his publications, a love letter from an anonymous student, these were the modest surprises he hoped the mail would bring. For people who no longer pray, the mailman is the true providential deliverer, the last emissary from the beyond, the only angel to alight on a rung of the career ladder. With a little bit of imagination and a minimum of effort, Eduard thought, the post office should be able to make allowances for its metaphysical mission. A modest ceremony at the doorway, a bit of glitter and tinkering of bells, some silk braid or even a purple robe affixed to the uniform would help a lot.

But even if one dropped demands like that and insisted only on the official duties, the man assigned to Eduard's neighborhood was clearly miscast. If this person had any metaphysical contact at all, it was probably with ghosts from the most recent German past. He looked as though he had stepped down from the pedestal of some heroic Nazi sculpture by Arno Breker and slipped into the gray uniform of the Deutsche Post: the dark Teutonic forehead, the heroic chin, the dumb determination in his eyes; you could almost hear him marching in step and singing the Horst Wessel Lied.

One Saturday, ten days after the semen test, Eduard stopped the man on the street and explained that he, Eduard, considered himself the victim of a one-sided delivery route. After so many years couldn't the mailman begin his rounds on the other side? The answer was unintelligible but clearly garbled. For a brief moment Eduard saw his opportunity: evidently the hated carrier consumed one bottle of high-proof spirits for every dozen addresses. But no sooner did Eduard begin to imagine his complaint to the postal author-ities than the whole project foundered due to his aversion to denunciations. This quintessentially German crime was per-missible only against Fascists, if even then. The mailman's resemblance to the Arno Breker hero did not constitute suf-ficient proof, and besides, if it did, it fit too many uniformed people. But the thought that of all people it was this model Aryan who would deliver the urgently awaited verdict on his potency—this thought alone caused Eduard to break out in a cold sweat. The only way he could hope to receive good news from this particular mailman was to close his eyes. The mere touch of the man's hand seemed to turn all letters into funeral announcements, demand notes, forfeitures, and pe-nalties.

Eduard was prepared for the worst when this grim reaper of postal sorrow appeared at his door one morning asking for a signature. Before he released the piece of paper, the carrier demanded to see identification.

But you know me, said Eduard, annoyed.

Doesn't make any difference, mumbled the mailman.

In his rage Eduard couldn't find his passport and instead presented the mailman with an opened envelope bearing his address.

I.D., please!

I don't know you either, I've never known you at all! Eduard cried out, you don't exist, you're gone, I swear it!

Unmoved, the man wrote out a collection ticket and handed it to Eduard. Eduard read the entry above the hours for pickup: ". . . excepting date of attempted delivery."

9

FOLLOWING HIS MORNING ENCOUNTER with the mailman, the rest of Eduard's day passed just as unpleasantly. Betty claimed she couldn't decipher his numbers, his sevens looked like ones and his sixes were easily mistaken for eights. Moreover, many entries in his lab journals were incomplete. He offered to help her read them, but she cut him off. Nothing would be gained by her mastering his handwriting; other readers less well predisposed toward him also had to make sense of his notes. Even though it was getting late, this was obviously not the day to drive straight home after work.

Things were hopping in The Tent. Theo was standing at the bar arguing with various visible and invisible opponents.

What do they mean "360 innocent passengers"—that's a strange adjective to use: the opposite wouldn't make any sense at all: "360 guilty passengers." Go ahead and compare the two, here, right under "civilians, innocent."

Eduard recalled the headline he had read that morning at the newsstand: KOREAN AIRLINER SHOT DOWN BY SOVIETS and guessed what Theo was going on about.

It was murder, cold-blooded mass murder! shouted Theo's opponent, with a conviction that drained his face white. But Theo seemed unmoved.

The jumbo jet which had ostensibly "strayed" was being

observed by an American surveillance aircraft flying at an altitude of sixty thousand feet, he insisted, the jet was really taking a planned detour to enable the CIA to test the Soviet defense capability. What would the Americans have done in a similar situation—imagine a Soviet reconnaissance plane flying over Key West or approaching Miami—do you think they would have politely looked the other way?

Eduard was never sure whether Theo really believed what he was arguing at any given moment. He had noticed his friend's habit of taking the most extreme viewpoint on any given situation, as a matter of principle, in order to achieve the greatest possible distance from his speaking partner and challenge whatever his opponent—or he himself—considered absolutely certain. A city which could boast two irreconcilable versions of the news seemed the perfect place for Theo's conversational strategy. Often all it took was for Theo to argue the Eastern perspective in the West and the Western perspective in the East in order to achieve his goal. Naturally the Wall itself hardly ever came up in the various discussions and debates that went on in The Tent, but its shadow was long enough to reach the farthest corner of the most out-of-the-way pub; its presence was like that of the Old Testament God, who has no name and whose likeness may not be replicated. For Theo, the state on the other side of the Wall, which kept expelling him like an indigestible stone, was a hated object of love, with whom he lived in a condition of permanent separation. But even the violence of the rejection contained a devotion he missed in the West. Over there he was feared; here he was simply around. It irritated him that you could say whatever you wanted in The Tent with impunity, that there was no one there who was at least writing things down. Again and again he would strike out against an imaginary limit; but the more violently he struck, the further that limit seemed to recede.

Have you all been brainwashed? he went on. Why is it you believe everything the CIA tries to pass off on you? Your touted freedom of the press is really nothing but propaganda, with the mass approval of the readership!

From the other end of the room someone started to clap, a few guests rose from their tables and moved closer, half a dozen speakers demanded the floor, finally the level of noise showed that something was at stake once more. It had been a long time since a headline had caused such an uproar.

It was an attack, said somebody, a carefully planned, secret attack on Soviet security. Nonsense, countered someone else, knocking over a beer glass, the North Koreans were using the Americans to shoot down 360 South Koreans. The Soviets, exclaimed a third party, shoving the second away from the bar, are a peace-loving people and have no desire to shoot. But unfortunately they don't understand much about antiaircraft technology, and in their haste they mistakenly fired live missiles instead of warning flares. Their equipment is corroded, their personnel drunk, it's a wonder their planes even fly!

You're all crazy, a woman wearing black leather pants began to scream. You're murderers yourselves, it doesn't matter to you in the least if 360 people get bumped off just like that; the main thing is that you have an explanation why! With your beards and rimless glasses, you're all still the same, still in love with death; the Germans never change, you have Fascism in your bones, and your mania for explaining things, your twisted thinking, your pseudo-sensitive, acquired stutter, it's all a disguise. You still are and always will be mass murderers! I'm going.

Theo seemed satisfied with the chaos he had created. He took Eduard by the arm and dragged him away from the bar to an empty table by the window.

Have you seen André?

Eduard made a vague gesture. He realized Theo wasn't expecting him to answer the question.

As far as I'm concerned I've broken off all contact with him. Recently he's been putting on such airs, don't you agree? He gets one or two good reviews of his piece for percussion and orchestra—which incidentally I find pretty disgusting—and suddenly thinks he's a genius.

Do you know it? asked Eduard.

No, I don't, said Theo with a disarming smile, but I don't like it. His last work for four trombones with orchestra was enough for me, with all those cheap effects. What I can't abide anymore is his megalomania. He wants to put his two cents' worth into everything, he corrects every single line I give him. I can't judge how good his French is, but he doesn't have the slightest feeling for German. He should write his own libretto.

Eduard mentioned André's impending wedding, but Theo's mind seemed elsewhere; after a few sentences he wasn't even listening anymore.

Did you ever run into the wedge-wolf yourself? he asked. I mean the man André was talking about. I'm just about convinced he's expanded his field of operations to the other side of the Wall.

Eduard looked at Theo in disbelief.

What happened? he asked.

The whole thing's ridiculous, it's unbelievable, Theo said. No, forget it, it's impossible to even tell the story.

Pauline? asked Eduard.

Theo stared in front of him, then jumped up, bought a cigar at the bar, and artfully puffed a few Arabic letters into the air.

It just can't be, he said, and began.

Theo had begun his marriage experiment immediately after the three friends had last met. The well-known signs of weariness were already long in evidence—an apple core left lying around set off a sudden fit of rage, one of Theo's hairs found in her hairbrush made Pauline want to vomit, she began to close the bathroom door. Theo, on the other hand, resisted sharing first the bedcovers, then the bed. Difficulties with work were accompanied by allergies and rashes; a ballpoint pen lent but never returned awakened urgent thoughts of separation. Traditional cures offered no improvement. The favorite Western household remedy, "temporary separation," was impossible due to the housing shortage. The only family counselor Theo knew was the official at the housing bureau, whose constantly shaking head prescribed only one cure: forced marriage. Psychoanalysis was not available, since the party refused to recognize the existence of the unconscious. A shared trip to Poland, distraction provided by a new love, the flight to same-sex partners or animal companions— they'd both been there and done it in seven previous marriages, all told. Convinced that the only way to save their love was to try something radical, something utterly new, they decided not to sleep with each other for an entire year. Not that they agreed to total abstinence; the vow of chastity was confined to the marriage. Both were of the opinion that if their union was worth continuing, it could withstand occasional affairs.

Pauline did make one condition which puzzled Theo: she

insisted on strict spiritual loyalty. An "alienation of the soul" would hurt her far more than any sexual escapades. For some time she had had the suspicion that the inner center of his feeling and desire had been displaced. The frequency of his visits to the West strangely contradicted his monotonous assurance that the visits weren't really worth it. He could no longer put her off with his bloodless formulas about West German "post-Fascism." She wanted uncensored reports, details of experience. Judgments and opinions bore me, she claimed, I want to hear stories. And in case Theo's intellectual and other appetites should take up permanent residence in the West, she expected to be told.

Theo had agreed without really understanding what she meant. For two months the spouses lived together in chaste harmony. The new rules led to strange and often embarrassing developments. The attempt to change erotic habits back into taboos *a posteriori* kept ending in relapses, and often their reflexes failed to keep pace with their intentions. They had the least trouble honoring their agreement in bed. In fact, they even felt a salutory effect from not having to prove themselves to each other every night. Controlling the intimate rituals of married routine proved far more difficult. Time and again Theo would greet Pauline by placing his hand distractedly on her buttocks, and time and again Pauline would push his hand away. Alternatively, Theo found himself forced to resist Pauline's bad-mannered habit of opening his zipper out of sheer boredom as they watched the Western evening news. In turn, she would forbid him to join her in the shower uninvited. But the first results were gradually becoming visible. They managed to reverse the erotic indifference of the nudist beach, which always takes over whenever two lovers set up house, by consistently keeping themselves covered. At night Pauline switched off the light before she undressed, and for the first time in his life Theo discovered both the sense and the virtues of a bathrobe. After some time the two lived in their shared apartment like two strangers who had been thrown together by some catastrophe such as war, earthquake, or atomic meltdown.

So skillfully did Pauline keep herself hidden from Theo that it was weeks before he again caught a glimpse of her naked, when he secretly peeked through the crack of the opaque glass window in the bathroom door. Her appearance blinded him, the whirling image pulsing in a thousand points excited him, he suddenly felt as if Pauline had been painted by Monet.

As grotesque as the experiment the two were conducting may have seemed, it was successful. Long unlearned feelings of shame sprang back to life, mutual respect grew, and a lost feeling of longing, even of excited expectation, occasionally resurfaced. Before falling asleep they would read Chinese love stories aloud to each other, and they began planning a trip to the province of Guangxi. To the astonishment of his envious colleagues in the League of Authors, Theo canceled a trip to the West for which he had just been granted permission. He secretly returned to a genre he had abandoned years before, the love poem, and found his verses bearable even after repeated reading.

The experiment was in its seventh week when Theo found a handwritten letter in his mailbox. It had been postmarked in the United States and was five pages long. An unknown person named Olympia mentioned a reading Theo had held in New York and an experience the two had shared right after the event, which involved rolling around the floor between the bookcases in the library of the Goethe Institute. Theo dimly recollected a similar episode, but believed it had taken place in the German Embassy in Stockholm. After an introduction like that, he was prepared for a feminist attack in the grand American style. To his surprise the author of the letter had nothing bad to say about the incident and proceeded to the real object of her letter. In animated, practically error-free German she offered an appraisal of his lyrical work along with a review of his love life. It appeared that Olympia had arrived at the conclusion that Theo was living a lie and as a result was writing one. Using selected passages she proved how Theo had betrayed his talent early on, with his second volume of poems; that deep down he was extinguished, fossilized; that his poetic hocus-pocus was really a pose and his socialist conviction a product of sexual hangups; she called him a "sado-Marxist." What struck her most about his latest work was the surfeit of rack-and-ruin metaphors, a rumbling, grumbling historical pessimism which claimed to hover high above the ideological borders between East and West but which upon closer inspection was firmly rooted in a mentality she branded "enlightened Stalinism." This and other signs of his irresistible decline she traced to his less than resolute choice to abide in a country where coded speech counted as art and a ban on publication served as proof of a book's quality. His real work still lay ahead of him, as he had yet to write about the most important things, namely, those events that concerned him personally, or if he had, it was only by omission: here she mentioned his first wife's fleeing to the West, his time in jail, his doubts concerning the idea of socialism.

Theo knew of actors, directors, and friends of the arts who regularly received mail from possessed admirers. The world was full of lunatics who, for lack of better options, lavished their need to communicate on random celebrities. He, too, had occasionally received "fan mail"—mostly negative—and had as a rule read it aloud to Pauline before tossing it in the wastebasket. Usually the accusatory letters ended with variations on the theme: "You must wonder why I hate you so passionately"—often accompanied by a request to pass on a first work to a publishing house.

But this letter was different. If Olympia was a megalomaniac, she was one with an astounding knowledge of detail. Theo had heard amazing stories about the ingenuity of American students; nonetheless, it remained a riddle how the distant letter writer had come in possession of so many of his texts and facts about his life. He almost had the impression he was the subject of a dossier. It was also conceivable that she was exacting her revenge for what happened between the book stacks in the Goethe Institute by writing a dissertation on him. As naïve and American as Olympia's attack was, it touched a chord. Theo had no doubt whatsoever that he might be falling for a trick used by gurus of all disciplines to attract disciples. For a temperamental person like him it was impossible to remain indifferent if a complete stranger said to his face: You are living completely wrong. It was not so much the diagnosis he found seductive as the implied promise that he could start all over again.

Against his custom he wrote a few lines back. He apologized for his behavior in the library. Books, anything printed, and especially completely white paper had an uninhibiting effect on him. As far as his Marxism was concerned, he considered the prefix "masoch-" more fitting. To be sure, he, like Olympia, was convinced that the socialism administered by

the stiff-necked fossils in his half-country would have to disappear. But for all that, he was more interested in the mistakes of history than in its success stories.

Olympia's second letter surprised him by taking a new
tone. She had hired a Chinese expert in California to construct a horoscope from his date of birth. Theo discovered
that according to Chinese astrology he was a dragon and
Olympia was an ape. The attached documents contained a
great deal of flattering material about his character and future prospects, but above all about the association Dragon–
Ape: "A couple no one will ever forget!" according to the
Chinese expert. "Together they propel each other from victory to victory, from success to success, they toss each other
flowers and love each other passionately. The dragon is en-
raptured to find a companion whose megalomania matches
his own . . ." To find out definitively whether a meeting between them had been preordained or not, she needed exact
information concerning the hour of his birth.

His mother had a hard enough time remembering his
name, Theo wrote Olympia, not to mention the hour of his
birth, so it seemed that whatever the stars had decreed for
Olympia and himself would have to remain forever in the
dark. As he was pasting the stamp on the envelope he heard
Pauline in the hallway. For no apparent reason he stuck
Olympia's letter in a book by Ernst Jünger which he had
smuggled in and kept hidden behind a row of books the Party
censors found more palatable. Later on, his secrecy annoyed
him: this gesture made him accomplice to an affair in which
his involvement thus far had been limited to that of addressee.

In her next letter Olympia suddenly started describing her
own love life. She suffered from an emotional division which

supposedly affected only men. She could be attracted either to the mind of a lover or else to his body, but seemed unable to get excited about both at once. For the last two years she had been living with an American professor of literature, a wonderfully talented and considerate human being. They had just agreed to get married when she met a man on campus she could only describe as a body double of Arnold Schwarzenegger. Without any intent or purpose she had engaged in a heavy flirt with this muscle man, and wound up helping him finish a paper on James Joyce—the man was much better equipped to tackle his opponents on the football field, which was why he had been accepted at the university in the first place. One night, at two-thirty in the morning, Schwarzenegger had knocked on her door, staggering drunk, and thrown himself on her. Although, technically speaking, it had verged on rape, she had to confess that she spent the most erotically exciting night of her life with Schwarzenegger, who, incidentally, after the first display of strength turned into the cuddliest teddy bear. "What should I do?" asked Olympia. "My professor now considers me a monster, my parents are threatening to disown me, my girl friends don't say hello, my psychoanalyst is talking about a split personality." Maybe it wasn't mere chance that she was opening herself up to a man from the East. With Theo she had the feeling that she could find both empathy and sexual audacity, tenderness and perversion, sophistication and exuberance.

Although Theo found Olympia's confessions more entertaining than her analysis of his work, he decided to send her a distancing letter. Her Schwarzenegger story revealed a certain courage, but it also angered him. He wrote that he was unquestionably not the man she was looking for. In fact, he was bound to disappoint her both with the size of his muscles as well as his knowledge of James Joyce—and had no aspirations to develop either. Consequently he was doomed to fail her fantasies in both extremes. Since she appeared to be writing a dissertation on him, it wouldn't be all that difficult for her to visit him and see for herself how mistaken she was. Incidentally, he completely understood her cuckolded professor. He, too, had something against women who, while holding high the banner of emancipation by day, at night succumb to the first best primate. In the P.S. he asked her to send a photo: just for my locker, he wrote.

In the next letter Olympia introduced herself to Theo from head to toe, though in writing only: she had not enclosed a photo. She described herself with an openness Theo couldn't believe. "I'm not even sure you like large breasts," she confessed, concerned, and: "I'm afraid I'm a whole head too tall for you! We'll have to hug each other on the staircase to touch in all the right places!" A masterpiece of sassiness. Theo didn't believe a word of it, but Olympia's self-conscious innocence charmed him. If he followed her description he was dealing with a happy mixture of Gertrude Stein and Marilyn Monroe. Apart from that, her self-portrayal displayed a sense of humor. She was already looking forward, she wrote, to the painful sprainings their difference in height would inflict upon them. For in reality she considered Theo polymorphously perverse, a highly talented lech, a frustrated Bataille, in truth, the dirty young man of the GDR. Naturally this aspect didn't show in his work. As a rule German literature showed a remarkable avoidance of anything impure, deviant, abnormal, or, pathetically put, evil. She had faith in her own ability to become Theo's muse in developing his talent for the obscene. But she was also afraid she might lose herself in a labyrinth of desire. Once certain boundaries have been crossed, there are no paths back into the garden plot of matrimonial cohabitation. By way of conclusion she conjured various scenarios—from romantic to absurd—as to how and where they would make love. They all showed a taste for improbable places.

During this time Theo went out more often than usual with Pauline. Having exhausted the thin volumes of Chinese romances, they were now reading French classics out loud to each other, including Stendhal's essay "On Love." The only thing that disturbed the idyll were Pauline's outbursts of sarcasm. It was enough for some long-legged blond creature to walk into the restaurant and out of the blue Pauline would start asking Theo questions: How did he like her, what was stopping him from getting up and trying his luck? Where did she even get such an idea, he hadn't even bothered to look at her! Pauline would smile as if she knew better. On the other hand, she refused to submit to the "interrogation" he wanted to subject her to after he saw her one day sitting in their own hangout, deep in conversation with a stranger wearing a parka; moreover, she found his alarming attention toward this "guy from the West" paranoid. Another time she annoyed him by observing that while their experiment probably wouldn't make their marriage any younger, it might at least lead him to a younger woman. But more than all her taunts and gibes, it was her kindness which most perplexed him, phrases like: I'm only asking, I can be allowed to risk a thought, too, can't I, just for once? Finally she wanted to know why Theo, who was always walking off into the Western sunset, never thought of simply staying there? No, she wasn't asking about plans, just about secret desires, the hintermost thoughts creeping around the cortex of his brain.

It irked Theo that Pauline was suddenly playing devil's advocate, since he felt the answers to all these questions were clear. Like most of the couples in their circle, Theo and Pauline considered themselves partisan cells fighting on two fronts: against the home-grown monster of socialism and the Darwinist alternative in the West. Some of Pauline's questions reminded him of Olympia's American directness, and he wondered whether he had left one of the letters from overseas lying on his desk for too long. If Pauline had read it, then she was right to be annoyed: in that case she would have known only Olympia's ungrounded declarations of love but not Theo's replies.

Theo decided to break off the relationship with Olympia —which he would have characterized as purely sexual— immediately and open Olympia's next letter right under Pauline's eyes and destroy it.

Instead of a letter he received a telegram: WEDNESDAY, 3 P.M., PRESSECAFÉ! LOVE!

At this point in his story Theo suddenly grabbed Eduard by the arm and pointed to a figure in a long, flowing silk coat standing outside the wall of windows. The man was peering searchingly into the interior of The Tent and for a moment he turned his face with its three-day growth of beard toward them, then quickly spun around and went on.

Was it him?

Who?

The wedge-wolf!

When André had told them about the wedge-wolf Eduard had thought he had recognized a loner whose workings he had himself once observed in The Tent. However, that man's body was a good deal slimmer and his beard a good deal thicker. Eduard shook his head and turned back to Theo, but his friend had already jumped up and run outside. At the door he turned around again.

I swear it's the man I saw plotting with Pauline at the table, he cried out. The bastard with the parka.

Through the window Eduard watched Theo running after the man with the flowing coat. When Theo called out to him, the man turned around and picked up his pace. Eduard saw both men run around the corner. He waited for another half hour, but Theo didn't come back.

10

THE REGISTERED LETTER they handed him at the post office was not the one he was waiting for so urgently: Eduard recognized his brother's handwriting. He had to try several times before he finally got through to Dr. Nastase, who immediately excused himself, much to Eduard's surprise. The doctor had been trying to reach Eduard for days. A mistake had occurred in the laboratory, inexcusable but quite explainable due to the popularity of the name Hoffmann. Two different patients, whose names each contained two f's and two n's, had two completely different results, and the lab could no longer say for sure which test was which. In order to exclude any error, both Hoff-menn would have to repeat the procedure. Eduard claimed he couldn't make the new appointment time suggested by the lab and postponed the date by several weeks.

"The breakthrough," wrote Lothar, "came from someone who despite being a close relation was always kept at great distance. Please don't jump to any premature conclusions when I tell you that the new evidence comes from Franz, our father's younger brother, who probably considers me a more likely addressee than you."

Eduard had a hard time remembering what his uncle looked like: thick glasses, a friendly face, slightly bloated but constantly smiling; a man who, although he was in reality three years younger, always looked three years older than his older brother—it was strange, all Eduard could remember about his uncle were those traits which compared unfavorably to his father, perhaps because he knew his uncle more from his father's descriptions than from his own observation. In any case, it was true that he, as an older brother, had no clear impression of Franz, his father's younger brother. Was sibling rivalry an inherited trait?

At the funeral Eduard had been struck most by Franz's conspicuous lurking in the background and his speedy getaway after the first cast of the shovel. And yet this same furtive Franz apparently had had enough time for a graveyard chat, younger brother to younger brother, for a sudden disclosure:

"After my talk with Franz I'm sure we now have a reason —if not the decisive one—for Father's premature death, a reason rooted in a traumatic event that occurred decades ago and which was constantly repressed. I don't have to tell you that our mother was romantically involved with other men from the beginning of her marriage on, and this with Father's knowledge, and probably even his approval—after all, Father never made a secret of it. However we might judge his tolerance, his claim that his wife's affairs never caused him any pain always struck me as dubious. The 'understanding' he showed for his wife's romances must have been too much for him, the more so because, when you consider that our mother's lovers were all what you might call Father's ideal superiors—successful men he knew well and even admired, with his pitiable faith in and worship of genius. The pianist who sent Mother flowers and tickets to his concerts, the author who edited her poems, the miracle doctor from Munich with his clientele of VIPs—all stars in their respective fields. Naturally he could comfort himself with the well-tested fact that his wife, oscillating between euphoria and depression, always came back to him. But was this certainty a guarantee of psychic survival for a man in those years of absolute patriarchy? Didn't he ever have his suspicion that he might be loved and used only as a provider and not as a man?"

What's going on here, wondered Eduard. Is it possible that two grown-up children are investigating the premature death of their mother thirty years after the fact, in order to ascertain what role she might have played in their father's death thirty years later?

"Why is it that our mother's death always remained as dark and mysterious as her unsteady life? Why did we always feel we weren't allowed to ask questions, why doesn't either of us have a photo or at least a clear inner picture of her when she was sick, when she was bedridden? It was Franz who led me to the explanation for this blank page in the family history, and I hesitate to call it surprising. For thirty years Franz has wondered that the following question was never answered: How could it happen that a sick woman, admitted to the hospital with a suspicion of tuberculosis, could up and die just fourteen days after the first symptoms had appeared? Such a rapid progression for a disease known for its protracted development contradicts all medical experience.

"Franz thinks the only explanation for our mother's death was that she took her own life prematurely. This suspicion is further supported by the fact that there is no death certificate to be found among the family papers. (Franz remembers the puffed-up face of the deceased—poisoning from tablets? And why did that 'friend of the family' with his Steinerian bullshit give the eulogy instead of a minister?) I'm sending you copies of Mother's last poems and letters, in which I detect an overwhelming death wish lurking just under the surface of the metaphors—I'm practically convinced she finally succumbed to it. This event, which Father kept concealed from us, and ultimately from himself as well, kept his life suspended in a tension which finally snapped. For thirty years he hid the trauma of a terrible failure under the mantle of his optimism: in the end neither his love nor the children provided a sufficient hold on his wife. When her hunger for love came into greater and greater conflict with her maternal duties, she quietly stole away."

Eduard sat without moving, completely at a loss, an electrical storm raged in his brain; all his circuits were shorted. Tear the letter to shreds or read it over again? Something struck him as completely out of joint, brilliantly twisted, but he couldn't put his finger on it. Electromagnetic waves ran from Mother's grave to Father's deathbed, currents of impulses raced back and forth across the space of thirty years, giving new meaning to an old text, and this reading was supposed to be the truth? Lothar seemed cognizant of the implications of his hypothesis: If his suspicion was correct, their father had kept the secret of their mother's suicide until the end. The whole notion struck Eduard as absurd, it didn't jibe at all with his image of Father. And what accounted for Lothar's accusatory tone in relating the story of their mother's suffering? According to this reconstruction, their father as well as his children were victims of a neglectful mother, who had denied her own family the barest minimum: loyalty and security.

For heaven's sake, Lothar! Look in the mirror! Staring you in the face is a well-balanced being whom your mother brought into this world, admittedly as the second child. Despite whatever harm she may have caused you or possibly even me, you can't claim that either one of us is a mental or physical cripple. We'll soon be older than she was when she died, what do we want to blame her for now? What chemical imbalance can bring a grown man to interpret the putative suicide of his mother as a hedonistic derailing, as a cowardly desertion? In case the young woman, beset with too many children and lovers, did indeed take her own life, what can her sons, now grown up, possibly show her except sympathy and curiosity?

This holding to account, this pronouncement of guilt, this unmasking! You, me, we, the sons and daughters of the Nazis, all suffer from an innocence complex. It's true: never before was there a generation so tempted by history to declare their parents completely guilty and themselves completely innocent. But what does that give us—apart from eternal immaturity? Even now, long grown up, we grab our parents by their hair and drag them along with us, holding them accountable for the fact we failed to become what we wanted to. We compete with one another as to who is the most damaged. Whoever can most fully explain his biography, his weaknesses and defeats, his suffering, his complexes as a series of wounds inflicted upon him by society deserves the crown of victimhood. A second violinist explains effortlessly why he didn't become a Menuhin: his parents didn't realize his talent and develop it in time. A tennis player who never made it beyond the minor leagues explains that he loses matches because in responding to his father's mania for authority, he is unable to summon the will for victory, and so on. Even if we succeed in proving that all our weaknesses are effects of a polluted environment, or the delayed results of a past still not overcome, sooner or later, at some point in our lives, we will have to accept them and recognize them as our own. When will we finally stop . . .

But it didn't stop: "If my reconstruction is correct, then apart from the obvious shock it may also provide you with a certain—perhaps unwished-for—relief, because it contradicts the legend that you were the preferred one, the most beloved, the star of the family. With her last decision our mother showed that you meant just as much to her as Father and I: to wit, nothing worth living for!"

When Eduard let the letter drop from his hand it suddenly conveyed another message. Wasn't all of Lothar's fanatical delving and researching really a yearning, a grown son's wooing of his parents, a final plea for love and acceptance, a need for understanding and reconciliation, which Eduard didn't miss in the least? And didn't this lack of need prove Lothar's thesis that the older brother could be assured of affection which the younger brother still struggled to obtain? Wasn't Eduard's readiness to accept their father's death the laziest way to show his mourning? Was this how the privileged expressed pain?

Among the enclosed papers Eduard found copies of two articles from professional journals. The first contained a devastating critique of Professor Bouchard's twin project. The author referred to more recent Finnish research which demonstrated that not only talent, but also heart attacks and other diseases of the circulatory system, could not be proven to be hereditary. All in all the article branded Professor Bouchard's Minnesota project as "racist" and ended with a sentence heavily underscored by Lothar: "There is not the slightest evidence that would indicate a genetic foundation for any behavioral trait except schizophrenia—whether intelligence, bad behavior, or aggressivity." The second article described a research project in Milwaukee Eduard had never heard of, headed by a Professor Rick Heber. The Milwaukee Project supposedly demonstrated that children from the American slums, when placed in similar nurseries and taught like children of the white upper class, quickly attain the same level of achievement.

11

EDUARD HAD SHOVED HIS BROTHER'S LETTER back under the mountain of mail, but during the next days and weeks it exerted an unexpected influence. Without realizing what he was doing, Eduard began arguing out loud to himself, trying to refute Lothar's hypotheses; finally he decided to undertake some research of his own into their mother's death. He knew exactly where to begin. According to the rules of science, the only reliable method for proving a theory false was to begin by assuming it was true. The path toward knowledge in the natural sciences was in the long run a method of error investigation: every researcher spent some of his time scrutinizing newly proposed, surprising solutions for particular problems, in order to discount them as humbug.

In his search for a possible witness who might provide a counterproof, he remembered a friend of the family who also lived in Berlin, a man Eduard hadn't seen since he was a student. Dr. Mertens had been his mother's last lover. Eduard decided to look him up and interrogate him. The address in the telephone book showed that Mertens lived in the same wealthy district where Eduard had in vain looked for a semen laboratory a few weeks earlier. On the phone, Eduard had the impression that Mertens had to stifle several cries of amazement and probably an incredulous snicker to boot as he listened to the suicide theory.

What a strange story, he said finally, I think I might be able to add a thing or two!

Eduard's suggestion that he visit Mertens at his home seemed to bore the man. They agreed to meet in The Tent, which Mertens apparently knew.

Summertime had emptied the city, the hundred thousand dogs had disappeared with their owners. A strange ritual: just when the weather within the walls was getting pleasantly warm, the inhabitants abandoned the city and set off for the unbearably hot regions of the south. This was Eduard's favorite time in the city; all of a sudden you could hear the echo of your own steps on the sidewalk. The gutters were full of rolled and dried-up leaves which suddenly seemed to burst into life whenever the wind from a passing car picked them up and sent them skipping across the lanes, like animals of the asphalt with a pronounced death wish. The windshields were blind from the drippings of the linden trees, which had been trickling down on them for weeks. The doors to most shops were closed, everywhere hung handwritten notices announcing a return which seemed beyond the realm of the believable.

A summertime calm reigned in The Tent; none of the few scattered guests looked up as Eduard sat down at his favorite table. When the waiter pointed to someone waiting at the bar, Eduard was shocked. There, waving in his direction, was an elderly but still handsome man, whose stooped posture bore witness to a very tall man's lifelong habit of having to bend over to hear what his partner was saying. Eduard searched the strange face for some trace of the love the man had borne for his mother, some line or wrinkle she had left on him. Mertens smiled without any sign of embarrassment and excused himself for not bringing his wife.

She forgave me long ago, he said with a slight lisp. But in her presence I would have probably still felt the need to excuse myself. Eduard recollected vaguely that Mertens had just become engaged at the time he met Eduard's mother. He suddenly realized that at that time his mother's lover had been as old as Eduard was now, and that his mother had been about the same age as Klara.

Mertens took out a dilapidated pocket calendar. The rumor you mentioned is easily disproved, he said. Fortunately I have a terrible memory for numbers, although incidentally not for feelings. Because of that, for decades I've been writing all sorts of things into little calendars like this. As you can see, the format doesn't allow for any real diary entries, it's more a registry of feelings than a record of events, I call it my private crib sheet. A fight with my father, the royalties for my first publication, how much a pound of butter cost on the 1st of September 1947, the day I ate meat for the first time after the war, the beginning and end of a minor affair, and of course all possible birthdays and deaths. In the process I discovered that our linear calendar is completely unnatural; human memory doesn't measure time in days and years and the stars probably don't either. Nevertheless, with the help of this crude device I can provide a fairly exact account of your mother's hospitalization; the dates are all written down.

Mertens leafed through the pages of the leatherbound calendar so that Eduard could see them, but he did not let the little book out of his hand. He opened it to August and reconstructed the last days of his love affair with Eduard's mother, holding the pages close to his eyes, which at times seemed disbelieving or even shocked by what they were reading, but would then for unknown reasons regain their calm.

"Admitted 8/3 to the regional hospital with suspicion of pneumonia," "last vis. w/A." Yes, I wrote the date of death underneath "last visit": 9/26. Now add it up, from the day of her admittance there are seven weeks and four days. Your mother was not bedridden for two weeks, like that malicious Franz maintains, but for a full seven weeks, which is easily long enough for a tubercular patient to die a natural death.

He deciphered a few notes from the middle pages: "106 degrees," "spoke her mind," "one lb. apples." During the last ten days I saw her almost daily.

Two weeks before the end the nurse had taken him aside into the hallway and instructed him to bring the patient whatever she desired and he could obtain, she would never leave the ward. It's possible that Eduard's father did not then know what her condition was. But it was impossible to deceive his mother, she could read her fate in the mirror, her premonitions were mathematically precise. As early as two weeks before her death Mertens had wanted to take leave of her, because he did not feel equal to the task she had set, to the complete ruthlessness of her passion. "Cowardice in the face of love" she branded his behavior, and her words tormented him for a long time. But he could no longer bring himself to walk past her husband day after day, coming in as he was going out. On Mother's deathbed Mertens had fought with her tooth and nail.

With animated movements he leafed up and down the pages, as if he wanted to check the feelings as well as the dates, feelings he hadn't allowed to speak for ages, but the word he was looking for was not recorded.

As he talked, he began to change. Eduard sensed that the old man's body straightened out, his forehead grew smooth, the age spots on the backs of his hands disappeared. He saw in Mertens's eyes the frivolity and cowardice of a forty-year-old who was remembering a great feeling, a last burst of exuberance before the shell began to grow. It was as if Eduard were holding a remote control that allowed him to rewind the life film of his mother's lover to the point where he was sitting across from someone his own age, almost as an accomplice.

She wasn't beautiful, Mertens explained, judging by the standards of his generation—the long-legged femmes fatales with the veiled gaze and smoky voice from black-and-white films. At first glance she actually seemed small, almost homely, too skinny to lose your head over out of sheer desire, but she exerted an unusual attraction in any company. She could make a man feel that he had previously made either a half choice or the wrong one, that he had missed what was most important. Small talk, or what used to be known as "conversation" before everything became Americanized—that was impossible with her. She was constantly putting him on the spot, subjecting him to tests, making him answer with the first thing that came to mind, not allowing him to think things through. Once she stole a bucket of syrup in the grocery store and shoved it under Mertens's coat: he had to smuggle it out while she bought laces for her boots. It wasn't just need that drove her to this; it was the adventure that counted. Who'll be the first to jump from the running streetcar. Anyone who let a tethered German shepherd scare him off a potato field was a wimp, whoever let steps approaching on the street interrupt an embrace was an unworthy lover. From the beginning he knew the only way he could keep this woman was to share her with others. When did she find the time to write her poems? She sat at the sewing machine for nights on end sewing things for the farmers: a baby's sleep suit for a sack of potatoes, a suit for a pair of children's shoes. Sleeping was a waste of time, you had to "grab what you could from the provisions of the immeasurable."

At the time Father was providing for the family by substituting in different clinics; he had to take work where he found it and was often away for weeks. Whenever Mertens came to visit—bringing a gift for the children, a hand puppet, a ball—he felt overwhelmed. Sometimes, in the night, he would start up: "A child is crying!"—he couldn't distinguish Lothar's and Eduard's crying from that of other children. At those times her face would cloud up. Then she would burst out at him: Why did he worry about her problems; he was a man always taking a break, that's all, someone constantly fleeing something, simply looking for a worthy excuse for his absence. "There's no bad conscience if you really love," she said. Not even with regard to one's spouse? She never had any doubt about her own love, but the idea of exclusive loyalty was completely alien to her. Her exclusivity was for the love, not the individual man. No one person was made for another, she claimed.

Those were the first years after the war, there was no order—internal or external. Everything had collapsed, nothing was left standing; one-time houses were now façades, former windows were sockets gaping in the dusty gray sky. They were living in the void, and the mistrust of any remnants of tradition which had survived the war was enough to encourage any mad folly. Never before in history, Mertens thought at the time, had the Germans been given such a chance. In Germany, hopes had always grown on ruins. Hunger begat hallucinations he had never known; anyone who could conjure up a bag of dried fruit was capable of inventing paradise.

At the time he was subletting a little room in Z, where he edited the cultural section of a daily paper. One night he met Eduard's mother at a party. In his fourteen square meters he and five friends, including Eduard's parents, were celebrating survival, it was his first postwar party. Thanks to his good connections with a butcher's daughter he was able to offer goulash and two bottles of wine—which he had "organized": the jargon of the time declared thievery to be a natural right. They talked and drank until midnight; then the party got a little out of hand, which was unplanned but inescapable since there was no streetcar, let alone a taxi. Only bicycle thieves had bicycles. Since it was technically impossible to get home, they stayed together in the cramped room, philosophizing, flirting, embracing one another, and after the candles had burned out they went to sleep, on top of each other, next to each other, an orgy forced by circumstances. The shortages unleashed an existential light-headedness, free from any plan or lascivious design.

That first night he noticed Eduard's mother was unhealthy; she coughed badly, her cheeks were glowing, her motions seemed strangely slowed. When he visited her later her condition had worsened. Back then Eduard's father was building up his practice in Z. Mertens had more time, so it seemed completely natural that he undertook to pick her up and accompany her to Z. All their friends realized his help was not exactly without self-interest, and Father also knew of Mertens's relationship with his wife, just as he probably had been aware of all her previous affairs as well: his wife had never spared him this knowledge. Mertens on the other hand kept bouncing from one excuse to the next, so that his bride-to-be remained uninformed. Eduard's mother took whatever time she made for him as her natural right. Whether Father suffered because of this, whether he simply hid his jealousy or whether he was generous beyond all measure, Mertens couldn't say. With his utter imperturbability he created for his wife a security none of her lovers could have offered her. This self-possessed composure apparently never left him. He never asked Mertens to explain things, even as they passed each other on their way to see the dying woman.

From the day the nurse explained Mother's true condition, Mertens began to curtail his visits. He read the nurse's instructions as a discreet request to give precedence to the father of the dying woman's children. Eduard's mother immediately saw through his newfound reticence. None of it mattered to her, the doctor's warnings, the nurses' looks, even the steps along the corridor he seemed so afraid of, nothing and nobody could ever bring her to forswear her passion. He fled her room without looking back. From that day on he was afraid of her.

In the days that followed he lurked around the grounds surrounding the hospital, avoiding her window. He wanted to stay close but invisible. As he made his secret rounds he waited for the event that would take him to her for the last time.

In the end it was Eduard's father who informed him of her death. The friends spent the whole night together beside the deceased. He, Mertens, stood there deaf, without feeling, as if he had no right to his pain. Father had said, with tears in his eyes, "She is so beautiful; you also knew her well, didn't you?" Mertens only grew stiffer, he felt he was in no position to defend himself. Suddenly Father hugged him, as if with this gesture he recognized his friend's love as well as his grief, as if he felt the only fellow mourner who could understand the extent of his loss was the man with whom he had had to share his wife. In complete harmony they sat beside the bed of the deceased and told each other stories of what she was like when still alive.

Eduard saw Mertens sink back into his chair; over the next seconds of silence the years seemed to repossess him. Before him sat an old man. It was as if Mertens had bent over someone he had once loved and whom the crystal ball of memory had kept eternally young. But in the end all this image did was reflect his own deterioration.

12

AT THE NEWSSTAND, headlines announcing a new act of terrorism caught Eduard's eye. Once again the victim was some functionary whose worst crime consisted in occupying a fairly high position in the institution where he was employed. He had been executed, one shot to the back of the head. The attacks seemed to follow a ritual: Every year some youth was chosen from the "military-industrial complex" to be sacrificed to the dragon god of the "International Liberation Army." The ceremony was usually performed just when the newspapers had resumed their periodic speculation that terrorism was dying out.

The article wouldn't have kept him there any longer if he hadn't noticed a surprising phrase in the letter claiming responsibility, which the newspaper had printed below. Among various clichés such as "one of the most important agents of international monopoly capitalism" and "a key functionary in the hierarchy of imperialism" one expression stuck out like a sore thumb: "The pilot fish who swim ahead of the school have no brain, and thus no conscience. Guilt within the system is too vast, it cannot be parceled out individually . . ." Wasn't this a thought of Theo's, however vulgarized? How did it get into the letter?

What can I do if they read what I write? Theo responded

casually when he met Eduard that evening. That's the way it is; once a sentence is published it becomes independent. You don't think I'd be a ghostwriter for amateurs like that.

For the time being Eduard felt reassured. He was certain that Theo would never let himself be seduced by terrorism; he might at most succumb to the appeal of a female terrorist. Nevertheless, there was something about Eduard's relief that seemed to irk Theo, although Eduard himself had no intention of getting caught up in one of his friend's anarchistic mind games.

Every profession, no matter how significant or insignificant it might be, had its advisors: financial planners, entrepreneurial advisors, design consultants, government counselors, cultural guides, environmental-impact assessors—terrorists were the obvious odd men out. Any society that has managed to maintain a healthy dose of mistrust in its public institutions actually needs a handful of terrorists. Only the most sanctimonious souls would leave earthly justice in the hands of journalists and officials from the Department of Correction; German justice in particular needs an emergency road service always on hand, always at the ready in case of a breakdown. Just take the thousand judges from the Nazi "People's Courts"—not one of whom was ever brought to trial, let alone sent to prison. Or the countless SS men who held high positions in both successor states to the Third Reich. Hunting them down, extorting confessions, and then releasing them was a task for self-appointed investigators. Even if they remained unpunished, they would still be found out, unmasked, and their reputations ruined. Half the world would sigh with relief and hardly even try to hide their secret joy at such an operation. Both German states were practically begging for terrorists with a trusted reputation. But it was precisely this profession which lacked advisors. The result: inane activism, shoddy language skills, formulaic thinking, ill-chosen victims, logistic bungling, an absolute dearth of professional standards. Vast amounts of energy were frittered away, operations were planned and executed in an amateurish manner, public relations were a disaster. With the exception of the nearly forgotten Lorenz kidnapping, not one single operation came close to fulfilling the requirements of contemporary, state-of-the-art terrorism. Had the terrorists consulted with him, Theo would not only have provided them with a new concept, he would have given them new goals as well. For example, he saw no reason at all why terrorism should exclusively target the West. An entire apparatus of official state oppressors lived on the other side of the Wall, and the neglect the terrorists had hitherto displayed toward the East bordered on the criminal.

This last sentence in particular astounded Eduard. He was surprised Theo would include the first socialist state on German soil in his proposed platform of terrorist reform. Theo conceded at once that personal motivations also affected his thinking—a fact he considered completely legitimate. Terror with no private motive for revenge was a sterile institution.

What happened? asked Eduard.

If he had read a published account of what he had just experienced, said Theo, he would have dismissed it as the malicious invention of the hostile Western press. Today his only objection to the generally insightful and clairvoyant horror tales printed in Western newspapers was that neither the authors nor their readers took them seriously.

He shooed away Eduard's question concerning the wedgewolf, whom Theo was last seen chasing around the corner of The Tent. That was a harmless passerby, Theo answered. Unfortunately even he, Theo, was a victim of the projection promulgated by the East German state, which attributed any and every symptom of internal breakdown to the workings of some enemy from the West.

Theo stared ahead and made no effort to explain what he meant. After a while he stood up, walked over to the bar, bought a cigar—which took some effort to clip and light— and resumed the story of his marital experiment.

Once Olympia had announced her intention of appearing in the flesh, nothing but complications ensued. Theo went to the Pressecafé at 3 p.m.—as Olympia had dictated—if only to catch a glimpse of the author of all the strange letters. Expecting someone to recognize him and approach him, he stood for a while in the doorway, but no one paid him any notice. He spent the next half hour sitting by himself at a table, drinking bad coffee and reading the Party newspaper, which did little to improve his mood. He decided he would never again make an appointment with an American woman writing her dissertation.

The next day a second telegram arrived: YOUR NAME: CLOSE SESAME. I WON'T GIVE UP. FRIDAY, 5 P.M., STAGE ENTRANCE DEUTSCHES THEATER. Theo suspected that Olympia, in all her American naïveté, had given his name at the border and had been refused entrance.

All further contact remained written. Hardly had Theo positioned himself at what he considered a safe distance from the stage entrance when the doorman came running up to him with a piece of paper. "Don't give up!" Theo read, "Sunday, 2 p.m., Tierpark, by the apes." The handwriting on the note was not Olympia's. Apparently she had an accomplice, an envoy of love.

But the pattern of near-misses continued. Instead of Olympia all he met were messages, which directed him to increasingly absurd meeting places, like some wide-ranging treasure hunt. Through his searching looks and questions he made the acquaintance of women who bore some resemblance to Olympia's self-description. His approaches elicited laughter, sometimes horror, and on one occasion a slap in the face.

If it were only a matter of meeting Olympia, Theo would have let things rest after the first missed rendezvous in the Pressecafé. But each new cryptic message only strengthened his conviction that the state authorities were trying to thwart his meeting with her. His suspicions gained further support when he tried to cross the border into West Berlin, just on a whim, and was rebuffed without being told why. He began to develop a complex: If, as Theo had begun to assume, an entire ministry was plotting to prevent an innocent professional conversation between an author and a foreign student of German literature, then it was a matter of self-respect to make this meeting happen, come what may. In the end, Theo was prepared to invoke the Helsinki Convention to uphold his right to meet with Olympia.

But one day at five o'clock in the afternoon, as he waited in the pouring rain outside the Potsdam observatory, Theo gave up. Soaked to the skin, feeling the onset of a flu in his bones, he asked himself what proof he had that Olympia even existed. Apart from letters and some notes scribbled in an unknown hand he had no tangible evidence.

That night he was awakened by a phone call. Among the voices of the countless people with whom he shared the line, he could distinguish a husky and strangely close female voice asking for his name. He recognized Olympia at the first word and was enraged to observe his heart was pounding. He interrupted her long-winded excuses and explanations and gave her an ultimatum. Tomorrow, at 2 p.m., at a place she knew and could reach without any difficulty, otherwise nowhere and never in this life. Olympia chose the Pergamon Museum.

Pauline had been fast asleep when he hung up the receiver. But the next morning she seemed upset. She asked hostilely what could bring Theo to the Pergamon Museum, which he otherwise avoided as a shameful monument to German "excavation imperialism." Theo explained that a somewhat high-strung doctoral student from New York wanted to interview him there; she didn't know her way around. But Pauline refused to calm down. He knew very well that the Pergamon Museum was a playground for informers, she yelled. This infuriated Theo. That Pauline in her jealousy was hiding behind the Stasi, of all people, was not worthy of her; if you let your life be ruled by suspicions like that, you might as well not leave home.

But it was impossible to talk with Pauline anymore; in her fury she even offered to sleep with Theo, right then and there and against all agreement. The long abstinence must have affected her wits, she said. This ostensibly therapeutic motive turned Theo against her completely; he slammed the door behind him.

At the museum Olympia could be found neither in Asia Minor nor in Assyria. Theo had the feeling he was being watched, but since this feeling was almost always justified, he decided to ignore it. He was poring over the booty stolen by the royal Prussian excavators in Turkey far beyond his interest when someone called out his name. A tall woman was walking toward him from the market gate of Miletus, which stood about twenty meters high. He didn't doubt for a minute that it was Olympia. Even in her trench coat and gym shoes she seemed like an ancient goddess who had chosen to pick up a quick and somewhat ungainly disguise at a vintage clothing store on Bleecker Street in New York. A loose coat trailed down to her heels, revealing only her long, slender neck and a face so symmetrical and masklike it seemed not to belong to a mortal. Only the full mouth, with its pale lipstick, called to mind the vices Olympia had confessed to him.

Hurry, we have to get out of here, they're watching us, she whispered, and stretched her white arm toward Theo. That same moment two men wearing parkas darted between them, grabbed Olympia by both arms, and tore her away from him. She called out something he didn't understand, and for a split second Theo felt she expected him to instantaneously transform into the Austrian muscle man with the flamethrower—but then she had already disappeared. By the time he reached the exit, all he could see was Olympia's profile racing away in the back seat of the Wartburg.

Pauline listened to Theo's report of the incident with a terrifying indifference. She was no longer able to help him, she said, since he with his addled brain had dismissed her advice as jealous ranting and raving. What advice? yelled Theo. She had begged him, answered Pauline, to stay clear of that ostensible doctoral candidate named Olympia—"It's obviously a made-up name, you shouldn't have to be told that!"—it's a conspiracy, a trap, the woman's a Stasi puppet, paid to slink into the mental world of a poet with a writing block.

Theo contacted a friend in the Politburo and demanded information as to the whereabouts of an American doctoral candidate who had been taken away before his eyes at the

Pergamon Museum. His contact communicated to him that there was nothing to be discovered concerning this incident, wherefore he urgently advised Theo to assume that it had never occurred.

Several days later Theo found a letter in his box which was undoubtedly written by Olympia, albeit in haste and unstamped; her accomplice must have smuggled it over the border. Olympia's message was more confusing than anything she had demanded of him to date. After the meeting in the Pergamon Museum she had been interrogated for hours and then deported. But she wasn't going to allow herself to be intimidated by the watchdogs who had thus far managed to keep them from meeting. She had devised a little performance she planned to produce on Friday at 4 p.m. in an apartment in the western half of the city close to the border: Harzer Str. 5, fourth floor. Theo would surely find the ways and means to watch the show from one of the apartments opposite. She advised him to bring binoculars.

Theo had already fallen so deeply under the spell of unknown attraction that he immediately fetched a map of the city. In his madness he even failed to find it suspicious that he knew someone in the block of flats diagonally opposite the named address. Like a schoolboy going to see an X-rated movie, he sneaked over to the apartment belonging to his acquaintance at the appointed time. Whereas Dr. Schauer had hardly recognized him over the telephone, he now received Theo with the exuberance reserved for a long-lost son. During the last few years Theo had avoided him; it was well known that apartments like that, so exposed to the West, were given only to people with an outstanding class consciousness. Theo hypocritically expressed his agreement with a letter Schauer had recently sent to the editor of the Party paper, and listened to his host's officially sanctioned Party nonsense while sipping first-class Italian coffee and Irish whiskey. Every now and then Theo would nod his head; in reality he was trying to figure out how he could get into the room that faced west. He was still looking for an innocent ruse when Schauer suddenly stood up and with a conspiratorial smile led him into his bedroom. At the window Theo noticed a device which any astronomer would have envied: a telescope capable of enormous magnitudes. Theo was confused; now he was no longer able to ignore the suspicion that he was a pawn in some game directed by an unknown hand. Schauer showed him how to focus the telescope and, as a test, allowed him a peep into the restaurant of the Western radio tower. When the weather's good you can see the food on the plates, he claimed. Theo explained he was interested only in the house directly over the border.

What he discovered there, hugely magnified, astonished him only because it was so familiar. The still life on the wall, the houseplants, the glass display cabinet with its porcelain pieces, the plastic armchair, the lampshade, the entire interior could have come from a people's department store somewhere in the East. Then he saw a pair of suspenders over a stomach, thumb and forefingers leafing through a newspaper; he never quite managed to bring the entire man into focus, only fingernails, underarm hair, nostrils. A slow pan revealed a gray volcanic landscape, and it wasn't until Theo looked with his naked eye that he realized the telescope was pointed at the building's outside plastered wall. In the next window there was nothing moving; the only light came from a flickering TV screen which was showing the same program that Schauer was watching. Finally Theo focused on what he wanted to see, the third window, but it was covered by a curtain. He glanced at his watch, the time had just expired. His nerves were shot, the prospect of some revelation in the window behind the wall had robbed him of all reason. He stood that way for an eternity and was not in the least distracted by the ringing which called Schauer to the hallway.

When the curtain was drawn back and the window opened, he recoiled. There before him stood Olympia in a white coat, so largely magnified he felt like a dwarf. Theo was now utterly convinced he was hallucinating and decided to call an ambulance, albeit not until after the hallucination was over, for the message Olympia was sending him from the other side of the political firmament was not to be missed at any price. Olympia's hand first waved to him, then began to unbutton the top buttons of her coat and drew back the left side. Underneath, on Olympia's naked skin, in letters which Olympia's breasts curved into fantastically florid scrolls, he could read C O R—the following M was half covered and required some guessing. The title of a love poem in his first volume of poetry. His verse about the diving bird which the Chinese fishermen send to catch fish after placing a ring around its neck had been understood as an allusion to the suppression of freedom of the press and reprinted underground. But before Olympia could reveal the rest of the word, she was torn back. Two men in parkas jumped out from the dark of the room and pounced on Olympia by the window. Holding her firmly by the neck and arms, they jerked her aloft and pinned her, stomach down, against the window frame. A tiny push from behind would have been enough to send her falling. Olympia defended herself desperately, Theo thought he could hear her cries for help. Just then a hand loomed in front of the telescope and capped the lens. It's all a figment of your imagination, there isn't any Olympia, said Pauline in a determined voice.

Completely crazed, Theo shoved her away so forcefully she fell to the floor. When he again looked through the eyepiece, Olympia and both men had disappeared, the window was closed and draped, everything looked exactly the way it had when he had started watching. For a while he felt as if the whole time he had been gazing into the eye of a video camera which was showing a film he had made himself. Only a crack in the glass of the window opposite bore witness to the struggle which had taken place.

When she came to, Pauline's disconnected confessions enabled him to piece together the entire unbelievable story. Yes, it was Pauline—who else?—who after a tipsy conversation with a girl friend had hatched out the whole plan: Pauline had dictated all of Olympia's letters to Theo, her friend had organized the mailing from New York. She wanted to test not only Theo but also her own intuition, inasmuch as she had manufactured the phantom image of a fantasy woman from clues she had culled from Theo's poems. She was surprised he didn't catch on with the Schwarzenegger story; she couldn't imagine he would fall for such a vulgar projection of male fantasy. Because Theo persisted in overlooking this and all further signals, the two accomplices continued. Together they concocted Olympia's visit and the missed appointments and wondered at Theo's patience. But then a new director had suddenly taken over. When Pauline had seen a real live Olympia, made to measure, so to speak, approach Theo in the Pergamon Museum—naturally she had been there as well—she was horrified. Apparently the Stasi had observed the entire exchange and recognized its chance. The intimate provocations and offerings which only Pauline could have invented offered an ideal opportunity to spy on Theo, to collect material against him which could be used for blackmail. What could be more obvious for the organs of state security than substituting a real Olympia for the one Pauline had designed? They appropriated the imagined character, which Pauline had invented out of reckless bravado and curiosity, and furnished it with a body in order to obtain more promising confessions from Theo. They even staged an arrest, in order to undermine Pauline's foreseeable warnings. The next act, Pauline concluded, would have comprised a meeting on the other side of the Wall, a night of love with a hired Stasi puppet, who would have given an account of every whispered word.

And the scene at the window, the men in the parkas, the attempted defenestration?

Well staged, you have to admit, Pauline had answered, and closed the curtains to Schauer's western window.

How do you really know, asked Eduard, that it wasn't vice versa, that the living Olympia isn't real and Pauline's "literary invention" isn't made up? He had asked Pauline the same question, answered Theo. The Stasi is banking on precisely this doubt, was Pauline's reply. He, Theo, would have to decide for himself whom he really believed.

↑↓↑↓↑↓↑↓↑↓↑↓↑↓↑↓↑↓ 13 ↑↓↑↓↑↓↑↓↑↓↑↓↑↓↑↓↑↓

THE VERDICT ON HIS SPERM was pronounced over the telephone. Dr. Nastase described the results of the second test as "somewhat complicated," nothing could be concluded one way or the other. As Eduard himself had surmised, the quality of his semen left something to be desired.

Quality? asked Eduard.

The concept was not to be taken as a value judgment: the mobility of the spermatazoa which were examined was so low as to make insemination unlikely. On the other hand, it was not impossible that one "candidate"—here Nastase mentioned a statistical percentage with figures beginning after the decimal point—"just might reach its goal."

The whole description sounded like a city marathon, where only one of the participants manages to stumble over the finish line, half dead and far too late.

Now, he didn't know, Dr. Nastase continued in a businesslike tone of voice, anything concerning Eduard's motives for the test and did not wish to speculate about them. On the one hand, in case this happened to be one of Eduard's reasons, he could not provide him with any hope for offspring. But neither could he relieve him of his duty to take precautions, since as is well known, the biological test could not measure psychological factors. Dr. Nastase then excused himself for giving the diagnosis over the phone and signed off, not without reminding Eduard about the missing insurance form. For the record he promised to mail Eduard the written findings.

Eduard's bewilderment was kept in check only by his indignation at the form of the communication. A diagnosis like that was simply not delivered by telephone and certainly not in the jargon of a sports reporter. He imagined Dr. Nastase in his whitewashed room, wearing perfectly creased, snow-white pants and a Lacoste shirt over a broad chest, toned taut and muscular by some luxury sport. On his very first visit he had suspected Nastase of being a charlatan. Go, get out, first impulses should be trusted. If Nastase agreed to meet on the tennis court, Eduard planned to take game, set, and match away from this star member of the male team, this champion who served super-fast balls by day and highly mobile semen by night, both right over the net.

Besides, he couldn't do anything with a diagnosis like that. Not one practical bit of advice, no suggested pattern of behavior came of it; he was at best at a scientifically well-founded loss. How should he now treat the whethers and hows of prophylaxis? Should he from here on out declare condoms unnecessary, with the argument that he was only "a little bit potent"? Or should he use them, hypocritically, to come across as a complete man? In reality he was no wiser than before, but the miserly percentage to which his capability of producing children had shrunk shook his fantasy life from the roots up. Was it really impossible for him to have children? Judging from the unease unleashed by this thought, he had to conclude that—despite all his claims— he had actually always wanted children. Evidently he had based his temporary decision against progeny on the cer-

tainty that it was revokable at any time. Now that this certainty was gone, his "renunciation" lost all its appeal. To
heroically renounce a possibility which never existed seemed
embarrassing at best.

The test results began to disrupt his sleep. All he needed
was to erase the difference between improbability and im-
possibility and his dreams of flight turned into nightmares of
falling. The measure of his self-esteem approached his
chances of producing a child. How would the result affect
his relationship with Klara? She was over thirty, her willingness to postpone having children was biologically restricted.
And what if she suppressed this basic wish out of love for
him? He couldn't accept a decision like that, it would place
him forever in her debt. A heroic option began to take shape:
rather than accept such a sacrifice, he would leave Klara to
her own best fate.

All of a sudden he remembered a different percentage,
which easily dwarfed his personal fertility rating: 10 to 15
percent of all German marriages remained involuntarily
childless. Statistics are the best psychiatrists; they lead any
and all invalids to a large group of fellow sufferers and offer
them inclusion. Whatever might be wrong with you, you
aren't alone; get a grip on your problem and let it be grasped
by others; the minute you confess it on the talk show you
already have company, you're actually part of a huge minority! Ten to 15 percent of all marriages—no stadium, no city
in the world could accommodate a complete assembly of the
Infertile. Once a problem has been statistically compre-
hended and acknowledged as having a certain size, an entire
army of prodigiously inventive happiness-engineers is mobi-
lized to solve it. Molecular biologists like himself as well as
sperm banks now offered the possibility of parenthood to

members of the club Eduard had just joined. The stories of
Jacob and Rachel, of Abraham and Sarah, the famous childless heroes of the Old Testament, Henry VIII's beheading of
Anne Boleyn because she bore him only daughters, the gnawing, scarcely expressed self-doubt of J. W. von Goethe, all
but one of whose children with Christiane Vulpius died of
some unexplained genetic disorder, Napoleon's insanity in
divorcing Josephine—unnecessary tragedies! Feelings, conflicts, entire spheres of human life had been swept away by
the geneticists; thousands of pages of literature, including
any number of Shakespeare's dramas, had been rendered ob-
solete by the advance of enzymology. One statistic alone con-
tested the promises of the reproductive technicians: 90
percent of all mothers who experienced in vitro fertilization
claimed that the influence of the "wish child" on their marriage had generally been an unfavorable one.

Eduard excluded all thoughts of a technical mobilization
of his potency. If he defined his defect as the task for a
lifelong work of mourning, a certain mental greatness was
guaranteed, although the problem itself remained unsolved.

Of course his relationships with other women would
change as well. The right to an occasional affair—which he
and Klara had each reserved—would now become a kind of
duty. Would not his incapability of producing a child tax his
capability of producing pleasure? There was no question he
would have to fill the space suddenly emptied of the risk of
causing pregnancy with new, yet unknown desires. Somewhere he had read that the removal of this risk lessened the
pleasure. No, it was worse, he hadn't read it; it was Laura,
Laura the much desired, Laura the bold, a pleasure expert if
there ever was one, who had told him of this surprising discovery. She had been smitten, so to speak, by a percussionist

in a jazz club and had taken him home after the concert. But after the chosen one had whispered, between caresses, into her ear that she didn't need to worry because he was sterilized, she immediately went stone-cold sober. She packed him off to his drumsticks as quickly as she could. By the same token, since she hadn't for a moment thought of making the unknown man a father, she was surprised by her own reaction. Evidently where love was concerned it made a difference whether this danger was only avoided or completely absent.

Eduard suddenly saw himself in the position of various women he knew who were his own age; who, after having talked their partners out of any hope for descendants, went and made some accidental candidate a father. Indeed, now he would support any pregnancy at all, even the most unhoped for.

When that Saturday morning at the baker's he met the uniformed dream Teuton, the bearer of all postal misfortune maneuvered Dr. Nastase's letter out of the mail pouch with deadly accuracy. With the unopened envelope in hand, Eduard rang Klara's bell. She opened the door in her robe and took the letter as well as the rolls, as if both belonged to her breakfast in bed. But it's for you, she said after glancing at the envelope.

It's for both of us, said Eduard.

He opened the letter and held the document in front of her like a schoolboy showing his mother a catastrophic grade that required a signature. Klara didn't show the slightest curiosity and remained uninterested after he explained the numbers. Defiantly she tossed back her hair, took the paper out of his hand, crumpled it up, and tossed it in the wastebasket.

That's all a lot of computerized nonsense, said Klara. Surely you don't believe that. The only place this question will be decided is in my body.

Eduard was speechless. With all due respect for Klara's intuition, she was no match for an electron microscope. How could she in the name of a strong feeling declare a procedure invalid that generations of researchers had developed over so many sleepless nights of trial and error? This was revenge for his tolerating her many instances of disrespect for the exact sciences. Her lack of faith was supported and spurred on by brazen, homespun theories taken from the alternative lexicon, and she did not hesitate to use them to insult his colleagues. Just recently she had flabbergasted an entire tableful of cocktail-drinking zoologists with her views on Darwin. Klara disputed outright that humans were descended from apes. A polite silence unfolded, the men who had themselves approached her as primates donned embarrassed professional smiles, but Klara was not to be stopped. She didn't doubt there was some relation, but the theory that *Homo sapiens* was directly descended from the apes was in her opinion full of holes. What actually spoke against the assumption that there might have been an independent race of humans living alongside the apes from the very beginning? Why did everything complex have to derive from something simple, higher orders from lower ones, the universe from the void— all male logic, linear thought. Couldn't intelligent beings exist at the same time as unintelligent ones, was it necessarily true that every mutation could be explained by its utility in the struggle for survival? For example, the claim that the female bosom developed as a copy of the female buttocks, since the erect gait meant that the front side of the female body had to be similarly sexually attractive—absurd, bad literature. You zoologists are all alike! Here the experts struck up a grateful gorilla laugh, as they unabashedly gazed deeper into Klara's décolletage. With this theory Desmond Morris really went off the deep end. One colleague even took up for Klara's fundamental critique: a deep-sea fish had recently been discovered which according to the laws of evolution couldn't possibly exist! Nonetheless, the impression of unshakable dilettantism remained in the room, casting its shadow even upon Eduard: There's a man who's lost control at home.

He shook his head when Klara opened his belt and dragged him by the buckle into the bedroom. His reflex to defend the honor of science could not withstand Klara's assault. She skillfully played Eduard the test victim against Eduard the director of the experiment, the sperm donor against the researcher.

At that point everything might have happened as it usually did. After a period of experimentation they had developed certain traditions in their love play, which was less directed to innovation than to mutual success. Besides, in this field Klara didn't tolerate much debate: there was only one position in bed which was totally equal, she said, the one where both partners lie next to each other with complete impartiality.

In practice this morally unobjectionable position was difficult to maintain, and what usually happened sooner or later, more often sooner than later, revealed the dirty traces of a basic drive which was never easily reconciled to the demands of an enlightened consciousness. For instance, Klara had surprised herself as well as Eduard with the confession that the maligned missionary position stemming from the colonial period still seemed quite viable.

Klara closed her eyes as if she wanted to give herself completely to the images in her garden. But the moment her eyes no longer held his gaze, something happened to him; suddenly he had the feeling he had dropped out of the human race. He looked at the tender fuzz on her upper lip, the line of her neck, her collarbone, the hollows of her shoulders in which he had so often hidden his head and forgotten the weight of his body, the high, white foundations of her breasts, the swing of her hips, the magic corner between her legs—all gone, the enchantment broken, no one there, the party isn't answering. It was as if he was no longer subject to the entire basic system of signals. The desires which this system had steadfastly, almost automatically released over so many years suddenly struck him as the remembrance of a time when living beings prepared to crawl from the ocean onto the dry land.

The spell which had befallen him still plagued his perception during the days which followed. On the street he saw an unknown woman walking in his direction whose appearance turned the heads of all male passersby within a fifty-meter radius. Eduard reacted by being shocked at the members of his gender. How was it possible that *Homo sapiens*, which had emancipated itself in all other areas from its tree-climbing relatives, was still stuck in the lowest level of rutting behavior? How was it that the species still followed in endless obedience the same three or four body signals with a turning of the head, a rush of blood, and stupid bits of speech? Take any warm summer day: was it not painful to see dozens of men, completely independent of their IQ, suddenly lose all reason and dignity when confronted by a pair of naked female legs? This ratlike obedience to simple visual stimuli, this traffic-light behavior, was an offense against the entire sex! And how much time, how much patience had he himself wasted sitting at school desks and on café chairs, staring into the blouses of women in front of him, waiting for the moment when some chance movement of the body might grant him one more centimeter of visibility. As if people didn't know what a breast looked like, as if every tightly fitted skirt were hiding the undiscovered secret formula of the world. And how pitiful was the special expertise that this drive to unveil had developed among his fellow males! There were approximately three billion amateur genealogists running around the globe, each one ready at any time to provide an exact identity kit for the body that came with a certain décolletage, a certain moving drape of skirt, a certain twist of female ankle. What was so exciting about these points of eternal stimulation? Two protuberances, where the male was flat, and a crevice where the male protruded. For almost 2,500 years these facts had been carved in marble, painted in oil, photographed true-to-life. Couldn't one expect the male specimens of the species to finally register them not with excitement but with the appropriate boredom, and so make way for at least some modest innovations in their sexual drive?

He spent the next evenings in his own apartment. He was determined to devote some time following up his doubts concerning the sexual drive of the human male. Stop his ears, switch off the man-woman circuit inside his cortex, take a position high above the belt.

For several weeks the TV programs had been under the

sign of soccer, it was the European Cup, and political news was crammed into the time-outs. There were the usual broadcasts of war, catastrophe, and epidemic. All over the world small, tenacious wars were being fought, but far away; the anchorman listed the casualties with the indifference of an accountant, a statistician of distant horror, compiling the misery of the world in a pleasant voice with perfect pronunciation. His singsong produced in Eduard a sleepy attentiveness which, even if it had reported a meltdown in the atomic power plant thirteen kilometers away, would have allowed him to gently drift to sleep, untroubled save by childish nightmares of pursuing policemen. The wars, like the victories and defeats of the European Cup, seemed to fall within the competence of the television reporter, who compiled the highlights for paying subscribers. One day, thought Eduard, the programs could be switched around, then the television would show live coverage of the final match between the superpowers and during the time-out relay the tournament scores. "Imagine there was a war and no one came!"—what a nostalgic slogan. In wealthy Europe, stuffed to the brim with atomic rockets, such a war, to which one could come or from which one could run away, was no longer conceivable. The only imaginable war, the final war, would hit the large majority of Europeans just like a soccer match; at home, beer in hand, right in front of the color TV. And right after the news this war would be over.

How realistic was this fear of a final, third war anyway? The rich countries had almost succeeded in eliminating war by overarming themselves. Within their borders war was conceivable only as the greatest possible accident; it had been reduced to a vestige of risk, a position behind the decimal point. War was a disease which had been overcome, like

cholera or the plague. Indeed, it afflicted only the under-
privileged nations who had no atomic weapons at their disposal. Since 1945 the poor regions of the world had seen
more wars than ever before. Was the fear which motivated
the Europeans truly a fear of war in the first place? Was it
possible that it hid an utterly new fear, the fear of inevitable
peace? Since time immemorial, war had been the steady accompaniment of human history, and apart from pious utter-
ances there was little that spoke for the idea that all these
wars were always only a consequence of external circumstances which were in contradiction to the "true" nature of
mankind and thus would disappear when the circumstances
did. But what if the drive to make war was an internal one,
was it then conceivable that its "renunciation" might proceed
without a violent internal upheaval? Would renunciation of
war not change all other human capabilities in ways yet unknown? How would a society as used to and even obsessed
with war as Europe come to terms with the idea that war
was fundamentally no longer possible? Where would the energies hitherto spent on warring find their outlet? They certainly wouldn't vanish overnight. Was it then conceivable
that such an immense change could take place without a new
ordering of feelings?

Shortly before the whistle announced the second half—
"We return to the stadium just in time"—the announcer
compiled the current images of the day: burning houses,
children's bellies bloated with hunger, a quick snapshot of a
dying black man's face covered with flies, cut, the camera
now had a different corner of the earth in its viewfinder, this
time people were drowning: "The rescue ship cannot continue operating due to lack of funds. It has pulled ten thousand boat people from the Sea of China, in which a quarter

million people have drowned since the end of the Vietnam War . . ." That was followed by a highlight showing an easily remembered number to which to send contributions.

The news disturbed him, a forgotten rage swelled inside him. That it was possible to mention this horrible number just like that, so casually! For the fifteen minutes before the match resumed, thousands of starved, burned, and poisoned people were providing half-time entertainment, just like the cheerleaders in an American football stadium. Don't wait for the next news item, and forget the whistle! Put your cigarette out and take down the number to send in your contribution now!

The next morning, after he had filled out a money transfer form from the Deutsche Bank, Eduard had only a vague recollection of the unease he had felt the day before.

FROM HIS SEAT AT THE BAR, Eduard witnessed an unusual pantomime through the glass wall of The Tent. Illuminated by the headlights of the passing cars, a man on the other side of the street was banging his left heel against the curb, as if he were rehearsing a tap dance. Not until the man managed to waltz his way through the cars to The Tent did Eduard recognize André, who continued to mutter curses and inspect the sole of his shoe as he said hello to Eduard and Pinka.

They say it brings good luck, said Pinka.

Then every inhabitant of this city should be a millionaire, André replied. Have you ever watched how people bounce and prance along the sidewalks? The way they proceed jump by jump, with their eyes glued to the pavement? The whole city is one big latrine for dogs.

Pinka laughed and sat down with them for a minute; she told them about a citizens' initiative called "Pure Soles," which was fighting for a proposal that would make dog owners responsible for cleaning up what their canine friends deposited on the streets. The issue had sparked more spirited public discussion than most political debates. Alarmed citizens from all districts of the city banded behind the little heaps left by their loved ones and fought for their dogs' right to shit wherever and whenever they pleased. Local television stations showed teary-eyed owners holding their four-legged friends close to the camera. The proposition was repeatedly sent back to committee and never came to a vote.

André nodded absentmindedly; the last sentences had gone right by him. Nor did Eduard's question about the upcoming wedding appear to interest him. He peered around The Tent in search of someone he knew or would like to know—but none of the faces seemed enticing enough for him to get up and exchange a few sentences. Finally his gaze lit upon his own reflection in the mirror behind the bar. He examined himself closely; Eduard had the impression André was observing a stranger.

Have you ever imagined your last day on earth? he asked. You get up, and then what? Shower, shave, fresh underwear, why not, you wouldn't want to go to your grave unwashed. Whom would you call, if anyone?—after all, the person you're going to miss most is yourself. What about the mail? All of a sudden it's so easy to take the raise in rent, the phone bill, and all the other preprinted junk and throw it unopened into the trash! And even the trash bin can go on stinking one more day. You're free to leave, all you have to do is get up and go! Wait, there's a melody playing inside your head, you can't go without hearing Don Giovanni's final entrance one more time: "No man has called me coward, and shall not while I live." But no, this one-more-time and for-the-lasttime are for people who believe that after the show is over they'll go to bed and wake up again the next morning. You go out without locking up. Everything is possible: You could still take a cab to the airport and fly to Seville, you could still fall in love, you could still father a child. Most likely you'll sit down at the café on the corner and order a cappuccino.

Something just might happen . . . You spend the day with this tiny hope, and that makes you lose track of time.

All of a sudden André's face showed a weariness which no amount of sleep could help.

What good does it do to ask yourself these questions? asked Eduard.

It happened again.

The quiet in André's voice drew out Eduard's fear. He recalled the night they had met, the square marked on André's chest with a felt pen, his precise, professional explanations, three months of radiation and chemotherapy, various operations. André's cool, composed account of his illness and all the craziness it entailed had rendered Eduard speechless. André had analyzed his condition like a patient who has acquired the knowledge of a specialist but who nevertheless refuses to allow this expertise to talk him out of his will to live. He treated his illness as a public matter; he very calmly discussed his chances of survival without any shame that some chance bystander might overhear. Why whisper: he who accepts the outcome has nothing more to muster against the illness.

By observing his doctors he realized that it was ultimately up to him to make the decisions regarding his therapy. He scoured the professional journals to keep abreast of all the new findings around the globe. Budapest, Paris, London, these were the loci of André's hopes. Eventually, after he had conquered the disease, he made his friends guess as to which of his characteristics had been the decisive one: his courage, his openness, his capability of detachment, his restlessness, his frivolity which never left him—one way or the other he seemed to have escaped his enemy. His carefree resumption of his old lifestyle, which threw all caution to the wind, caused his friends to forget that in the struggle with this illness there could be no final victory.

I have to go, André said abruptly. Are you coming along? I'd still like to see some women.

The sentence sounded awkward, an overly literal translation of some foreign expression like *voir des femmes.*

Eduard was too surprised to say no. Certainly he was not about to let André wander the streets alone. André looked over his shoulder at him as Eduard leafed through the bills in his wallet.

I'll cover you with my card, said André, but don't forget: debts for love are like debts for gambling—holy. And anything borrowed will be paid back, if necessary to my heirs, with interest.

André curled up on the broad leather seat of the Citroën like a sleeping child. It was still night in the inner city, but a pale light was seeping in from the horizon. It erased all the wrinkles and shadows on André's face, which was stuck to the back of the seat, white and flat as a piece of paper. The streets were empty, the façades of the houses appeared hollow, like a film set after shooting; the large car glided along like a giant prop being pulled across a stage in front of a painted backdrop.

Looks like it's after hours, giggled André. If we have any choice at all it will be a desperate one.

Suddenly André was wide-awake and determined; he made Eduard cruise around the same block several times. Finally they caught sight of two female shapes standing in the entrance to a building that opened out onto a large, vacant square. It wasn't clear whether they were waiting for the last clients or the first bus. André signaled for Eduard to stop.

Eduard peered into one lighter and one darker face: both

women apparently used the same lipstick, which only accentuated the real difference in the color of their lips. Both were
quite tall. They emanated a strange glitter; Eduard couldn't
decide whether it was coming from their silver eye shadow
or from the eyes themselves, with their look of inviting disdain. The meeting on the empty square was a little unreal,
artificial, as if a thought, a fleeting fancy of the brain, had
been dipped in a solution of reality. In the light of the movie
marquee next door, with the sunrise just breaking over the
horizon, the two strangers seemed more beautiful and desirable than any woman he had ever met. The brunette was
wearing a long dress which reached up to her neck; she
seemed younger than her colleague and let her do all the
talking. The second one was blond and wore a negligee
which was two sizes too small underneath her summer
jacket. The women silently assessed the two clients and communicated with glances that seemed to say it could have
been worse.

Together or separate? asked the blonde. She had a slight
accent Eduard attributed to one of the Eastern languages he
didn't speak. André looked at him with curiosity, obviously
he wanted Eduard to supply the answer.

Together, said Eduard, although he had no clear idea what
that might entail.

As they followed the two women upstairs, André nudged
Eduard with his elbow and asked with his hands which one
Eduard had chosen.

Out on the street the more noticeable blonde had seemed
the more desirable. But now that all he could see was the
backs of their knees, he could no longer recall what they had
looked like from the front.

The blonde, he said.

Me too. How are we going to do this?

Let André have his way, that would be the least he could do, thought Eduard. Three steps later, on a landing, he sensed another reaction: the blonde or nothing. Never before had a client been armed with a lamer excuse: Really I was just accompanying my friend, he's terminally ill, you see . . . André had addressed him as an accomplice, not as a nurse; he would immediately see through any decisions made out of consideration for himself and he would never forgive Eduard.

I say let's let the ladies themselves decide.

André laughed his assent. Fair but sneaky, he teased. As a blue-eyed German you're banking that you have better chances.

My eyes are green, answered Eduard.

The room was as big as a ballroom, the windows overlooked the large square illuminated by the blinking blue light of a furniture store. The alcove housed a large double bed; another, narrower bed was next to the wall beside the door. Glossy photos of half-clothed, buxom stars adorned the walls; the entire interior was obviously geared to the clients' taste and not the tenants'. Both women sat down in the middle of the room and wanted to drink something. André ordered champagne.

The blonde clonked off to the hallway in her high heels and came back with a bottle in a silver bucket and the credit-card recorder. André haggled with her a little in order not to seem like a complete fool. A meditative silence ensued when he positioned the pen next to the blonde's red fingernail. Of the three digits Eduard could make out only the first, which was a five. Once the check had been signed, both women stood up simultaneously. The clock is running, thought Eduard.

What's the matter, suddenly shy? asked the blonde.

Not at all, just a little betwixt and between, said André. Since we're both equally enthusiastic about each of you, we'd like to have you choose between us.

The two giggled, whispered briefly among themselves; something like surprise or confusion spilled over their faces. Evidently the proposal went against the rules of salable love. It demanded a form of involvement not covered in the contract. All of a sudden the blonde took Eduard by the hand, presumably just because he was sitting closer. That same moment André stretched his hand out to the younger one as if his secret wish had been fulfilled.

Eduard missed André as he followed the blonde to the back of the room; now, for everything that would follow there was no other director than himself. The blonde looked at him as he unbuttoned his shirt, bored—this was a style of love where women undressed more quickly than men.

So what'll it be, asked the blonde, garters, leather, or the rough method—for a little extra?

Eduard glanced over at André, but his friend was already beyond these choices. At the wall, in the light of the marquee, Eduard saw an isosceles triangle formed by one pair of legs and a head which was bobbing up and down. Isn't he afraid of anything, thought Eduard. Perhaps André outwitted his illness by avoiding the places where it felt most at home; perhaps he escaped his pursuers by plunging headlong into dangers of his own choosing.

Garters, said Eduard, and was amazed to find he wasn't embarrassed. As if courage were called for as well as decisiveness, he summoned a distant memory, when a seductive, unobtainable relative unfastened the garters from her stockings right in front of the adolescent boy, and then sent him off to bed. The blonde nodded absentmindedly and grabbed one of the plastic bags next to the bathroom door; suddenly she seemed very tired. Out of all possible repertoires, named or unnamed, he had evidently chosen the most common. As she fetched the accessories out of the bag, he was amazed to see all sorts of torture equipment: leather armbands with silver buttons, a leather mask, leather gloves. In disbelief he watched as the blonde glided a whip over her fingers. Suddenly she laughed out loud, shook her head, then tapped her forehead as if she had been caught making a mistake, went back to the bathroom, and returned with the wishbag he had chosen.

With a few tricks the strange woman metamorphosed into the image in his head. But every one of her sentences began to bother him, every discrepancy; and anyway, it was all happening too fast. As he tried to coax the scene in his memory to the point where it had always broken off, he suddenly heard André clapping his hands next to him: Come on, we're finished, let's go!

Eduard was enraged, but he couldn't help laughing; it was too late to ask for a little patience. Paying his compliments as he dragged Eduard to the door, André took his leave, as exuberant as a schoolboy following a successful prank, and his good mood infected Eduard. On their way downstairs he claimed to have immediately recognized that Eduard, the ostensible winner, was in reality the loser. He, the loser, had been lucky to wind up with the brunette.

Let's drive around a little more, said André, when they were again sitting in the car.

Eduard headed for the autobahn. When, at 100 miles per hour the heavy car began to vibrate, Eduard saw a wanton gleam light up in André's eyes. He wasn't afraid anymore, André yelled. Once he had been in an airplane when a storm caused a free fall of a few hundred meters; he was the only passenger who kept on looking curiously out the window. Without warning he placed his left foot on Eduard's right and pressed down on the accelerator. When the needle reached 115 mph the bushes and shade trees on the edge of the road seemed overcome by a torrent which was bearing down upon them with terrific force. Eduard followed the last exit before the border and took a narrow lane down to the lake. They stopped at a place where the dirty sand of the shore touched the asphalt. A few trees were standing in the knee-deep water and casting their shadows on the dark surface of the lake, which was moving quietly, as if remembering the wind of bygone days. A thin band of haze shrouded the opposite shore, Eduard and André opened their doors wide and leaned back in the plush seats of the Citroën, and watched the sun build a shining street of light across the water. Annoyed, André imitated the basses that were pounding out through the stereo speakers and switched off the radio.

Can you hear how this music can't hold its own against the silence? he asked. Then he intoned, in a surprisingly high and strong voice, the Mozart theme "Kneel and pray God for pardon," signaled with his hands for the orchestra to enter, and continued with the counterpart, "Let dotards talk of kneeling," until finally with one voice he improvised the trio: "Pray to Him!"—"No!"—"Pray!"—"No!"—"Pray! Pray!"— "No, no!"—"Your hour of doom has come!"

André cawed more than he sang; you couldn't hear him

produce melodies and notes, but you could hear his idea of the melodies and notes, of the musical machinery in the battle between the Commendatore and Don Giovanni, and André's idea of this work was so overwhelmingly beautiful that Eduard couldn't hear enough of it. Right in the middle André broke off, quoted some nonsense out of Mozart's letters, and as Eduard watched his friend improvise Mozart with gestures, notes, phrases, the Citroën was transformed into a Viennese coach—Mozart had always driven a Citroën, and it was Mozart to whom Eduard owed 250 marks for a night of love.

15

IT WAS HARD to recognize the same old André beneath the tuxedo he was wearing, only his conspiratorial glance as he greeted his friend recalled the night creature of Eduard's acquaintance. He showed no trace of his illness, the wedding seemed to electrify him. He took Klara's hand and greeted her with a kiss.

Actually we would have made the perfect bridal couple, he said, and clasped her hand tightly, as though he were waiting for her to answer yes. You know how when you're in love it's so easy to fall in love again right away. It's the same way with getting married. People should do it every year!

Theo had varied his usual attire by a single component: over his trademark T-shirt he was wearing a wrinkled linen sports coat instead of his usual leather jacket; otherwise he looked the same as always, not even the boxing shoes he had brought back from his last trip to New York were missing. To be opened after the honeymoon, he said as he handed André his wedding present, a sealed envelope bearing the label "The Rake Reformed—final version."

The ceremony took place in a converted S-Bahn station. André had hired an army of door openers, coat checkers, and waiters, as well as a combo of nimble old men whose repertory of hits spanned three generations and several continents. Meetings of the Conference on Security and Cooperation in Europe were arranged in a similar manner, André explained, and listed the countries and cities from where the guests had traveled.

In the brightly illumined station Eduard saw André's relatives, both old and new, standing loosely grouped in conversation; the room was abuzz with a dozen different languages, several shades of skins and three generations were all represented. At the other end of the hall Esther, clad completely in white, was surrounded by her family; Eduard recognized her father—who was wearing tails—from the fiddler's patch of red on his neck. The bridal entourage also included a dog, who was orbiting the entire group like a gently swaying satellite.

André was still holding Klara's hand as he introduced her and Eduard to his parents. Eduard looked into the bright eyes of an aging bohemian, whose lips carried the same seductive smile as his son's. André's mother, though petite and more fragile, seemed somehow to have both feet planted more firmly on the ground, a counterweight for two men inclined to float away. As he watched his parents exchange civilities with his friends, André looked proud, or even in love, so it seemed to Eduard. For their part, they treated André with the care parents reserve for a brilliant but ever-endangered child. With a rush of envy Eduard told himself that this family had evidently never experienced the same generational strife which had alienated him and Lothar for so long from their parents. In André's case the question What did you do then? could only be rephrased as How did you escape? Or maybe he was romanticizing André's connection to his parents? Was it possible he bore an entirely different burden, of never having been able to completely break from home?

Only gradually did it dawn on Eduard that for the first time he was in a largish gathering made up mostly of Jews. During the 1920s an occasion like this would have been an everyday event; now, almost forty years after the German crimes against the Jews, there was something ephemeral about the whole affair, something almost unreal. It was as if they were restaging a memory which could find no handle or hold in the present. In a few days the guests would again depart for wherever their families had saved themselves a half century earlier, and suddenly Eduard realized that even André and Theo were living on borrowed time in the city where he felt at home. Both kept the passports of the countries where their parents had found refuge; they themselves moved around like resident refugees who refused to be deceived by a forty-year calm, two somewhat pampered, watchful sons, always on the alert for the moment their "mother tongue" might suddenly reactivate the words of murder and deportation which had been temporarily suppressed.

Unintentionally André's father had entangled himself in a conversation with Theo about the situation of the Jews in the other Germany. Whether he wasn't mistaken in assuming that the official anti-Fascism there served as a magical cloak of invisibility which the Germans across the Elbe used to cover up their own guilt in the Holocaust? After all, their government had thus far refused to pay any reparation; the East German state had never even managed to recognize Israel's right to exist. Theo's reply was remarkably toned down, his answers sounded like excerpts from an encyclopedia, evidently he didn't want to spoil André's wedding. Eduard felt an elbow in his rib cage; André was looking on concerned: with remarkably accurate aim, André's father had asked Theo about the one topic which—next to the *Don Giovanni* project—was the subject and source of endless conflict between the two.

André never let anyone have the slightest doubt that he was Jewish and accepted the extra attention this communiqué was bound to trigger with great poise and charm. It was not in his nature to be mistrustful, and in principle it was all the same to him how the children of the perpetrators dealt with their complexes. The main thing was that they treated him well or, better yet, that they loved him. As far as he was concerned, he approached every German of his generation with a presumption of innocence, at least as long as the person in question didn't prove him wrong. André reacted vehemently whenever he came across the contention that the victims of yesterday had become—in the Israeli-occupied areas—the perpetrators of today; he never let anyone get away with this all-too-transparent attempt at passing guilt. But the opponent who upset him most in these matters was Theo. Certain views which André considered anti-Semitic struck Theo as worth investigating; the latter generally accused André of reacting too quickly with this label, claiming that he unnecessarily dramatized everyday nuisances and annoyances which could happen to anyone else. During such debates Eduard almost always sided with André, whereupon Theo would claim that it was only his typical bad conscience that was speaking. With all due respect for your scruples, unfortunately they lead to a paralysis of thought. Time and again Eduard found himself in the unlikely situation of staunchly defending the Israeli position, while Theo would subject it to scathing critiques. He considered the

founding of Israel in Palestine a great misfortune, the Jews
would have done better to erect their own state right in the
heart of their conquered enemies, in Bavaria, for example.

André succeeded in averting the conversation that threatened to engulf his father and Theo by asking both to sit down
to dinner at the family table and seating them as far from
each other as possible. Esther's family had already taken its
place in a closed formation along one long side of the table.
So it happened that both families were sitting opposite each
other. Esther's relatives had donned costumes the like of
which Eduard had recently seen onstage as part of a Che-
khov play—Yuri had undoubtedly picked up a large part of
them at miraculous discounts at flea markets around the city.
Esther's mother, who seemed oblivious to the concepts of
dieting and cholesterol, was bejeweled to bedazzle; she bore
with great dignity necklaces and bracelets whose sheer
weight would have been enough to make André's mother
buckle. With his wild white hair and well-rounded belly, Yuri
looked like a circus trainer about to announce the entrance
of the elephants. By contrast, André's very properly clothed
relations came off as being color-shy and a little undernour-
ished. Only connoisseurs would recognize the great French
and Italian couturiers by the cut of their dresses and suits;
their gestures were restrained, and the volume of their conversations was kept at chamber-level, so that whenever dialogue spanned the table it was as if a string quartet were
attempting to communicate with a brass band.

The mere sight of the new relations from the East must
have been a shock for André's father, for he donned a prophylactic smile the moment Yuri opened his mouth. For his
part, Esther's father watched open-mouthed as his new relative sniffed the cork of the wine bottle he had asked the

waiter to bring him. For a long time André's father seemed
to ponder the news heralded by the cork's aroma; then a
critical wrinkle appeared at the end of his elegant nose, and
he pronounced that the wine was past its prime. Yuri was
thrilled to discover such expertise in his new Western relative: André genius, father also genius, what fantastic family,
he said as he refilled the glasses with vodka.

André's father smiled with unruffled composure as Yuri
clinked glasses. Then he turned back to Theo, who seemed
to interest him the most, and offered a new topic of conversation: Don't you agree that utopias are modern society's
most dangerous enemy? Isn't it true that the people of Eastern Europe, and above all the Poles, are all trying to free
themselves from the utopias which had been foisted upon
them?

Theo evidently felt no inclination to get sucked into an
argument about utopias, so he responded rather lacklusterly
that capitalism, which claimed to follow the laws of nature,
never managed to work without a social idea as a corrective
measure. It was possible that the capitalist countries of the
West were the only ones who had profited from the experiment of socialism.

André's father could not refrain from commenting on this
opinion and suddenly seemed bent on bringing the Eastern
relations into the conversation. With friendly curiosity he
looked toward Esther's parents as if he considered them the
only informed judges of the debate.

He would advise distinguishing, he began, between the
loss and the erosion of utopia. The former concept had a
moralizing undertone: one was immediately inclined to
mourn the misfortune which had so undeservedly befallen a
dear friend named utopia. But in reality this utopia had not

experienced any misfortune at all, it simply had not with-
stood the test of time and thereby proved itself to be the true
misfortune.

While Esther translated, her parents hung wide-eyed on
the lips of this worldly philosopher from Paris. But Yuri must
have misunderstood something. Probably thinking that André's father had just given his wedding speech and that it was
now his own turn, he got up, banged on his glass, and raised
a toast to the wedding couple. Then he immediately bent
down, pulled a violin case from under the table, and signaled
with his bow. As if he had conjured them out of thin air, a
band of musicians wearing Gypsy dress appeared in the
room, overran the stage, and started the wedding music with
a brisk *tutti*. Esther tried in vain to restrain her father; Yuri
had just taken over the podium and after a few measures
reached his fastest tempo. Like a Ping-Pong ball supported
by a jet of water, the rotund man pranced up and down, his
white hair flapping across his face strewn with sweat; he
stroked his violin with such power that at the end of each
piece entire fringes of hair were dangling from the bow. In
his booming bass he introduced the pieces: "Sirba," "Song
of Vladimir," "Peasant Pictures from Russia," "Odessa Melodies," "Happy Prayer." All followed the same basic rhythmic
pattern; each began with a slow theme that accelerated faster
and faster, until it broke out into a St. Vitus' dance.

Encouraged by the applause, Yuri again left the podium
and played his way over to the families' table. In front of
André's parents he dropped to his knee in order to attain the
greatest proximity to their hearts and ears. But it was not
until Yuri changed the program and struck up a Yiddish song
that the first signs of emotion appeared on André's stone-
faced father. When Yuri finished playing "Yiddishe Mama"

with surprising tenderness, André's father removed his glasses and wiped a few tears from his eyes. In this moment of silence, so it seemed to Eduard, the entire gathering forgave Yuri. Unfortunately, he read the thunderous applause as encouragement for further encores. Hearing his cries of "*Oppa, oppa*" and "*Passa, passa,*" one section of the Eastern relatives could no longer stand being confined to their chairs and a few began to weave improvised dances between the tables. The entire program had run amok: the order of speeches, the serving of the courses, the various performances of André's artist friends—it took almost violent means to enforce the order of ceremony. Two hours after the wedding dinner the entire gathering was in a general state of scatter.

André's father paced restlessly up and down among the tables, slapping his head as if he were looking for gentle words to pronounce a devastating verdict. Finally he turned to André: East is East and West is West, even a wedding ring cannot revoke the compass.

16

DURING HIS LAST LECTURE of the semester Eduard was bothered by four students wearing Mickey Mouse masks who sat in the second row. He had grown accustomed to freshmen performing any number of activities in class: knitting sweaters, darning socks, trimming their fingernails, or practicing Yoga, but never before had they turned his lecture into a children's party. He coolly asked what the performance was all about. Instead of answering, the four unrolled a banner: "Stop the mouse concentration camps! Freedom and happiness for all lab mice!"

The first sentence was absolutely inappropriate—for carnival pranks as well as animal-rights activism. He called on the protesters to remove their masks and explain their slogan. No reaction, not a word—the four seemed to think their highly legible words needed no further commentary. No one else in the auditorium chose to speak out, so Eduard decided to keep his cool and not play into the hands of the protesters with an angry reaction. I'm sure you realize I don't have anything against protest at the university—back then we used to— Stop, forget the back then. Anybody who knows me knows . . . That's even worse . . . I always considered protests against animal testing entirely legitimate, always said that approximately 80 percent of such experiments are unneces-

sary. But what I can't abide is your masking your faces, this
flirt with illegality, this hiding behind a banner, don't give
me this kind of spineless, simplistic slogan, don't you trust
your own arguments? And the words "concentration camp"
cannot be tolerated as a means to convey your protest. Evidently you don't have a very clear, well-informed picture of
what went on in the German concentration camps, otherwise
you yourselves would have found them utterly inappropriate.

Besides, the correct target for the protest is the cosmetics
industry, the pharmaceutical industry: approximately three
million animals a year lose their lives in the private laboratories; the institute uses a few dozen at most.

Uses, cried out an unmasked student, so riled up his face
had turned white; that's the language of the Wannsee
Conference!

It took Eduard some effort to control himself. This comparison was also absurd, but that didn't stop him from cor-
recting himself. Okay, approximately two dozen mice are
incarcerated at the institute, misused for experiments, and
murdered. And as much as he disapproved of this—there was
no fundamental solution for the problem. Science had not
arrived at the point where it could completely forgo experi-
menting with animals, since the effects of many substances
could not be reproduced by alternate methods such as cell
cultures or organ isolation. He considered animal testing in
the cosmetics industry uncalled-for, but unfortunately it was
indispensable in the struggle to understand and overcome
life-threatening diseases like AIDS, cancer, or multiple
sclerosis.

Maybe the fault lay in his telling; in any case, Betty had a
good laugh when he described the incident to her. And the
fact that most of his colleagues considered the appearance

of the Mouse Power Faction a teapot tempest made him even more anxious and provoked him to find common cause with the mouse protectors. In disqualifying their protest had he not resorted to the same arguments his professors had used fifteen years earlier in dismissing the student revolts of '68? "Protest, by all means, just not in this form . . . You're targeting the wrong person; the industrial complex, on the other hand . . ."

Of course, the animal activists' unwillingness to discuss things ran contrary to his experience as well as his standards, but where did he get the right to canonize his own generation? Besides, he had a pretty good memory of the disgust he had felt when he first jabbed a needle into the living body of a mouse, the sense that he was committing some undefined wrong, that he was abusing some unwarranted power. Gradually, in the name of research and by dint of habit, he had come to suppress this feeling, but the question as to why the adult world believed that human beings alone among the animals had a natural right of inviolability remained unanswered. Wasn't his reaction in the classroom an outgrowth of that early distress he had ultimately overcome? Did he feel taken by surprise because other, younger people had taken the reflex he had suppressed and posted it on a banner?

General sensitivity seemed to increase with each new generation in direct proportion to average body size. Of course, human sympathy for animals was every bit as selective as it was for endangered examples of its own kind, and in the animal kingdom, too, unknown wannabees vied with star celebrities for international attention—but the sympathy itself was clearly expanding its range. Eduard's peers had once focused their feelings of solidarity on big animals such as whales and elephants. Obviously their criteria in making this

selection derived not only from how endangered a given species was but also how attractive. In principle there was no
compelling reason why less impressive species such as potato
bugs, cockroaches, or mice should suffer worse treatment.
Christian ethics, which proclaimed mankind to be master
over all the animals, were already precariously perched on a
very shaky moral foundation; the idea of differentiating according to the degree of relation to humans was even more
tenuous. Why should, for instance, horses, cats, and dogs
enjoy a greater right to life than the so-called lower orders?
The circumstance that mice were clearly smaller, uglier, and
more numerous than whales gave no one the right to inject
them with viruses and kill them. In the meantime, a generation which had grown up under the tutelage of Mickey
Mouse had now come of age. Walt Disney's animation had
made this nimble, talking mouse the unchallenged star of
children's fantasies. Was it not conceivable that someday this
most popular of prophets would spur his fanatical and eventually even armed disciples onto the streets and into the fray?

He hadn't mentioned to his class that he felt his own work
threatened by the animal activists: he had to resort to animal
testing for his project on multiple sclerosis. For their part,
the activists had neglected to spell out the implications of
their demands: a ban on animal testing either meant abandoning any attempt to discover the cause, and one day the
cure, for diseases like multiple sclerosis or else it meant con-
templating human experimentation, following the example of
the Nazi doctors. Society could not defend both values
equally unconditionally: the animals' right to human protection and the right of sick humans to a cure. Whoever wanted
to exercise one right was bound to injure the other. Evidently

humans were not granted a life completely free from guilt, at least not in this world.

But none of these ruminations helped him overcome the apathy he was feeling toward his lab work. Weeks had passed and he had yet to move beyond the first basic steps in his MS experiment. He hadn't even managed to isolate the virus he was looking for within the tissue. He was considering a new approach, but his brain was utterly drained from corrections, critiques, and routine paperwork, and his ideas struck him as commonplace, mechanical, devoid of inspiration.

Nor did his self-imposed sexual abstinence help. The broadened view, the emboldened spirit, the liberated flow of ideas—all the payoff promised by the prophets of abstinence—were missing. Evidently the urges which had been forced underground had organized their resistance and were now deploying an unremitting stream of partisans into Eduard's cerebral system to sabotage all his plans for work. Their most successful weapon was Dr. Nastase's test result: why analyze foreign cells when you can't even explain your own?

For several weeks two women in long skirts had been following the Tamil rose sellers in The Tent along their endless procession from table to table. But instead of hawking wet long-stemmed roses, they were peddling the future. Their *modus operandi* was to first catch the eye of a solitary patron, then make a beeline for him. Once in his face, they would apprise him of his fortune, which always turned out to have a Bulgarian accent: It's better no travel in August. Very big crisis!

Next they would sit down, grab the hand of their still-undecided customer, and examine it closely, all the while thoughtfully shaking their heads. Hardly anyone managed to retrieve his hand, and whoever didn't plug his ears at the very first sentence would invariably want to hear the second. But that is precisely the moment when soothsayers around the world break into an unintelligible murmur—it's impossible to get another word out of them unless you pay. Naturally the Bulgarians let you haggle: for a third of the requested fee you could peep into the next millennium. And although these two women looked neither especially old nor particularly wise, they had managed to attract a rapidly growing clientele. The popular verdict was that these fortune-tellers were Bulgarian, after all, and where fortune-telling is concerned, there's no better place in the world. Exactly why this particular art flourished in Bulgaria of all places was as great a riddle as palmistry itself. Because Bulgaria lies under the sign of the soothsayers, answered the women.

After taking his twenty-mark bill, one of the two women gazed into his hand for several minutes, studying his Heart Line. Look for yourself, she said at last, beginning is good, but then . . . up here, down there, even in middle.

Eduard had never noticed the pattern below the bases of his fingers: what the woman called his Heart Line did indeed begin very solidly before branching out into three clearly distinct parallel arms, each of which in turn sprouted numerous hairline branchettes. The fortune-teller showed his hand to her companion, who immediately let out a stifled cry of shock. Eduard had the impression both women were reluctant to break the news to him that the best thing for him to do was simply relinquish love altogether and leave it to more competent individuals.

You cannot live with one woman, for you it is impossible, she said, always there are three.

Three women?

The Bulgarian palm reader nodded, full of sympathy, and folded Eduard's hand as if she wanted to spare him the remaining details concerning his terrible fate.

He sat there, upset; it took him a while to put his thoughts in order. Naturally he didn't believe in chiromancy for a minute, but then again he was reluctant to exclude the possibility that there might be something to it which would someday find a scientific explanation. Apart from that the diagnosis didn't cause him any great despair. If it was true that his Heart Line excluded the possibility of a strictly monogamous lifestyle, it was a defect he shared with about two-thirds of his fellow males. According to a poll of 2,467 individuals, 68.7 percent of all men had cheated on their partners at least once, and the corresponding percentage of women was only slightly smaller. Because the study had not included *ménages à trois*, the statistics failed to take into account the complex matrix of disloyalty that would ensue if someone in that situation decided to spend a night with a different couple.

Over the next days he discreetly checked the crucial line on his friends and acquaintances. The handshake so popular among Germans provided the pretext; he simply transformed it slightly to suit his purposes. He grabbed the person being greeted by the wrist and drew the palm decisively up to his eyes. Theo's Heart Line simply dissolved at the base of his ring finger, while André's resembled an exploding shrapnel bomb. In no hand did he discover anything remotely approaching his own line, so Eduard had to grow used to the thought that he was on his own; he would have to come to terms with the fate inscribed in his palm without any guidance. The assignment at hand, as it were, was to discover exactly who his three fates were. If he attributed the middle line to Klara, the two outside branches remained unnamed, and it was now a matter of identifying these two strangers. As long as he was destined to be unhappy with three women, he at least wanted to make their acquaintance.

In studying the literature he discovered that the lines of your palm don't change overnight. The Heart Line is something you're born with, a large handicap given before you start the game; it's already inscribed and impervious to any influence of will or circumstance. There was nothing that indicated Eduard was destined to take a trip around the world. In all likelihood he had been struggling with his romantic destiny for a long time; he had probably even met the bearers of his ill fortune without recognizing them.

That same afternoon he rang up Jenny. It was impossible to reconstruct how they'd started talking to each other in the first place: a series of misunderstandings concerning a film whose only salient characteristic was that Jenny found it exciting while Eduard felt bored to tears. Although she could not remember the title, the director, or the story, she could recall in unusual detail specific images and entire passages of dialogue which had escaped him completely. Evidently she had focused exclusively on the montage and derived her own conclusions from that: the car with its bright lights at the edge of the picture, the boy in the background in front of a house—she had completely missed the basic plot. Was it that she saw more than most people? Evidently they'd watched two different films with the same title.

He wouldn't have devoted any more thought to their disagreement if her opinions hadn't provoked him—Jenny always had strong opinions about everything. She claimed, for instance, that a single surprising image, a sequence never before seen, was enough to justify a film, and besides, the only films that would create such a lasting effect were the successful ones. So what if the dialogue was witty or the story well constructed—what will ultimately become of the film? Bare bones, a skeleton. It's like your biology teacher using charts to explain the difference between a man and a woman. The details are what make or break a film, the visual surprises you can latch on to, not the movie as a whole.

Eduard disagreed with her just for the sake of argument. The only trouble was that in doing so he involuntarily verified her claim. In a short time he had completely lost the main thread of Jenny's arguments and was able to focus on only two details: Jenny's Egyptian neck and her eyes, which seemed to peer from very far away. Apart from that, her skin irritated him: it was too flawless, too porcelain-pure, it belonged in a fairy tale, it was an affront to common sense, so much innocence and purity couldn't possibly exist. If you were to run into a Botticelli angel wearing leather pants and holding a glass full of vodka, the first thing you'd do is question your sense of reality. You wouldn't want anything from her, maybe just to touch her arm once to check whether such a creature really was made of flesh and blood.

They didn't fit each other at all. Jenny's speech was insolent, even hurtful; from time to time a haughty smile would creep across her lips. Her hands didn't suit her arms, her fingers were enormously long and almost coarse. Worker's hands, thought Eduard. Her clothing, too, contradicted the message sent by her neck and skin: men's jackets with padded shoulders, flat shoes, male shoes on female feet. Rings, armbands, chains, lipstick—any hint of feminine ornament or glamour was militantly avoided. Possibly her eyebrows had been plucked a tiny bit and highlighted with millimetric precision, but perhaps it was nature who had drawn this arch of unearthly perfection.

After their first encounter they had parted with the unstated promise of letting it go at that. But over the next few days Eduard noticed that the thought of Jenny was boring away inside his brain like a tiny drill, leaving a trace of fine powder. Somehow she had succeeded in annoying him; he only hoped he had managed to annoy her as well and that they would have another occasion to annoy each other.

She wasn't surprised when he showed up at her door, and he made no attempt to explain his uninvited appearance. Had he misheard or just forgotten that she was a city planner? Since he was neither a senator nor any other key figure involved in awarding large municipal contracts, Jenny suggested the next best motive for his intrusion: lobbyist, fan, and spokesman for her ideas of redesigning the city. Eduard told himself that he probably wasn't the first who had to put up with this casting. Apparently Jenny had learned to deflect the interest of her male onlookers from herself onto her projects.

Her apartment was a living sketch. Everything was fast-paced, temporary, tailored for immediate departure. The large windows were bare, the boards painted white, the furniture from the flea market, the cupboard doors ajar, the tubes in the bathroom all uncapped. On the floor a mattress and at eye level a first-generation color TV. Months later, when Eduard received Jenny's first postcard, it reminded him of this apartment: rough poetic bits tastefully composed on the card, the syllables weren't spelled out completely; Jenny even treated words, above all long ones, as unnecessary bal-

last which cramped her style and were therefore best discarded.

What at first confused him about her designs was their
scale. Unflaggingly she carried in rolls of paper the size of
columns, which she spread out on the floor and unrolled,
using Eduard as a paperweight for the lower right corner.
Her ideas about architecture and urban planning were every
bit as far-reaching as her sketches. She believed the law
should be expanded to cover a new punishable offense—
"architectural crimes." You can always get rid of a politician,
but it's not that easy to vote out criminally ugly houses and
uninhabitable districts: they stick around for fifty to a hundred years.

As she stood there in front of him with three new paper
columns, Eduard felt something happening inside him. Although she was almost entirely hidden behind the rolls, he
suddenly sensed a painfully clear, bodily image of her. He
was moved and excited by the idea that someone with shoulders that narrow was so determined to make her way through
life lugging these mighty sketches: Jenny, a female knight
setting out to battle the construction mafia, armed with
lances made for giants.

The bed was the only place in Jenny's apartment where
you didn't have to stand. While she was making coffee, Eduard turned on the TV, which first emitted some ominous
ticking and then took two minutes to produce a picture.

A man from a primitive tribe in Africa sets out to hunt.
Because this will require several days, he first needs to discover a source of water, which only his involuntary companion, the ape, can show him. But how is the man to catch an
ape unaided and unarmed? Inside a fissure of a cliff, our
hunter searches for and finds a beehive. Using sticks and

stones, he closes it up until only his hand will fit inside. Now he must wait; he lies down beneath a tree and sleeps. Eventually the ape, addicted as it is to honey, will discover the hive, but while the animal is satisfying its sweet tooth, its leathery hand is stung by the bees so often that it swells and gets trapped inside the narrow fissure. The hunter's moment has now arrived: having fashioned a noose out of roots, he captures the ape, opens the fissure, and tethers the animal to a tree. Again he waits, through the night and into the next day. He lets the ape swelter in the noonday sun until it grows weary with thirst, then at last he unbinds his accomplice. The ape will now look for water, and with all its apish instincts it is sure to find it. With tired bounds the thirsty animal trudges forward, the hunter close on its heels. Together they arrive at a hidden spring. Now at last our hunter can devote himself to the real purpose of all these preparations, the hunt.

It was at Jenny's that Eduard first became acquainted with the Animal Film, an underrated genre in Jenny's view; German TV didn't have much more to offer—you know most of them are old BBC reruns, anyway. If the people who made feature films and documentaries paid as much attention to the human species, and approached it with the same capacity for awe, then maybe there'd once again be some reason to watch human films instead.

While other couples might make love to the strains of Verdi or choirs of Tibetan monks, for Jenny and Eduard the Animal Film became an indispensable accompaniment to their passion. They forgot themselves to the thunder of buffalo herds, the singing of whales, the rattling and rustling of desert snakes, the flapping and cawing of voracious vultures, and it was presumably these sounds which caused him to make light of Jenny's warning: I don't have any safe days, I'm fertile thirty days a month.

What to say? There's nothing to worry about? Or maybe: I've been sterilized?

I'll be careful, said Eduard.

Maybe it was part of her design philosophy that Jenny hardly ever undressed completely. She let the immediate position of her body decide where her desire would originate. Eduard was taken aback to find that underneath all the men's clothing her skin just kept on going, as it were—what did he expect, anyway, calluses? Freckles? Weals? In the counterglow of the African TV sun, the colorless fuzz on Jenny's stomach vibrated and trembled like a fluorescent script of hairline letters. It annoyed him that her skin hardly ever showed any sign of moisture. As if her pores refused to open for something as pedestrian as sweat. Even the hollows of her body were utterly free of any odor. Whatever glistened on her ribs or buttocks was never the result of her own exertion. Or was she just lazy in bed?

With quick, expert movements she did what was necessary to make a man rigid, to set things in motion. Sought and found the position which required the minimum movement on her part. Drawing on thousands of years of intuition and experience, she knew exactly which buttons activated the machine of desire. Or was she only forestalling any attempt by him to do the same; did she understand his motor better than her own?

The only thing he knew for sure was that Jenny was one hell of a mechanic. All of a sudden a dumb sentence—was it André's or Theo's—bordering on the macho popped into his head: Following the age of bosom fixation, the needle of the erotic compass was suddenly drawn to the backside of the planet. Progress or regress, it was definitely a Copernican revolution. Woe to the man who met a woman whose two poles were equally attractive—he was bound to wind up in the nuthouse.

Jenny lay on her stomach and Eduard learned new prayers. How was it possible that he had so long denied this most ancient god of sexual rapture? Had it really taken him half a lifetime to discover pleasures which most fellow males probably stumble onto when they're taking their first steps? Herds of zebras galloped across the ticking TV screen, spraying tiny droplets of sweat on Jenny's back; lions hunted and slew the fleeing game; and while a tropical downpour pounded the desert, Jenny evicted Eduard with a giggle.

Over the weeks which followed the first Animal Film, his visits began to assume the rights afforded by precedent, a right based on habit and not on contract, a state of affairs they each interpreted differently but neither chose to define. Jenny never asked where he was coming from or going to, not to mention when they might next meet. And she veiled her own intimate life with the same discretion—at least that part in which Eduard was not physically present. The question posed by the wedge-wolf, to tell or not to tell, seemed for Jenny to have been answered without it ever having been asked. Evidently she believed in keeping things quiet to the point of denying them. Occasional signs and clues—a letter on the bed, a shaving brush in the bathroom, a new bicycle —"A friend gave it to me"—led Eduard to infer that he was not her only lover. But Jenny left him alone with his conjectures and could not be induced to talk, not even about earlier lovers now long gone. Her first lover remained as shrouded in secrecy as the one she was presumably with at present, and she left it to Eduard to decide whether he preferred to think of her as a wanton or as a nun.

AT ABOUT EIGHT IN THE EVENING, on his way home from the institute, at a traffic light that had long turned to green, Eduard experienced an epiphany. While an angry driver honked at him from behind and a swerving cyclist stuck a raised middle finger through his open window, while the windshield wipers screeched in vain at him that it had stopped raining, it suddenly hit him: the dusky pattern on the last X-ray film he had tossed aside without paying any attention appeared before his eyes, fantastically magnified, as wonderfully legible as if a giant had scrawled it in the evening sky. When another angry driver began to lean on the horn, Eduard spun around at the crossing and raced back to the institute.

Checking his vision against the film itself, he ascertained that his mind's eye had correctly captured the salient features of the X-ray film. The DNA sequence bore a marked resemblance to other viral sequences. He noted the order of the letters and fed them into the computer. That same night he took out the bottle of champagne he had been keeping on ice. He was as good as certain he had identified the virus responsible for multiple sclerosis.

Later, when he recalled the circumstances of his discovery, he was unable to decide whether the breakthrough was due to his brief attempt at asceticism or the subsequent expansion of his love life. Whereas poets had had their passions scrutinized in great detail, the love life of scientists had never been studied at all, since no one thought they were capable of having any. But fellow professionals were well aware of certain specific coincidences. Albert Einstein postulated his general theory of relativity when he was twenty-six years old, having just fallen in love with his future wife, whom incidentally he also had to thank for the mathematics involved in his stroke of genius. Erwin Schrödinger—according to one biographer—reputedly sketched out his wave theory while on a ski trip with a lover, during a "late erotic explosion over the Christmas holidays." Watson and Crick had themselves described their own emotional turmoil at the time they discovered the double helix: two pubescent students plagued with acne, erotic fantasies, and a near-pathological ambition made the second most important find of the century.

Whether it was pure chance or prophecy fulfilled—at the same time he was getting to know Jenny, Eduard made the acquaintance of a woman who gave the third branch of his Heart Line a name: Laura. André had introduced them; she was an opera singer of Italian descent. When Eduard first laid eyes on her he immediately recalled André's remark that being in love is a generous feeling, whoever has fallen in love with one person can easily do it with someone else right away.

Laura's first visit to his back-building apartment was stored in his memory under the headings "Desire," "Conflict," and "Black." Desire for conflict, conflict over desire, conflicting desires, desirous conflicts—the first two words were both very malleable, they offered an endless number of combinations, what was rigidly immutable was the color black. Laura's hair was of a black that did not occur naturally in his part of the world. It made her rather dark skin seem pale, as if illumined by an eternal moon. Her wide-open eyes, agape with an insatiable curiosity, promised unexplored pleasures—and unknown strife.

Whenever and wherever they met, they began each encounter with a delicate pricking, a verbal acupuncture. With sure aim, Laura pushed her invisible needles into his nerve centers. The Nordic man, his haircut, his very German precautionary neurosis, the German fear of living, Eduard's opinions of Italy—any occasion was a good one for voicing irreconcilable differences of opinion. Nor was his own field of inquiry safe from her attacks: on the subject of twin research, she defended his brother's views with great verve. At times her spirit of contradiction reminded Eduard of Theo, an observation which promptly led to another argument. Only in a culture as dependent on consensus as the German could a desire for difference, a taste for the extreme, cause any amazement at all.

As fearless as she was in battle, she was no less fearless in love. Her desire, insofar as it extended to Eduard, excluded the bed as venue. Telephone booths, bathrooms, cinema seats, his old Citroën—Laura preferred any and all to a bed. Perhaps her rejection of traditional locales was a veiled protest against her own desire. Maybe the occasional excesses with Eduard were actually an affront to her idea of love, so that she felt obliged to offend public opinion as well. For whatever reason, Laura was an enemy of every predictability, desire needed to come over her with the power of a natural phenomenon, neither the place of encounter nor its course could be subjected to any rules. Indeed, Eduard never knew what to expect from a given meeting with Laura; in her eyes expectations existed only to create disappointment.

The border café where Laura liked best to meet him was situated on one of the easternmost points of the Western Hemisphere. From the window seat you could see the passports of the transit travelers and the shaved necks of the East German border guards. The crossing hadn't lost any of the glaringly illuminated gray first portrayed in *The Spy Who Came In from the Cold*. Compared to the wattage consumed by the café, the neon light of the border crossing seemed designed to save energy. When Eduard raised his wineglass to his lips, he had the momentary impression of being able to see the bones in his hand. Laura across from him—black scarf and coat, black eyes and hair, black the lightest fuzz on her lip, shaded by her nose, her small teeth phosphorescent in the light of the border. Even without makeup she seemed to glow, her cosmetics were innate.

She began by entangling him in a riddle which he solved miserably. Eduard the bean counter just couldn't figure out the math. A ferryman is given the task of conveying seven sheep and one wolf safe and sound to the other side of the river. But only three animals fit in his boat. In which order using which combinations does he complete the task? His brain was a mess, he had to be reminded of the fact that wolves are inclined to eat sheep. So the ferryman can't leave any of the sheep alone with the wolf, not even for a second . . .

As he was trying to solve the riddle, Laura took off her pullover and his attention was captured by the two lively creatures lurking under her tight satin blouse. Soon all he could think of was how to throw overboard ferryman, sheep, and wolf so as to climb into the boat alone with Laura and sail for some other distant shore. Inside his brain, each of the riddles held the other in check.

And you claim to be a biomathematician?

A molecular bio-futurologist, said Eduard.

A dark Mercedes pulled up to the border outside. A woman lifted her hair to expose her ear, which the official ear fetishists examined for several seconds. Laura suddenly felt a chill and wanted to get out, anywhere. In this part of the city getting out meant performing a slalom down a flat stretch of serpentine road which followed the crazy course of the Wall with hairpin turns every hundred meters. At one such curve, where the street followed one of the Wall's switchbacks along a ninety-degree bend, the car's rear wheel landed on the sidewalk, so that Eduard had to slam on the brakes. Laura suddenly felt enthused about the barren landing, there wasn't a soul in sight, she didn't want to drive anymore but get out and go on foot instead.

In the luminous neon sign of a publishing house from the other side of the Wall, the words "People" and "World" stood next to each other without any connection, the light for the conjunction had fallen out. Scanning the horizon, they could make out the silhouettes of the unlit tenements sprinkled randomly over the unbuilt ground like gravestones belonging to a bygone race of giants. High above the clouds, the onion dome of the TV tower hovered like a spaceship.

They followed the footpath which ran along the Wall like a narrow mole run. To their right was a rank growth of pioneer plants, flies whirred, invisible rodents whooshed across the path. Only an electric crackle interrupted the eerie silence across the Wall, or now and then the distant barking of a dog. Laura stopped and leaned against the Wall. "Three years of Holger are enough," Eduard read over her shoulder.

The Wall bowed in at this point, the semicircle looked like a generously planned, windowless apse whose western half was missing. In the turret above, Eduard could see the illumined cabin of a watchtower and, inside, the back of a man's capped head. As a rule the border guards kept their backs turned toward the front, the enemy always came from within.

Laura stood in the shadow of the border lights. He saw the sharp line of her nose, her mouth, now also black, the arches of her eyebrows. A stray beam of light from the watchtower imbued her skin with a bewitching glow, her high bosom shimmered through the sleeve of the sweater she had slung across her neck. He touched her and she let out a deep groan. From that point on she was deaf to any disturbance; no crackling, no spotlight, no siren could scare her.

This is childish, an adolescent game, political kitsch!

With one movement Laura freed Eduard's penis from his pants and held its tip in the light of the border. She forced him against the Wall and pinned a scissor hold around his hips. The concrete structure held, but Eduard's knees were getting softer and softer. A few dry leaves rustled like wood catching fire somewhere, or was it a footstep? Both the footpath where they were standing and the Wall itself belonged to the other city. All of a sudden he remembered there were supposed to be invisible, seamless doors inside the Wall, which could be opened only from the other side. He had heard of three prisoners whose freedom had been bought by the West German government, who as soon as they had been released in the West had gone to the Wall and given vent to their hatred with a can of spray paint. Completely unnoticed, East German border guards had slipped through one of the secret doors and hauled off one of the sprayers.

Somebody's there.

You're not romantic at all, are you!

What do you mean romantic, it's dangerous!

Eduard couldn't believe his eyes. Just to be contrary, with the carefree attitude of someone new to the city, Laura took off her shoe and flung it just like that over the Wall.

What are you doing?

I'm only proving there's no one there.

Scarcely had she resumed her position when something dark and about the size of a bird went flying by their heads and landed on the ground a few meters away.

The shoe!

So there is someone!

And what of it?

Laura was not to be stopped, and Eduard forgot all rumors of secret doors. Once again he had to acknowledge her ability to subjugate his instincts, to suppress his reflex of flight or fight in favor of a stronger drive. Yes, he would rather languish in a "People's" prison than seem petty at a moment like this.

18

ALL KINDS OF BUREAUCRATIC CHORES awaited him at the institute. Forms had to be filled out, the further steps of his experiment needed to be arranged. His discovery of the MS virus remained a hollow claim until it was verified by experiment. It was now a matter of transplanting the virus in the genome of a healthy organism.

Unlike clinical practice, medical research requires its practitioners to be versed in the art of communicating disease. The final proof that the source of a viral disease has been identified lies in the ability to evoke the sickness, symptoms and all. Before claiming its place among the healing arts, scientific medicine had to first show itself capable of doing this, using what might be called the undercover principle of infiltration; that is, the complete identification with an opponent in order to unmask it. Experimental infection differed from the natural in that out of an endless number of possible agents it sent as few as possible—ideally only one—on its destructive mission, and then apprehended it *in flagrante delicto.*

For the further progress of his experiment Eduard required a white female mouse which had been prepared for the necessary surgical interventions. Using a microscope, the virus would be injected into one of the mouse's fertilized egg cells, which had been previously removed. The egg would then be planted back inside the mouse. Only if the MS virus and the corresponding disease could be detected in a later generation would his hypothesis be confirmed. Because this type of surgical procedure was carried out by technicians trained in such skills, Eduard had nothing more to do than rely on them and wait.

During the lunch break, on his way into the cafeteria, he practically collided with the stair tripper. This student made him strangely uneasy; Eduard couldn't remember anyone who had rubbed him the wrong way like that at the very first encounter. What bothered him most was that this man looked like a youthful copy of himself. His slightly hunched gait, his forehead and cheekbones were undeniably Eduard's, and like Eduard he had the habit of running his hand through his short-cropped hair as though checking its thickness—except these all struck Eduard as oddly vulgarized copies of his own eccentricities. If this was an impersonator it was one with an evil eye, who mimicked only unfavorable traits. This Doppelgänger performed afresh all the ruses and bad habits Eduard thought to have put behind him. Eduard felt both drawn to and repulsed by a certain glint in the stranger's eyes.

Have we been properly introduced? May I help you with something? Eduard asked, since the person was standing in the door, looking at Eduard as if to challenge him.

The man shrugged his shoulders. Why the formality, man?

You're spying on me, you seem bent on catching me at something. What do you have against me?

How about a little fresh air, let's go for a walk, the man said, and pointed toward a small park in back of the institute. Eduard could have just turned around and left, but that suddenly seemed overly defensive. The stranger had put him in a position where it was hard to tell whether it was better to meet such an importunity head on or simply to ignore it. The smile with which he asked Eduard for a cigarette had the charm of a man who had grown up surrounded by women; there was something seductive about him, something violent. He puffed without inhaling.

I used to admire you, he said, without looking at Eduard. What happened to your rage, your restlessness, your sensitivity? Your manifesto about the ethical boundaries of genetic research, how long ago has it been? Ten, fifteen years? Sure, one can always recant one's opinion—the noblest human right is the right to make mistakes! But some reflex of recognition, some greeting for the other side of the barricade, was that asking too much? From you I would have expected a different reaction to our little protest in the auditorium. How can you just dump yourself like that?

Eduard sensed that the other person hated him, was bent on destroying him, but for the moment he wanted to know what he had done to attract the destructive energies of a total stranger.

On the other hand it's possible, said Eduard, that the human being walking next to you is the same as the one you once admired. It's possible that his face, his thoughts, his actions have all changed not only through the usual corruption of aging but also by the greatest straining of his will. You at least ought to entertain that possibility for someone whom you once admired. You should ask your former role model the reasons for his surprising degradation. Surely your desire to destroy is up to this little test of hardness!

The other person didn't look at him, only raised his shoulders a few times as if he wanted to stop his ears with his shoulder blades. Maybe this enemy had selected him completely by chance, following a new, ancient rite of passage: in order to be recognized as a warrior, you first have to throw a stone, beat a policeman, and take the scalp of a professor. Or maybe he was taking revenge for Eduard's having mellowed his once scathing critique of the "invincibility of science" and for the fact that the current version no longer corresponded to the image he had once revered. But none of that made any sense. This accuser was far too young to have known Eduard from his radical days; even today he was still half a child, just a boy with two days of scruffy growth instead of a beard. Lord have mercy if such children come to power. They pass judgment on you, finish you off, wipe you out with the best conscience, presumably all for your own good. The wrinkled old man with the scythe, this romantic image of death, belongs on display in the anthropological museum. Death in the twentieth century, mass death, is delivered by half-growns, by kids with sticks and hobby horses. The unwrinkled faces of the liberators.

How does a traitor like you live? the other asked. Not bad, I assume, as far as externals are concerned. Upper-income bracket, permanent relationship, next the alibi child, now and then a weekend affair. But what goes on in the space beneath the skin and bones? Don't you hear anything? Not a peep from earlier days, no noise from the barricades to haunt you every once in a while? In case you're interested, I can tell you the exact date when your decline began, and I will help you bring it to completion.

It was a mistake to have even entered into this conversation. The man had no concrete accusations, he was following a program of militantism that was immune to any objections. Probably all his opponent saw was a cardboard cutout, a stand-in for the entire scientific establishment. So why did all the gibberish get him so riled up? Did the misplaced accusation remind him of some future failure? Whence this willingness to accept guilt?

You don't mean me, I'm not the subject of your story, he said quietly.

The stranger was no longer there. Eduard saw him walking diagonally across the meadow, twenty meters away.

That night a dream offered a sequel to his encounter. Two visitors rang the door of a newly built apartment—a man (the stair tripper? Lothar?) and a woman he had never seen before. They politely informed him that they had come to ask him a few questions regarding his relationship to women, and gently added that he had no choice in the matter. As they were speaking, they let in a horde of silent men wearing diver's suits, led by his old mathematics teacher, whom the divers referred to as Thomas Mann. The men immobilized Eduard and held him fast.

Eduard insisted on his rights—to proper procedure, to refuse testimony, to a defense—and went so far as to challenge the court's authority but was told he wouldn't get anywhere with a shotgun argument like that. The man explained that those so-called rights were really relics of a bygone era, a past which had been overcome, and that the proceedings currently under way harkened to a higher law. Then the man unfurled a gigantic white sail and suddenly Eduard realized that in this stark, laboratory-like room he would be spared no bodily torment: everything would happen quietly and without passion, with efficient handholds and in the silence of torturers who were acting not out of personal interest but in the name of a higher goal.

To his own surprise he managed to escape; all of a sudden he found himself swimming in the middle of the ocean. But the divers were hot on his heels; they were wearing fins and would soon catch up with him. So he swam to the steep cliffs on the coast and dived beneath the dangerous rocks.

He surfaced in the middle of a cone of light that was spilling from a craterlike opening in the water, a long tube pointed toward the heavens like a powerful telescope. He took a deep breath and rested; he knew his pursuers would never find him here, and waited in his hiding place for an eternity.

But the water was freezing, and he had to dive back. When he again surfaced he saw his pursuers sitting on the edges of the cliffs like gigantic black birds. They gently took him prisoner, and escorted him to a natural arena in the rocks, where they placed him under guard in the middle of a stage. Eduard decided to render his watchman harmless, if need be to kill him. He fell on the man from behind and knocked him to the ground; they struggled and Eduard pressed the diving mask into his opponent's face until the man's lips ran blue; Eduard was already enjoying in advance the surprise of the prosecutor, who had undoubtedly thought him incapable of such an aggressive physical move. Then he slipped out of the arena, but was immediately recaptured, without force, and taken back inside.

The chief prosecutor, who for a second had assumed Klara's features, summoned one of Eduard's earlier lovers—Andrea?—to the witness stand. Dozens of women gathered on the stone steps, most of whom he didn't recognize. They were all dressed in black, their faces were pale and bitter, and they spoke in a babble of different languages. The woman who had first rung his doorbell made a formal an-

nouncement that the scope of the hearing had been significantly expanded. Not only his relationship to women would
be tried, but also his views in general, on the state, on scientific responsibility. To Eduard's amazement the murder of
his guard was ignored completely; evidently this counted as
a minor infraction compared to his other crimes.

Then he decided to take the stand himself, unsummoned.
He began to speak, and felt an unexpected power rising
within him; he felt capable of defending his cause himself
and successfully leading it to victory.

Why should I deny or even justify what I consider a service
rendered? It is true I did not bind myself to any of the accusers here present, but neither did I pledge undying loyalty.
Where is it written that a declaration of love given in the
rush of the moment is sufficient cause for a claim of per-
manence? Does the hour of passion mean nothing because
it is finite? Is the moment of fulfillment worth any less because it cannot be repeated? Ask the women who have come
to testify against me: In those same nights they are citing as
the basis for their alleged rights, did I betray their happiness?
As evidence of my innocence I submit to the court the shared
joy of the moment, and declare myself guilty if and only if I
was alone in my enjoyment.

But the more he spoke, the more he sensed he sounded
tedious and haughty, as if his words were an involuntary confession of guilt, as if in a terrible moment of blindness he
had delivered the prosecution's argument instead of his own
defense.

There was no more escaping, he had only to wait for the
verdict and then disappear, deep below the surface, inhale
the water, and flood his lungs.

ONE SATURDAY MORNING Klara tossed a train ticket onto his breakfast plate. Somehow the gesture reminded him of the abruptness with which she had retrieved her car keys from his predecessor. This was her way of leaving, her way of signaling to Eduard her final departure: without words, without warning.

With two fingers he extracted the ticket, which had taken on a bit of butter. Since his glasses weren't within easy reach, he held the ticket at arm's length—but all he could make out was the large print: PARIS.

You want to go to Paris? he asked.

Klara looked at him, her voice brimming with triumph and disdain.

With both of you?

This wasn't the best time to look for his glasses. A closer examination in the light by the window revealed that there were two tickets stuck together. The first had been issued in his name; the second was made out to Jenny Jarwin.

For some time Eduard had avoided looking at himself in the mirror, but at this moment he could see his face as clearly as if it were a photo in a glossy magazine: the face of a betrayer, a two-timing husband, a treasonous consul arrested one morning at breakfast who can muster no more than a stupid smile. Eduard had suggested to Jenny that she accompany him next month to Paris for the molecular biologists' conference. And he could guess how Klara had gotten wind of his proposal: it was all the postman's fault. The Teutonic slave to authority had been unmoved by any and all entreaties, so Eduard had finally filled out the necessary forms authorizing Klara to receive his mail. And of course the first item this champion among mailmen delivered was the registered letter from the travel agency.

It can't go on like this, said Klara. I stay up at night wide awake in bed, I waste hours thinking about you, all to absolutely no avail, I phone up The Tent and a dozen other of your favorite hangouts and the only reason I know for sure you're not running around with this lady is that she calls here and asks for you.

This was serious. Long before André's story about the wedge-wolf, Eduard and Klara had agreed to a practical rule: Anything on the side would be kept quiet, unless it began to move from the side toward the center. What wasn't clear was where the side ended and the center began. Now it turned out that the principle of keeping quiet offered absolutely nothing to hold on to in the moment of being caught. He stammered on helplessly, his ears burning red.

He could spare himself any explanation, said Klara, all she wanted was a decision. If, according to his definition, this was "only an affair," then it wouldn't be difficult for him to break it off. In case he wanted to continue seeing Jenny, he would have to give up Klara.

Klara had taken the initiative—an unquestionable strategic advantage in any scenario of separation. She presented him with a choice, determined its conditions, and gave him a deadline—and Eduard would have to do the choosing. He knew already that whatever his decision was, it was bound to be the wrong one.

He began to account for his behavior using words that sounded as if they belonged in a foreign-language dictionary. He spoke of being petrified. That he would be happy if he could say he wanted to elope with Jenny. Sure he was in love, but this being in love wasn't feeding off the hope for a new life so much as off the fear of the old one. He had the sense of living in a noiseproof capsule, immune to any danger of being disturbed, any threat of being shocked or shaken. The ridiculously armored knight they'd seen on their trip to Sicily in the castle armory had reminded him of himself; he remembered thinking that the iron breastplate was designed less to protect against the lances and arrows of external foes than to prevent the bearer's own feelings from escaping to the outside.

Ridiculous is right, said Klara, that's the only true word you've said yet, you can cut the rest of the babble. Her eyes were bristling with shiny, bright darts seeking their target. You call yourself petrified—putrefied is more like it, and I don't just mean your internal state. After all, wasn't he the one who kept haggling with her, getting her to shore back her feelings until the simplest declarations of love sounded like outlandish exaggerations? Or didn't he realize how quickly he had become the champion of feelings he once had so vehemently opposed? His tempestuous yearning for change was in reality limited to TV channels and women. My compliments on your meteoric career: the only thing left of his utopian visions were secret business trips for two—and of course the receipt for his accountant.

She can't be serious, getting political with me, thought Eduard, a digression in love does not mean a regression to the right. But she left him no time for heuristic hairsplitting; there was no room for misunderstanding, no chance to discuss the terms: Right this minute . . . If it's Jenny . . . then pack up, *tout de suite*.

Eduard walked out of the kitchen without saying a word. Only a schlemiel shows remorse when it's no longer asked for. As he picked up the things he had left lying around Klara's apartment and packed them into his leather bag, he felt like a soldier carrying out a senseless order. Was this the end? Should he break up over something as pitiful as this? Because of a mistakenly delivered ticket for a trip that hadn't even taken place? He had assured her he would never leave her for another woman, relationships always broke apart for internal reasons. But seldom did the immediate impetus for the split measure up to the relationship itself, hardly ever was the occasion as dignified as it ought to be. He stood in the kitchen, bag in hand, ready to go, ready to separate, a man "who knows how to draw conclusions."

I'll pick up the rest of the things later.

Go, right this minute, so things will be clear. "Clear"—the word was a trap, it contained a false decisiveness. Go? Where to? The "other love" for whom he was standing up so resolutely wouldn't keep him even for a day. The fact that he was now making a choice was really Klara's decision, Klara's victory; for the time being he preferred to await the consequences at a distance, a hotel would be best. But there he was, lingering around, like a graying salesman who knows he's bungled his pitch but feels the need to plod on.

Klara walked past him and thwacked him on the nose with the back of her hand, as if he were a punching bag just hanging in her way.

Go on, there's nothing more to be said, going and talking are mutually exclusive, there's no smooth transition from the parting word to the sound of a closing door. Go, open the door, shut it, don't look back, this is it.

He passed by Klara on his way out and noticed something melt inside in her eyes, a metal fiber unable to withstand the high voltage. Had he forgotten he had to avoid this *one* signal? Earlier quarrels had taught him that the sound of a closing door elicited an irrational reaction in Klara, a restraining reflex she could not control; not only Eduard but anyone who left in discord could set it off. A closed door meant danger, the fear of becoming inwardly blind; it was tantamount to staying behind, to being abandoned in a lightless room. But how to orchestrate a separation without a shutting door.

She stood between him and the door, half-turned, as if caught in a terror from long ago. Almost imperceptibly she shifted her center of gravity backward; for a second Eduard thought he would have to catch her.

This whole business with the trip really didn't suit him at all. A sudden fit of carelessness, an unarranged burst of enthusiasm she could imagine, but not this bureaucratic planning four weeks ahead, this advance booking of deceit.

For a moment Eduard felt relieved, vindicated, but unfortunately in the wrong way. In the grammar of Klara's feelings there were no means of expressing his misdeed. Still clinging to her image of a man who deserved her love, she braced for his attack. And Eduard said to himself that lovers who are incapable of committing the same crimes are no match for each other.

He pushed the door shut behind him.

As he made his way through the institute on Monday morning, he had to fight the ludicrous notion that the news of his breakup had already made the rounds. Wherever he nodded or waved his greetings, he was met by attentively restrained faces. Any separation always raised the question of which member of the former couple to keep as a future friend: from what he could see, his colleagues had taken sides a long time ago.

He was told that Betty wanted to speak with him urgently. As he knocked on her door, Eduard was secretly hoping for a private chat, an unequivocal intervention in his personal affairs. He knew he could trust Betty, who thought either in milliseconds or in millennia, to produce some oracular utterance concerning the final outcome of the association Klara–Eduard.

But Betty had other worries; she was upset about a communiqué from the ethics commission. They had felt obliged to inform her—"merely as a matter of procedure"—about an anonymous report concerning preparations for an impermissible intervention in the transmission of human genes. The suspicions, she explained, applied exclusively to Eduard's MS project and were of course easily refuted—she had done so with the appropriate stringency. But since they had to prepare themselves for additional questions, it would be best if from now on Eduard kept her informed of every further step in his experiment.

It was this last, really the most harmless of Betty's sentences, which made Eduard feel the most indignant. She knew as well as he that his project was exclusively designed to identify a virus; developing a therapeutic model was entirely out of the question. If she had already dismissed the accusation—as indeed she should have—as unfounded speculation, why insist on such petty control? Betty's desire to be involved on a day-to-day basis was a diplomatic way of declaring their relationship to be on a new footing. In the language of labor law this was known as "damaged trust." With a unionized rage in his stomach, Eduard marched into his laboratory. At the moment he had nothing more to add to his log for the MS project; as usual he was in a position of waiting. He filled a piece of paper with key words for a speech in his own defense.

When he examined the anonymous accusation in the light of his project, everything seemed clear. In the best-case scenario, Eduard's experiment could lead to proof that multiple sclerosis was caused by a viral gene which was passed through the hereditary genetic code. Not until this gene was determined would therapeutic intervention even begin to be a possibility. On the basis of Eduard's work, some research team would in all likelihood eventually produce an antiviral medicine capable of rendering the suspect gene harmless within the cells of the stricken patient.

Theoretically, however, if Eduard's discovery were confirmed, it might also lead to a different speculation: so-called genetic therapy. But the attempt to repair harmful genes in the embryonic cells of a diseased woman in order to protect her progeny from the disease encountered hitherto unsolved technical problems; moreover, it had already been dismissed by the majority of scientists, among them a certain Dr. Eduard Hoffmann, for ethical reasons, and besides that, it was illegal. In the concrete case of his MS project it would suffice to show that both therapeutic models, the permissible as well as the forbidden, went far beyond the bounds of his experiment.

The anonymous accuser, whom Eduard believed he recognized, could thus refer neither to real nor to potential transgressions: he was working with a generic suspicion. Eduard surmised that this was part of an undeclared campaign to overcome the past: people imputed to scientists the secret wish to carry on projects like Heinrich Himmler's infamous "Lebensborn Foundation" with modern means at their disposal, and to create the preconditions for a "biological elite." As it happened, it was the genetic researchers themselves who, in the hour their science was born, had launched a discussion about the dangers of the new area of research and proposed a moratorium. But in his country the debate had been poisoned by the accusers' asserting a kind of moral monopoly.

Eduard explained the heavy emotional charge carried by such accusations as part of a cathartic ritual. To avoid being sucked into the crimes of the Nazi generation, not a few of their descendants found salvation in a mania for innocence. People vied with one another as to who was the "true," the "more consistent," anti-Fascist; the most discreet way of misusing the word "Auschwitz" was to show that someone else had misused it, and one's own immaculate conscience was best demonstrated by detecting trace elements of Nazi thinking in others. These vigilantes were little concerned with exact knowledge, and most of the cries of alarm came from representatives of the philosophical sciences. What enraged Eduard the most was these colleagues' unwavering faith that they were better equipped to provide a moral assessment of genetic research. Did they have a greater, more direct access to ethical principles? They would have been better off notic-ing how politically outspoken so many natural scientists had been, particularly the first geneticists, from Joshua Lederberg to Jonathan Beckwith. There was no reason to assume that natural-scientific research and morality were mutually exclu-sive, that social scientists somehow made better people.

Whence this self-righteousness? The amateurs who were unleashed upon the world and who set into motion the great crimes of the century, along with their notions of "master race" and "new human being"—didn't they come from the other faculty? Wasn't it the Idea that had run amok, that had been elevated above all skepticism, beyond all doubt, until it was no longer subject to moral scrutiny? Wasn't it the Idea, thus privileged, that had turned even natural scientists into murderers?

20

EDUARD HAD TAKEN HIS TIME sending the letter about his talk
with Mertens and was amazed when Lothar called him. The
voice sounded nearby. A symposium on "ethical questions of
genetic research" had brought him to the city, haven't you
heard about it? Eduard concealed his surprise: of course it
stung that he had to find out through his brother about a
conference in his own field and on his own turf. Whoever
the organizers were, they evidently didn't consider him an
expert in matters of ethics. Or perhaps they had caught wind
of the anonymous accusation?

He calmed down when he discovered that the whole thing
was being organized by an interest group called Ethical
Science—Eduard considered it an honor not to be invited by
them. Experts merely smiled upon the group's speculations
about "engineers of class conflict," at work on breeding "as-
tronauts made to measure, human drones, and human
warriors." But Lothar didn't waste another word on the
conference—apparently out of consideration for his brother,
and Eduard for his part refrained from annoying him with
any disparaging remarks. They arranged to meet at The Tent.

Eduard was nursing a glass of Soave when he spotted
Lothar among the pedestrians on the other side of the street.
For a moment he felt as if he were experiencing difficulties

in optical transmission, as if his brain were running a flash-back. Remembrance was taking the place of perception. He had to struggle against the impression that the man who looked so lost as he stood in the middle of the street and tried to make his way across through the honking, braking traffic was really his father. The upper body a little too stiff, too erect, the careless attitude toward the automobiles, "those tanks on tires," the absentminded gaze fixed straight ahead, oblivious to any danger—had he always simply over-looked this paternal inheritance in Lothar or had it just be-come more visible after their father's death? He jumped up from his chair and waved energetically to his brother, as if he could somehow assist his passage through the enemy lines. Lothar recognized him and laughed; it was the natural laugh of a child, which Eduard hadn't noticed in his brother for a long time. Eduard followed his impulse and answered with the same laugh; he felt a strong sense of joy at the reunion, as if they had tossed streamers to each other over the rooftops of the cars, as if a childhood trust were renewing itself along an invisible line that stretched between the wav-ing hands. A few seconds later both smiles had grown un-certain, a watchful gaze appeared in their eyes, and adult patterns of reaction regained the upper hand. They greeted each other like former lovers who approach each other slowly, and from the distance recall the first meeting, but who, as soon as they sit down, remember the separation.

Lothar hadn't been surprised at Eduard's letter about their mother's presumed suicide; his own research at the clinic in question had led him to the independent conclusion that his hypothesis was incorrect. By-the-by, he did notice that in his attempt to save the "honor of the family," Eduard had over-done it a bit. Perhaps his own inclinations had led him to portray the *ménage à trois* in such a romantic light it almost seemed kitschy. With a little more detachment, even Eduard would have to admit that their mother was a highly complicated and selfish woman, whose romances must have caused their father no small anguish. And it was difficult to distinguish his heroic tolerance from sheer despair. Eduard had to acknowledge that his brother was right and suggested that both brothers were following a new division of labor as they continued to act out the roles of their father and mother.

But none of that concerned him at the moment, said Lothar. He had come across something about their mother's father which upset him much more deeply. With these words Lothar placed a copy of an article from a professional historical journal on the table. You probably don't remember him any more than I do, said Lothar. I think we only saw him a single time, and that was a few years after the war, when he deigned to visit us, by way of exception, of course. All I remember is that we were terribly disappointed he didn't bring any presents; after all, he was the only rich relative we had.

As far as the presents were concerned Eduard had an entirely different recollection. He well remembered a red toy car with a stick that could be shifted into four gears and even reverse. Lothar was bound to have received a present of his own, possibly one which paled in comparison to the older brother's trophy and therefore left no impression. In contrast to the homemade wooden toys of the postwar period, the chrome-plated, silently moving convertible had seemed to Eduard the wondrous creation of a distant, superior civilization.

Do you remember his first name? asked Lothar.

Franz?

Franz . . . Are you sure?

Franz, Hans, Ernst—in any case, something monosyllabic.

And apart from that? You were eight or nine at the time. What else do you know about him?

Reiner, a lawyer, deputy to the Reichstag during the Weimar Republic, something about Hugenberg and the German National People's Party, a peasant party—Eduard tried to piece together some dates. Green lederhosen. Right, now he remembered a gigantic pair of green lederhosen that he had discovered as a little boy while rummaging in the attic. Eduard had imagined that whoever could fit those pants had to belong to another race, a race of giants; there was enough leather there to outfit the entire family. Eduard had secretly removed the emblem from the breast band—a stag carved out of horn—and used it to decorate his own suspenders.

One day on the veranda a tall man, whose bones seemed to stick out of his wrinkled skin, came walking toward him. It's your grandfather, Mother had told them. Eduard greeted him with his hand on his chest, fearful that his grandfather would immediately recognize the carved stag emblem. How could this skeleton have ever fit the lederhosen in the attic, where had their grandfather left the missing two hundred pounds? He didn't dare ask.

Don't you find it strange that neither of us can even recall our grandfather's first name? asked Lothar.

Eduard disagreed. It was their grandfather who had broken off contact after his daughter had married "beneath her." It was true that the family had lived in the grandfather's summerhouse during the years right after the war, but the master of the place never allowed himself to be seen, nor was he ever mentioned in conversation.

So much for the official version, said Lothar, the fairy tale concocted by the parents to spare the children. Unfortunately, we have reason to suspect there were other, more ominous reasons to purge this relative from the family memory.

Some kind of loathing, some weariness prevented Eduard from picking up the article on the table.

What is it that brings us, he asked, choosing the binding plural at the last second, to delve into the personal lives and careers of our relations, just now? We never bothered ourselves with these things before, or if we did, we contented ourselves with convenient half-truths. All of a sudden the two of us, two children who've recently turned forty, are outdoing each other in bringing our ancestors to trial, even though they're half-blind, half-deaf, confined to wheelchairs if not dead.

What are you getting at? Lothar countered. Is a realization superfluous because we didn't take the trouble to discover it at the right moment? Can we spare ourselves the truth because it took so long to come to light?

Eduard's gaze followed Lothar's index finger and fell upon a half sentence marked with a ballpoint pen: F. Reiner, from the Office of Jewish Affairs . . ."

How had their mother's maiden name become associated with that dreadful office? Father would never have concealed that fact, someone in the family must have . . . Why wasn't the first name spelled out . . . How many Franz Reiners were there at the time? Did the text mention a birthdate? Besides, his name was Hans . . . These and a half dozen other defensive evasions ran through Eduard's head, and not one could banish the horror. Well done, Lothar, you've succeeded in planting another worm to gnaw away inside my brain.

Lothar had already asked himself all these questions and more, and had as yet been unable to answer them. The periodical had just come out. The comprehensive historic study announced by the author wasn't due to appear until fall. Lothar had written the author but had yet to receive a reply. What playwright could have conceived such a scene: forty years after the end of the war two middle-aged children were poring over an article, asking themselves whether the accomplice of Eichmann named therein was their grandfather.

F. Reiner, Officer of Jewish Affairs, had sent a memo to Adolf Eichmann informing the latter that he had "no qualms concerning the planned deportation of a total of 6,000 stateless Jews to the concentration camp Auschwitz (Upper Silesia)."

A message from their grandfather to Adolf Eichmann, discovered forty years after the fact, and not a hint, not a trace, of any reference in their family history, not even the famous embarrassed silence at the mention of the name, just a shrug of the shoulders and a vague smile of rebuke?

The rest of the text focused on the victims of the white-collar war criminal Reiner, nothing more on the man himself, not to mention his grandchildren.

And on whom should it focus if not the victims? Why should something change in your feelings or mine concerning the victims because of the name Reiner? Assuming we are related to him, should we rue his crime all the more or, equally absurd, suddenly come up with excuses to defend the man or keep things quiet?

Nevertheless, there remained the question, the simplest of all: When did our Reiner die, anyway?

Lothar looked at his brother attentively. Why do you ask?

Because, to be honest, I'm not entirely sure, but he might still be alive.

Would it make any difference if he were?

Eduard started thinking about that. Assuming that their grandfather and the Officer of Jewish Affairs were one and the same and still living, then—hopefully—he would be brought to trial. And his grandchildren would be forced to take a stand, regardless of what their own relationship with this grandfather might be. To say that they had seen him only once in their life would sound like a cheap excuse. Whether they wanted to or not, they would now, without any delay, have to take an interest in this relative. The grand-children of an expert on Jewish affairs named Reiner would encounter a new, hitherto-unknown pressure to justify what-ever they said or did. Even the explanation that they first found out by reading the newspaper that their grandfather had been actively involved in the "Final Solution" would sound suspiciously like an admission that they just didn't want to know about it.

In case it gives you any peace of mind, Reiner died a peaceful death eight years ago, said Lothar.

"Peace of mind" is the wrong expression, replied Eduard. He just thought that the crimes committed by a man named Reiner concerned the two brothers no more and no less than if the man had been named Schmidt or Müller.

Are you sure? Give it some time, said Lothar. In any case, he, Lothar, would follow up on the matter; they'd know in a few weeks whether the Officer of Jewish Affairs and their grandfather were one and the same.

On his way out Eduard couldn't help quickly handing Lothar some material in the matter of Bouchard which he had intended to discuss, but now, following the disclosures about Reiner, the subject seemed too far removed. According to Eduard's research, the Milwaukee project which Lothar had cited as a counter-model to Bouchard's Minnesota project had not produced any scientifically useful results. To be sure, the head of the project, Professer Rick Heber, had succeeded in showing some positive results from his program of "compensatory education." But after this promising start he had absconded to Egypt with all the project's funding. When he popped up in the U.S. again years later, he was arrested and tried. The last anyone had heard of him was that after serving time in jail he had moved to Texas, where he was now running a stud farm. Naturally—Eduard had noted on the margin of his small folder—that did not exactly disprove anything about "compensatory education" and its possible effects. But neither could Rick Heber be considered a reliable witness against Professor Bouchard.

Over the next few days he treated the whole Reiner affair like an unpleasant letter which can be answered at a later date.

But it proved impossible just to sit back and wait for Lothar to write. By a numerical coincidence, the entire nation seemed compelled just now, forty years too late, to peer into the abyss of its recent history, the period politicians usually described using the adjective "dark." Since he had come of age Eduard couldn't remember a time when the Nazi past had been discussed and debated in such depth and breadth —it was as if the tight seals on a vaguely bad conscience were about to come undone and unleash all sorts of new facts and figures which would finally demand an emotional response.

The debates and documentations were mostly broadcast

late at night on public TV. Eduard had developed the habit
of recording them so as to watch them when the occasion
arose. As he now opened the cassettes and rearranged them,
he realized that he had hardly seen a single one of the films.
Thanks to his computerized VCR, he could tape the films,
which supposedly interested him, without watching them.

The suspicion that he might be the direct descendant of
Officer of Jewish Affairs F. Reiner changed his perception
entirely. He already knew most of the facts the films presented. But there was one photo he couldn't get out of his
head: two SS doctors in Dachau, sitting on the edge of a
barrel-shaped tub, bending over the prisoner inside the cold
water with friendly, interested faces, using their professional
hands to feel and measure the man being tortured, while a
third doctor used his to hold the pen to write the protocol.

For the first time he tried to procure material about the
history of his own science during the Third Reich. Once
again he made the surprising discovery that historians as well
as the media had only recently begun to examine this subject.
The most exact, the most comprehensive portrayals had been
published in English and had yet to be translated. A colleague of Eduard's at a West German university had begun
to examine the role of geneticists, anthropologists, and psychiatrists during the Nazi period. Eduard asked for the paper;
he was staggered by what he read.

Almost all the laws which had been enacted or even
planned against Jews, schizophrenics, psychopaths, and "social aliens" stemmed from the recommendations of expert
scholars like himself. The majority of biologists, anthropologists, and psychiatrists of the time—honorable, in some
cases even brilliant, scientists—had served as propagandists

for the racial ideology. Moreover, a small army of well-educated assessors, physicians, technicians, and researchers had placed themselves at the disposal of the program of annihilation: the few who refused to be part of the murderous machinery were not made to suffer any disadvantages: there were enough others eager to acquire a position.

Josef Mengele was conducting a scientific project in Auschwitz about "specific endosperms" and "eye color." The heterochromatic eyes of murdered twins which he sent his professor, von Verschuer, were received by the latter with a note of thanks "for the rare and valuable material." The anthropological institute where von Verschuer had carried out his research had been housed in the same building where, two decades later, Eduard and thousands of other students had completed their formal matriculation into the university. To this very day there is no tablet, no clue that would recall the history of the building. Otmar von Verschuer and numerous other scientists who prepared the way for the Nazi crimes were able to continue their professorial careers after the war and retire with honors.

His eyes roamed the room as if searching for a place to rest, some object to prove he was living in a different time. He didn't have to defend himself against anything; he had nothing to do with Reiner from the Office of Jewish Affairs, or with his murderous professional predecessors. Even so, as he switched on the coffeemaker, he noticed the sweat was dripping down his back to his buttocks. Was it shock from the facts he had discovered? He had known the general outline, but he'd never had any cause to study the details, some of which would have been inaccessible, anyway. His new perception led him to conclude that he had thus far protected

himself against them. Insight into these issues always followed initial speechlessness and shame. Had it really taken
this Reiner from the Office of Jewish Affairs to awaken this
new curiosity? Lothar was right, he owed him an apology.
Even if the truth took forever to come to light, there was no
way to keep yourself closed to it once it did.

He was so upset he decided to call André and tell him all
about Reiner, in the hope of hearing some untroubled, if
need be even malicious, remark which would give him a little
relief. But as he picked up the receiver, Eduard told himself
that in this case he couldn't count on André's habit of making light of difficult situations, of taking hard things easy.
What was André supposed to say? That Eduard couldn't do
much about his grandfather? That if necessary he, André,
would testify on Eduard's behalf? For the first time ever,
Eduard had no idea what André might say, though he could
easily imagine what he might not say.

Call Theo? Until now Eduard had never had any occasion
to ponder the fact that two of his best friends were Jewish.
When it came up, he had explained that he had had no idea
about their background when he met them. They just seemed
more attractive, more entertaining, more talented than other
people. In hindsight the sentence struck him as telling, at
best frivolous. What if he had known about their Jewish
background? A man with a Reiner perched in his family tree
would find it difficult to say things like that, the same remark
would seem chummy. Was it really just chance, spontaneous
affinity, which had determined his selection? Suddenly he
started brooding about attractions he had always considered
involuntary. Now, with this Reiner on his back, he suddenly
saw the murdered relatives of Theo and André hovering over
their heads.

No, he'd rather not subject them to the whole business; why embarrass them, especially before his familial relations had been cleared. Of course, he was sure neither one of them would treat him any differently even if he did turn out to be the grandson of that accursed grandfather. They would take him in their arms and assure him of their support, without missing a great opportunity to tease him a little: Look, you of all people! And we believed in you! How about a little contribution to the victims of the Nazi regime? Here's our account number. By the way, don't take it too tragically! A grandfather like that can happen to almost anybody!

The discreet little word "almost" made all the difference in the world. Because a grandfather like that could not possibly happen to André or Theo. This was a difference Eduard could do nothing about, but it existed nevertheless, had always existed, and now it had become significant. How could Eduard have ever referred to any state of innocence if, forty years after the event, a newspaper article was enough to brand him the child or grandchild of a perpetrator? On the other hand, why should the descendant of a Nazi criminal produce any more scruples than anyone else? The argument of "biographical coincidence" went both ways. If guilt was not hereditary, neither was innocence.

Besides, it wasn't true that the issue had never affected his relationship with Theo and André. The business with Reiner cast new light on a scene from The Tent three years before. Eduard had gotten into a fight with Theo over nothing, and the more heated things became, the more Eduard kept forgetting himself. The dam within him suddenly burst and some long pent-up anger came gushing over him. All of a sudden he was lashing out at Theo for paying artful compliments to a critic whose most recent article Theo had just torn to pieces: the author in question had popped up at their table and sat down with them. By the time the critic parted from Theo, almost tenderly, Eduard could no longer bridle his indignation.

You're just a salon anarchist, a flatterer, you always talk about people in power differently behind their backs than to their faces!

A rage broke out of him. Sentences he had suppressed at other, more fitting occasions poured from his lips, he was getting in deeper and deeper. Later he was unable to explain how the most heinous reasoning, the argument which presumably had been outlawed forever, found its way into his accusation. Unannounced and practically uncensored, all of a sudden it was there.

When I look at you, the way you get in good with everybody, the way you schmooze, I can almost understand how people could come up with something like anti-Semitism. This fawning! All you're doing is proving the stereotype.

Until that moment, André had been enjoying the entire exchange, but then Eduard saw that the corners of his mouth were ticking nervously. Theo, who had just seemed on the verge of slugging Eduard, stopped and stared at him with a calm attentiveness, a kind of ethnological curiosity. In the silence that issued from his two friends, Eduard could hear the echo of his own sentence. From what part of his subconscious had this sentence come, and how had it got there?

Under no circumstances ever are you allowed to say anything like that, André said. Neither smashed nor sober and certainly not in front of us. Say that Theo is a careerist, say he'd sell his grandmother for a good verse, say that he's an unscrupulous bastard. But never say that he's this or that because he is a Jew.

Eduard's defense only made things worse. All he could do was explain his mistake as a spiteful reaction against an internal censure of thought and feeling. As long as a person suppresses an observation because he's afraid of being branded an anti-Semite, that person is trapped. He had only wanted to try out a sentence that he himself was afraid of.

What are you getting at? Are you trying to tell us that Jews in Germany will be discriminated against as long as people aren't allowed to make anti-Semitic remarks?

He has to be able to tell us what traits we have that stick out, mocked Theo, just like we have to be able to tell him that every now and then you can see a bit of Nazi in our beloved goy.

This distant scene suddenly began to torment Eduard. In hindsight, his friends' reaction seemed much too mild. His attempt to speak his mind with absolute impunity, because he could count on their protection, to say whatever popped into his head, with no holds barred, to utter even the sentences he feared most—showed nothing more than arrogance and ignorance of history. In this situation a simple admission of embarrassment was probably still the norm.

An entire eon seemed to pass before Pathology transferred a tiny white mouse for further observation. It belonged to the strain of mice that, according to his hypothesis, should have inherited the MS virus that had been injected into the grandmother.

Mechanically, almost without curiosity, he examined the first tissue samples. They showed unambiguously the anomalies characteristic of multiple sclerosis. The final certainty that he had discovered the functional mechanism for MS would be the appearance of the atactic disturbances which indicated the outbreak of the disease. These could not form until the little mouse was grown up. He named the mouse Lotte.

21

ON MONDAY MORNING he had hardly made it up the first set of stairs that led to his office when he was told that Betty wanted to see him right away. As he walked in she rose from her seat, as if whatever had to be discussed could not be explained sitting down. With brisk steps she led him to the scene of the crime—his department—the clatter of her heels accentuating the unpleasant atmosphere. She opened the door to the animal laboratory and turned to face Eduard as if he were responsible for the catastrophe which was beyond his wildest imagining: the cages were all empty, the wire doors had been opened, the inmates released. MURDERER! SADIST! STOP THE MOUSE CONCENTRATION CAMPS! FREEDOM AND HAPPINESS FOR ALL LAB MICE! had been sprayed on the walls. Eduard registered the emptiness of one cage alone—Lotte, whom he had been observing since her arrival and whom he had privately asked for forgiveness for the sacrifice he was asking her to make for the good of humanity and himself; Lotte, who had to bear the cross of multiple sclerosis in order to save mankind—Lotte was gone, she had risen and had taken to her paws. Eduard heard only fragments of Betty's reconstruction. Over the weekend a group calling itself "Viral Agents" had stormed the laboratory. Either they had a copy of the key or else Eduard hadn't locked up—I'll swear on whatever you like, I always lock up, out of fear of the viruses if nothing else . . . !

Betty cut off his stuttering with an angry gesture. How far along were you? Does the specimen have multiple sclerosis or not?

Because he still intended to run a control, Eduard had kept the last results quiet. But it was clear to him that a tentative nod on his part, which under other circumstances would have prompted every conceivable congratulation, would now suffice only to put Betty in a panic.

It does, he said. Most likely. But Lotte's sterilized. She can't pass on the disease.

He thought he saw Betty stifle a sob, but the guttural sounds coming out from behind her raised hand increased in volume to become the most unseemly laugh he had ever heard.

It's probably too late for congratulations, she said. Or too early! Maybe you should take a quick course in mouse catching! The whole morning I've been bumping into stone-cold sober people who claim to have seen white mice all over the place!

He looked at Betty bewilderedly. As she walked away, Eduard thought the tic-tac of her heels sounded like a flamenco dance.

Over the course of the morning he was able to reconstruct the crime from the body of evidence. It seemed the activists had released at least a few mice into the "wild." If the eyewitness accounts were correct, the liberators didn't deserve very high marks. Their attack had actually created the danger to which they wanted to call attention. A free roaming mouse with multiple sclerosis could conceivably infect an entire population: after all, the activists didn't know that Lotte was sterile. But it was also possible they were following the logic which states that the best way to warn against some impending disaster is to create it.

Seeing that neither rage nor passion brought him any further insight, Eduard forced himself to look at the entire episode from a greater distance.

Historically speaking, it was a sign of progress that people had banded together to defend the rights of trees, plants, and animals with the same fervor with which others fought for human rights. The only dubious thing here was the phrase "concentration camp," which was absolutely impermissible. Besides, it didn't follow at all that a militant sympathy with animals went hand in hand with love for humans. It was well known that most of the concentration-camp commandants and supervisors displayed a special love of animals. Once André had suggested that one reason why the Nazi doctors may have been so ready to perform their gruesome experiments on people was that they wanted to save animals from similar tortures.

As he stared into space, his head crowded with similar thoughts, a little patch of white whooshed along the edge of his desk and disappeared behind the printer. At first he attributed the apparition to a sunbeam which a moving branch had let into the room for just an instant, but the little streak of lightning had not followed a straight line; Eduard thought he had detected tiny deviations right and left—and he'd never heard of a light ray exhibiting voluntary evasive action. Now he thought he heard something rustling in the continuous paper which hung down from the printer to the floor. Very carefully he rotated his revolving chair 180 degrees so as to bring the whole room into view. A noise by the radiator drew his attention. What he saw there was too phantasmagoric to count as true perception, too much alive to be dismissed as a mere figment of the imagination. Sitting—or rather standing—there was his one and only confidante, the sole friend who knew of his discovery, the living proof of his hypothesis, the star of his future earth-shaking paper and a spectacular publication in *Nature*, the worthy occasion for the next Leibniz prize, possibly even for a trip to Stockholm—there was Lotte, standing next to the heating pipe, using her two front paws to hold on to the molding as she sniffed the paint.

How to catch a runaway Nobel Prize? Cats, traps, cheese, bacon—none of that was available. All of a sudden he remembered how a friend had once caught a mouse with the help of an open paper bag. Eduard took a large padded envelope from his desk and tiptoed on all fours to the radiator. Lotte didn't show the slightest sign of unease and kept gnawing at the white paint. As he watched her standing there, trusting completely in her own agility, Eduard grew more and more unsure. How did he know for certain that this white mouse was really Lotte? The unpracticed eye can hardly distinguish even common gray house mice from one another; with lab mice this interchangeability was by design. They were all descended from an albino mutation bred in China a thousand years ago. The Chinese preferred them because of their outstanding artistic talents and used them as circus mice; researchers held them in esteem because, after a thousand years of incest, the albino mice had virtually become a race of identical twins. Lab mice are defined precisely by the fact that you can't tell one from the other.

As Eduard crawled closer he had a strange encounter. For the first time in his life he believed in the forgotten language once shared by all living things, as described by American Indian lore and any number of esoteric sciences—or at least in a secret communication between mouse and man. For the wee beastie before whom he had prostrated himself as if he had converted to Islam seemed to hear his prayer. Gripping the wall bracket with its front paws, the mouse turned its back toward Eduard, completely of its own accord, to show him the little red L which he had marked with a felt-tip pen. He gingerly shoved the envelope closer, and just as if she were starting a race Lotte flitted, quick as a thought, right toward him, right between his arms and knees and right past the envelope. He threw himself flat on his stomach, half out of fright and half in the hope of blocking Lotte's way, but when he turned his head she was watching him from the opposite corner of the room. Eduard, who was still lying at mouse height, looked her straight in the eye and believed he saw something like a final adieu. Then she sprinted through the room, scrawling an indecipherable farewell on the linoleum tiles as if with a light pen, and disappeared behind the wall without a trace. Eduard knew that Lotte had parted from him forever and that no cheese or bacon would ever lure her back. She had vanished with their shared secret, lost in the vast hunting grounds of the heating system, and he gave her his blessing.

After her departure he felt a strange relief. He knew it wouldn't be easy to repeat his experiment anytime soon—there were too many hassles, too many unknown opponents, and if he didn't roll over and play dead for a while, Eduard could already see the headline that was waiting for him, in great big bold letters: GRANDSON OF RACE FANATIC UNDER FIRE AS COMMANDANT OF ANIMAL CONCENTRATION CAMP!

There are some challenges which are best met by taking a vacation.

At home he found a letter from Lothar in the mail. Just like their grandfather, the Officer of Jewish Affairs was indeed named Franz, but with the year of birth 1906 he could not possibly be their mother's father. Of course, this didn't mean he wasn't related to him some other way. As it turned out, the news no longer brought Eduard any relief.

How far removed does a person have to be for his descendants to be no longer connected to him? When does the connection begin? The important thing was that the Reiner in question might well have been his grandfather—by the same happenstance which now determined he was not. The possibility that they were related had triggered an anxious curiosity which had put his previous examination of the Nazi past to the test, and found it had been far too superficial.

So as Eduard read the letter, he experienced a strange reverse effect. Knowing in all probability that he was not related to Reiner-friend-of-Eichmann, he followed that man's career—as far as Lothar had documented it—with all the emotions of a horrified grandson.

Not until he read it again did he notice something Lothar had penciled in the margin: According to the files, Officer of Jewish Affairs Reiner was listed as holding the rank of Obersturmbannführer in the SS. The author of the study suggested that this error could be traced back to a case of mistaken identity with an "SS-Ostubaf. Ernst Reiner, born 18.7.1892, or with the SS-Ostuf. Franz Reiner, born on 26.4.1888.

"It was all a matter of luck," wrote Lothar, "no more and no less. So our Reiner wasn't a 'specialist' on Jewish affairs. We could still look into the possibility that we might be related—to one degree or another—to an SS-Ostubaf. named Ernst or perhaps an SS-Ostuf. Franz."

22

THE NEWS OF HIS SEPARATION from Klara spread among his friends like gas seeping through a hundred-room mansion. The smell seemed to attract his closest confidants as well as mere acquaintances. He steeled himself for a wide-ranging, reproachful silence. If someone failed to make the expected call or didn't keep an appointment, he read it as a sign that the person in question had taken Klara's side. Certain indications even led him to believe that their breakup had released a general sentiment which had been brewing against him for some time. He learned that Klara had been defending him lately against comments made by mutual friends who suddenly felt obliged to draw her into their confidence. People made predictions as to how his life would go without her. His most recent scientific success was several years back, his new project had given rise to evil rumors which would not quiet down.

But his suspicions invariably turned out to be unfounded. The missing phone call came an hour later, the person who stood him up in the café called the next day with an apology, always there was some innocent reason which, after the fact, made his fears seem like paranoia. Suddenly nothing happened anymore, no one drew away from him, he followed the normal rituals from one day to the next.

Lothar had asked if he could help with a friend's apartment or with money. Eduard was moved but declined the offer. To avoid running into Klara he had arranged to camp out for a while at an apartment which belonged to a colleague at work. It was a bachelor pad his acquaintance had first intended to keep as a workspace after he married, but he had never been able to use it for this purpose. One recently separated friend after another kept asking him for the key.

This emergency shelter was in the miserable condition tolerated only by single males. The place was full of empty beer cans and full ashtrays, the mattresses were saturated with cat piss, the industrial carpet was matted and clogged and littered with a decade of crumbs and spills. The first days were spent packing, hauling, cleaning out the old things and putting in the new, shopping for soap and detergent, extension cords, plugs, hooks, and paint. Occasionally, while letting down a box or bending over to pick up a rag, Eduard went dizzy and the whole world seemed to spin around him.

Betty had appealed to his conscience to start work on repeating his experiment, especially now, so soon after the attack by the Viral Agents. In the end she granted his request to take a leave of absence. He was at a loss what to do with all the time suddenly at his disposal; the drudgery of a ten-hour day in the laboratory soon seemed enticing once again. He had no desire whatsoever to go to The Tent. Even André and Theo seemed suddenly inaccessible. Eduard saw himself, too, from a great distance, coldly, through the eyes of a female enemy: a man not worth getting worked up about.

After a rain he looked out the window at the slick, dripping branches jutting into the sky; a few leaves had rolled up as if they were cold, others were already covering the ground.

He watched a man with a shovel kicking a maple tree, over and over, as if he were venting his rage on the trunk. It took Eduard some time to realize that this frenzied individual was wearing the uniform of the municipal sanitation department and that his kicking was intended to shake down the rest of the leaves.

Prescription sleeping pills failed to produce the promised effect. They usually kept him awake for hours, so that he wouldn't fall asleep until morning, when his three-phase alarm clock switched on the "Wake up!" mode.

Jenny and Laura called every other day, often one right after the other, but he kept both at bay with the same bulletins of woe. His telephone talk was all a variation on one simple theme, whose main motifs were phrases like "I can't today," "slept badly," "a little more myself." An ancient hit from the seventies kept echoing inside his head: "Fifty Ways to Leave Your Lover." Previously he had never even paid attention to the words, just reacted to the music, and all he could remember was the refrain. Now he felt obliged to learn all the lyrics, test each of the fifty ways, and pick the two best suggestions. But he never seemed to get past the refrain. He looked for the LP but couldn't find it.

He couldn't overcome the feeling that having split up with Klara he should also break off from Jenny and Laura. But because he didn't explain this to them, and simply continued to keep both at a distance, they took whatever he was prepared to give them and drank it to the dregs, exhausting him in the process. In the rare moments when he saw himself without self-pity or self-hate, he discovered that everything fit a simple formula: he was playing the same power games as any other playboy, a Don Giovanni accoutered with the halo of the sufferer. The man who evaded or withdrew and

refused to surrender evidently triggered an overwhelming reflex to search and seize.

Eduard generally spent his evenings in the borrowed apartment in the company of two-dimensional comrades-in-fate.
The television set populated the room almost daily with dozens of fellow sufferers all eager to confess. The whole city
seemed obsessed with the idea of "separation." Whenever he
switched on the tube, he found himself in the middle of an
expert panel discussing the most "humane" way of separat-
ing. Eduard followed this perpetual public controversy with
a disgusted curiosity. At times he could hardly resist the urge
to dial the number on the screen and seek refuge in the
plural.

The talk shows followed a strict ceremony. A group of "victims" sat across from two or three experts who asked questions and then abstracted the experiences into concepts. For
the most part they didn't want to admit that the victims presented their stories in the same jargon used by the experts.
An inventory taken of this exchange of experience would include words such as "possessive thinking," "fixation," "dependency," "addictive behavior," and—over and over—"in
this society," without ever specifying the other society which
the modifier implied. The gurus of the ongoing public discussion were the authors of bestsellers whose messages were
generally exhausted by their titles. The most important task
of the speech-shapers seemed to consist in developing formulas to translate every individual story into a collective
experience. As soon as the suffering person accepted the formula, he discovered that he had plenty of company and thus
was saved. From then on, he could look around any chance
gathering of people and calculate with statistical probability
the number of fellow sufferers.

The new concepts functioned as machines designed to annihilate experience. Dull-witted individuals who persisted in clinging to the details of their story discovered that they lacked the proper "problem consciousness." In fact, the consciousness was responsible for a good part of the problem. Experiences were considered understood once they had been recognized as "signs of sickness or dependency." The readiness to confess was repaid with the pledge of a cure, the promise of liberation. The entire performance functioned according to a principle which seemed counter to any real insight: social consensus replaced analysis, the patient was considered healed as soon as he accepted the interpretation of the therapist.

He constantly thought about Klara, whom he saw irregularly at planned intervals. Just after he had moved out they agreed to a kind of moratorium: they would first keep a distance and then go on a trip somewhere over the fall break. She spoke to him about the "work of being alone," about how much effort it took to discard certain habits she had acquired while living with Eduard and to replace them with other pursuits and interests of her own which she had either forgotten or allowed to atrophy. She had always been bothered by his haste, his lack of attention for the small things, his disregard for the moment. Lately she had been taking things slowly, trying gradually to resume her own pace.

How difficult she found it to place the sounds, to fix the images she was once again beginning to sense. She was also reading a lot, mostly books she already knew; she had to read and reread to remind herself who she was. In the process she noticed for the first time that most male authors of the nineteenth century had never even questioned their ability to portray female characters from the inner depths of their own feelings and perceptions. Where did this astuteness come from, this presumption that enabled these authors to present the most silent stirrings of creatures they knew only from their ability to sympathize or, if need be, from their own desire? And what had happened to this wonderful ability and presumption? Why was it that now men could describe only men, and women only women, with any degree of accuracy? What had happened between the sexes that they saw only the other in the other, and no longer themselves. Armored tanks passing in the night.

Wasn't his attempt at breaking out, the light-headed abandonment of his love, just a symptom of a much broader disintegration? she asked. A further example of the pusillanimity which had gripped an entire generation, this ducking out of the way of truly big emotion? The rebels of yesterday were the beaten and cowed cripples of today, so quick to skulk into their bureaucratic titles and three-room apartments. Where was the common language, the readiness to embrace risk, the will for real exchange? People bundled up their small, mistrustful love, or carefully packed their delicate separation and sequestered themselves inside their four walls, where they begot and conceived children behind closed venetian blinds. They married in secret, celebrating their union in court surrounded by two or three friends they could rely on to be discreet, and later spread the unhappy news on environmentally friendly paper. What was driving them back to the old institutions they had once despised, and which in their backward slide they robbed of all pageantry, pomp, and splendor? What was a wedding without ceremony, without pathos? Whenever asked, they would respond by citing tax advantages, by referring to their consideration for future children, by invoking the proven failure of other alternatives. It seldom happened that a couple explained their decision to get married with the only sentence which was really worthy of the occasion: We love each other and want to be together; in fact, to be precise, we want to stay together forever and ever!

Klara told him about a small, unpretentious painting she had noticed while preparing an exhibit for next spring—an Italian landscape from the Settecento. The eye followed a path up to a mountain village of crooked roofs and gables; it passed a mill and continued through groups of farmers until it reached a village square. Then it climbed a steep winding way that led up a high promontory, which offered a view of the entire medieval cosmos. The pinnacles and spires of the holy city shimmered in the distance, while on the horizon light struggled with darkness. If you gazed long enough into the depths of the picture you realized that not only did this sky vault the valley—it canopied the universe; the path didn't lead to some high mountaintop but to the reaches of the invisible, to the realm inhabited by the maker of all things. Klara felt that her eye was peering through the thin crust of reality into a room whose monstrous, invisible objects were becoming natural objects, things discernible to the mortal eye. She had missed such moments of peaceful submersion in the years spent with Eduard, also this way of viewing the world. His own view—not only of the world but of her, Klara, as well—was through the recording lens of a camera, not with the inner eye.

Her speech made him uneasy. His dreams, which he could practically recount verbatim, thanks to the recent quick rotation between waking and sleeping, warned of an impending headlong fall. He saw himself in the passenger seat next to Klara, driving in an open car down a winding road along a coast of cliffs. A marble city shimmered in the distance. Klara pointed her finger at the hotel where they would stay, and while he searched the domes and steeples for the roof she was describing, she put her foot on the gas and steered the car off the road toward the edge of the cliff.

One evening, when he showed up where they had agreed to meet half an hour late, just as he was parking, a car with no lights on made straight for him and whammed smack into his Citroën. Klara climbed out of her car with the anger of a driver who is absolutely convinced that any court in the world would find the other party guilty: for once she just couldn't stand his making her wait. She calmed down again as they both assessed the damage, and rather matter-of-factly discussed problems of insurance. The image of the dented Citroën, which they had taken on so many trips, etched itself in Eduard's mind: a car that had been in an accident, a car whose door no longer wanted to open, and the two people who had once sat inside were now standing in front of it, outside.

After one of Klara's visits he noticed a page missing from his address book—the one with Jenny's number had been torn out; another time he opened his journal only to find that his last entry had been followed by another one, written by Klara with a thick felt pen. Attacks like that led to paranoid visions which even he considered ridiculous but which nevertheless caused him to implement certain precautionary measures. Whenever he expected Klara to visit, he collected all keys, locked away all journals and address books, cleared his typewriter from the desk and hid it in its carrying case.

He could deal with her assaults; it was her vulnerability that made him helpless. He looked on in horror as she succumbed to the assault of her feelings almost will-lessly. In the middle of the night he would recognize her ringing by its frequent, urgent repetition; sometimes he opened up, sometimes he covered the reading lamp with a senseless haste and braced himself for a stone flying through the shattering windowpane: he was happy when he heard the Fiat underneath the window drive away. The next morning she would be standing in the doorway like someone deathly ill, her eyes aflicker, and casually invite him to dinner that weekend; she had just come across his favorite wine in the store, just happened to have prepared a meal. She denied having rung his bell at night, then admitted it with the smile usually reserved for confessing a pretty peccadillo. There was a hopelessness in her which shook him to the roots and didn't allow any feeling other than pity and self-hate. When he showed her to the door, he could read the words in her face: Why are you letting me change like this, it's all in your hands, what have I done wrong that you're letting me go like this? Whenever she looked at him she tried to banish any challenge from her eyes; after all those years she smiled at him like a girl checking out a new boy on the block. When he had closed the door behind her, he could see himself standing there, holding the butcher knife.

He sensed she hated herself for her inability to break off from him completely. She knew women who behaved differently in similar situations, who could turn away without compromising themselves; she saw how his nervous silence, his rejections always brought her to lower her demands, that she attained only tiny reprieves, but there was no more stopping things, no more room to maintain pride, free will, mutuality. She was breaking every rule of separation, flying in the face of the "good manners" which prescribed that pride should be maintained under any circumstance, regardless of who originated the breakup—never surrender, come what may. It was as if an intractable child had taken hold of her authority; it threw tantrums, it begged, it banged its head against the wall, and Klara seemed determined to let it have its way.

At times, when he wasn't defending himself against her, he sensed that she, too, was witness to her own attacks of frenzy. There was within her a superior court which knew all the rules and rendered assessments, except that this court was powerless to intervene. Perhaps Klara had even chosen to let the desperate, unreasoning creature inside her have its will. The more furious its behavior, the sooner its strength would be depleted.

Once when he was leaving her place, she gave him a small package she had accepted for him. He opened it, removed the book, and left the box. She punched him with her fist in his neck. That's too much, you can't just take the contents and leave the trash behind, I'm not your trash bin. He grabbed her firmly, and when she hit him again he began to beat her in a mindless rage. The anger burst out of him, he told her everything he hadn't said in the course of the previous hour.

When he was outside he regretted he hadn't said it all earlier, when he had his wits about him. Once people begin to draw boundaries, once they begin to enclose the open country, no land can be safely protected. And their preserve had dwindled relentlessly to nothing.

One evening he picked Jenny up from the airport. As he was leaving the parking lot a car came zooming out a few meters in front of him, so close that he had to slam on the brakes. At first he experienced the usual terror of anyone who has just narrowly avoided an accident, a short cramp which ultimately turns into the well-known shaking of the limbs.

The second shock stayed longer and came with the realization that it was Klara at the wheel of the other vehicle. She showed no intention of talking to him; evidently she had assumed the physical shock would lead to a psychological shakeup as well, over the wreck of their relationship. He didn't doubt that she was following the effects of her action in her rearview mirror; in any case, she drove so that her Fiat stayed just ahead of his Citroën. Eduard stopped the car and got out. He wanted to do what all reasonable men do when the arguments are all spent: keep calm, put things right, return to the level of rational discourse. Klara, too, stopped her car, but just as Eduard was almost next to her, she stepped on the gas, stopped about thirty meters down the road, and waited until he had returned to his car and started the motor. As he drove on he wondered how best to answer Klara using the language of driving maneuvers she had forced upon him. Stay behind her in the hope she might disappear from sight? Keep following an endless circle around the airport parking lot and wait for her to finally exit for the city? Catch up with her in order to get caught in a drag race? Ridiculous! The best way to show his detachment was simply to follow her slowly.

Eduard chose a pace which he believed meant "cool, calm, and collected" in the language of cars, but Klara adjusted her speed to his, she even forced him to drive below the minimum speed limit. If you want to get rid of me, her driving seemed to say, you're going to have to use your horsepower. They took the exit to the city and together they crawled along the freeway as if bound by an invisible towline.

Why don't you pass? asked Jenny. You're holding up traffic.

Instead of answering, Eduard switched on his hazard lights. The idea of his hauling past Klara with his face turned away from her tormented him; he didn't want to do that to Klara, nor did he want to grant Jenny such an automotive illustration of the current state of affairs. For what seemed a painful eternity the two cars dragged themselves toward the city; a cyclist could have overtaken them. Klara didn't signal whether she intended to take the exit into the center of town. She evidently foresaw that Eduard would gladly consider any detour rather than stay behind her. At the last moment she raced down the exit ramp.

Jenny only made his mood worse by her lack of concern in formulating the obvious: All's fair in love and war but nothing's guaranteed. Eduard had thought of this and a thousand other sage proverbs himself while his eyes were glued to Klara's bumper, and he realized that Klara was either reading his thoughts in her rearview mirror or else had said them aloud to herself a long time before. Jenny's remark only made him suspect that she might be completely incapable of a similar act of despair.

After they had finally found a place to park in front of her apartment, Jenny preferred not to get out. She felt a sudden urge to check out The Tent and sit awhile in the evening sun. Eduard was furious, what kind of an idea was that? After all, she knew The Tent was right in Klara's neighborhood, that they'd be in danger of running into her a second time. Or maybe that was exactly what she wanted? Jenny looked at him calmly—why on earth should she have to hide from Klara? Evidently she was launching a hard-line policy for combating terrorism which demanded that Eduard declare in public that the young state was prepared to defend itself valiantly against any provocation.

Even later Jenny steadfastly refused to show any interest in Eduard's scruples. And this time the ticking TV offered

no distraction as it described an American zoologist's difficulties with Guinean gorillas—nor did Jenny's lustrous skin.
He wanted to talk, he was in the mood for confession, but
Jenny was in a mood for sin, and Eduard's attempt to find
absolution in the pleasures of the flesh misfired completely.
Was not this the trial of any young love, the only reason
which justified smashing the old tablets of law—the fact
that the pleasure proved stronger than all scruples? In his
thoughts he was with Klara, and if he had ever doubted it,
he now knew that there was no going back, that he loved
her, her anger, her need, her inability to adjust.

Late that evening a call from Klara. No, she didn't have
any intention of excusing herself, she just didn't want to
leave the interpretation of her action up to him. As it turned
out, it was not a new means of conducting a conversation
but an attempt at catching him in one of his secret moments,
also a kind of retaliation. For a short time she had been on
top, it was she who had acted, she who was forcing him to
react. After she finally raced off, she felt a great sense of
relief, as if she had pulled off a very successful coup. He
should please understand the scene—and any others she
might create—correctly. They were not designed to get him
to come back; they were attempts to regain authority over
her own feelings.

Finally, she reminded him that she was driving somewhere
during the fall break with a girl friend. Did he still intend to
look her up as they had agreed?

He hid his surprise that the date had snuck up on him
and caught him unawares. Ever since he'd taken his leave
from the institute, he'd lost all feeling for the difference between work time and vacation.

On his birthday—which he was ringing in with a bottle of

mineral water and a sleeping tablet—early in the morning, the doorbell rang: a telegram. Just one sentence—albeit one in capital letters: I LOVE YOU! No signature.

The mindless joy which first overcame him quickly gave way to a feeling of discomfort. The telegram was a trap, there were at least three possible senders. The signature he had automatically supplied seemed upon closer consideration somewhat questionable. Klara wouldn't forget to put her name under a message like that, would she? Such negligence was better suited to Laura; in fact, she might have left it unsigned on purpose. Laura would expect anyone in the world who received an anonymous declaration of love sent by her to know immediately and unequivocally who had sent it. But it might just as well have been Jenny. Two things could be expected of a woman who refuses to write out final syllables as a matter of principle—either she simply forgot to sign or else she ran out of money.

But there was another conceivable scenario, which made all three women suspect; namely, that the sender had intended, even calculated, the confusion which was bound to result from an anonymous declaration of love; let the recipient decide for himself who had sent the telegram—whom would he prefer to have sent it? The telegram was designed to lock him inside a hall of mirrors in which he kept meeting only himself and the swirling chaos of his own feelings. Even the assumption that there was only *one* sender had now become dubious. Was it not conceivable that all three had conspired to send the telegram together?

III

⥮⥮⥮⥮⥮⥮⥮⥮⥮⥮⥮⥮ 23 ⥮⥮⥮⥮⥮⥮⥮⥮⥮⥮⥮⥮⥮

IT WAS DRIZZLING, the white umbrellas outside The Tent had turned a dark gray; beneath them two men in trench coats were sitting alone in front of half-filled glasses, gazing at the immutable sky. Eduard's favorite waiter had been replaced by a big blond bodybuilder who treated him as a newcomer: when Eduard tried to sit down at his usual table the waiter asked whether he planned on eating, and added that there was a special place at the bar for diet-artists and aficionados of liquid nourishment. Pinka, who could have shown the lout his place, was not around. Apparently she had attended the funeral of a friend, another proprietor and a pioneer of the café and pub culture for which The Tent had subsequently set the trend. That was the first time Pinka had seen her regulars at ten in the morning: there they stood gaping at the open grave, their faces deathly pale, their foreheads glistening with the cold sweat of alcoholics, their eyes glazed over with high-proof liquor instead of tears. Supposedly the sight had so sobered Pinka that she took off for a sunny island that selfsame day, without telling a living soul when or even whether she'd be back.

Theo greeted Eduard as if he'd seen his friend just the day before. He fished several loose sheets of typing paper out of his jacket pocket and started thumbing through them. For a while he appeared to have forgotten all about Eduard, but then he tossed the entire bundle on the table in front of him.

Theo had just spent nearly an hour at the post office, occupying the telegram counter until closing time, much to the aggravation of the people in line behind him. At first the woman behind the window had resisted his dictation, but her impatience soon gave way to a sympathetic curiosity. Stop? she kept asking. Nothing doing, he said, that's just the beginning, keep going without periods or commas. But this is a letter! No, it's a poem, a love poem, if you really want to know, he explained as she rang up the subtotal: eighty-three marks and fifty pfennigs.

The grand total came to 187 DM, the longest telegram she had ever sent. Three-quarters of an hour of capital letters had made her hand completely cramped and sore, but the second she finished the final stanza of the poem she sighed, moved—she, too, would be happy to get a telegram like that!

That woman's review, said Theo, was my most beautiful literary success to date.

Eduard leafed through the handwritten pages, often unable to decipher the words which had been jotted down as if in a fit of intoxication, but what he did manage to make out formed part of a declaration of love unlike any other, in free verse, the romantic undertones artfully roughened by a sprinkling of vulgarities.

His recent work, explained Theo, was exhausting not only his poetic powers but his cash flow as well, since it consisted entirely of lengthy telegrams.

A period of watchful waiting and tentative groping had followed Pauline's confession that she had been the architect of Olympia and the author of all the letters. Both parties were obliged to admit that each had broken their mutual pact: Pauline, by using a fictitious admirer to lead Theo into temptation, and Theo, by allowing himself to be tempted. The only ones to benefit from the experiment had been the secret police.

But this realization had failed to bring Theo and Pauline back together. Theo accepted invitations to the West more and more frequently; they were again letting him through at the border without the slightest problem—although still without telling him why. For a brief time he toyed with the idea of really meeting the woman Pauline had planted in his imagination. He had always been surrounded by women who were infatuated with his early poems and felt confident they would become the muse for the second volume, for which they waited in vain. But he couldn't stand being with any one of them for very long; he felt himself more bound to Pauline than ever before, he practically plagued her with attention. It was as if the mistrust which had inspired Pauline to invent Olympia had simply passed on to Theo.

Theo demanded a precise account whenever Pauline went out without him, then waited up for her late into the night and expected to hear the exact details of what and whom she had been discussing with her friends. Her "nights out with the girls" particularly bothered him; when she declined to be interrogated, he smelled a conspiracy. At the same time he overwhelmed her with tokens of his affection. In the middle of the night he would wake her up and tell her how much he loved her—in phrases which never repeated themselves —and when she, overcome with sleep, just rolled away from him, he would formulate her replies as well. At times even he suspected that his affirmations of love were in fact supplications. When Pauline asked whether his passion was really directed to her, the Pauline he knew, his answers were either excessive or nonexistent. She felt herself watched, cramped, led by the hand like a child, corrected in every sentence, even in every thought; he was constantly catching her making some mistake, he demanded that she answer him using his words, that she confirm his opinions, that she dress the way he wanted her to, perform only those motions he approved of; at times she felt as if he didn't see her anymore, as if he wanted to shape a creature entirely according to his own imagination, as if she, the living, ostensibly beloved Pauline, were only an obstacle to the execution of his design. Moreover, she could no longer put up with the full ashtrays, the little scraps of paper covered with scribbles that littered the apartment, the empty whiskey bottles, his reeking of alcohol at ten in the morning. Often all she wanted to do was get up and get out of the house.

Theo couldn't deny that he drank more than he used to and that his work was hampered by an inexplicable uneasiness; he was able to recognize all the signs of degeneration, but unable to change things. One morning—Pauline had returned from a girl friend's quite late and had once again been subjected to Theo's interrogation—she made good on her threat. When Theo woke from his alcoholic slumber, he found the bed beside him empty. Pauline had left without any message. After a morning on the phone Theo discovered she had taken a trip to an island on the Baltic with Theo's least favorite of her girl friends. That same day he wrote the first of his long telegram poems, which moved Pauline so much she decided to come back. She stayed a few days, then fled once again. This pattern kept repeating itself until both sides, worn out by the whole routine, admitted that their love could survive only at a distance. Pauline wrote that by putting Theo's loyalty to the test, she had let herself be guided by a completely false suspicion. In actuality he wasn't looking for another woman at all, but then neither was he looking for her, Pauline. What he was after was the constant renewal of a yearning which could be fulfilled only by the absence of the loved one. His most beautiful poems assumed an addressee who could be reached only by mail.

Eduard hadn't seen André or Theo since he broke up with Klara. He was shocked when Theo told him that André had been in the hospital for ten days.

The news that André had been forced to relocate the theater of war to a university hospital shifted the main focus of Eduard's attention. Thinking about André forced him to reassess what was important and what wasn't, with the result that his own needs began to seem completely incidental. At the top of the list of Most Important Things, as inalienable as a bill of rights, was the sentence: André cannot die.

He spent the next day trying to find out more about André's condition and his chances of recovery. The information he received led him into a maze of opinionated advice and secret tips, where everyone claimed to know the only way André could be saved: the one institute, the one professor, the one new cure. A colleague who swore by grains and dry heat tried to convince Eduard to take André to an oasis in the middle of the Sahara. A friend recalled a legendary inventor on the other side of the Wall who had built an apparatus for cancer patients which allegedly killed the cancer cells by overheating them—a cure which had been neither proved nor disproved by science. Laura gave him the address of a diviner who could search André's body and his immediate surroundings for hidden currents and rays which might be crippling his immune system. Others told amazing things about a Bulgarian substance derived from yogurt which was capable of reversing the metastasis until the cancer could be surgically removed. The most devastating blow for Eduard was the discovery that even the specialists, forced by their own repeated setbacks to pay attention, had no clear opinion to offer concerning these alternative procedures. Surrounded by computerized tomography, linear accelerators, and radiotherapy devices, they sat there and listened to the advice of their colleagues from the Stone Age.

Eduard had agreed to meet Theo in front of the clinic. The oncology department surprised him with its unconventional style, which was so cheerful it seemed to belong to some more southern clime. He had expected an oppressive silence, an overbearing odor of disinfectants, the sheen of freshly polished tiles, the muffled voices of the staff, which always reminded him of the murmur heard in Protestant churches on Good Friday. But there was none of this constant readiness for death he knew from other hospitals. No one lowered his voice, no one softened his gait, most of the doors stood wide open. It was as if André had infected the entire department with his happy-go-lucky attitude.

They had to wait in a corner between corridors. A patient about fifty years old was sitting across from them; Eduard couldn't take his eyes off the man's handsome, emaciated skull. He kept glancing at the large eyes, which seemed to bulge with constant fear. The disease was a gruesome artist who drew the same portrait of anyone who chose to resist it: the hairless skull, the translucent skin spread tautly over the cheekbones, the deep-set, darkened eyes.

André's room looked like the headquarters of a rock star on tour. Numerous bouquets testified to far-flung mutual affections, the phone rang every few minutes, a young conductor whom Eduard had often seen with André was filling in as secretary and was busy scheduling appointments. Even though he was now almost too weak to talk, André had not lost his talent for making other people so enthusiastic about him they would run his errands. The room was littered with open books, scores, and musical notebooks covered with ink. His desire to read, André explained, grew in proportion to his inability to take solid food.

He had become terribly haggard and gaunt and his face looked gray, all the highs and lows seemed to have been filtered out of his speech, his eyes stayed hidden behind a pair of glasses with colored lenses. The borsalino on his bare head cast a soft shadow on his hollow face, only his wonderfully distinct Jewish nose still stuck out boldly. He took off his rose-colored glasses so as to let Theo and Eduard look through them. There were times he could no longer bear the omnipresent white, when he had a desire for rose: a room in rose, nurses in rose, friends in rose, a desire for rosy prospects.

For a moment Eduard saw in André's eyes the old undaunted rogue, but his friend's speech scared him. He spoke with large, arrhythmic pauses, and when he stopped he inhaled deeply and then exhaled so audibly it seemed as though he were sighing. It was a sound Eduard had never heard André produce. Despite everything, he was still a lucky devil: out of all possible types of cancer he had managed to catch one which offered more than a 50 percent chance of survival.

The scar from his operation stretched from his collarbone to his navel. Dryly he explained the scientific charts that went with it—the X-rays, the blood tests, the histological findings he had asked to keep, all the testimonies submitted by his body as evidence in the trial of his life.

Let's go for a walk, he suggested, and locked his arms in Eduard's and Theo's. They stepped from the bed to the window, from the window to the door, then out into the corridor. André hung heavily in their arms, he kept catching his breath, his mouth displayed its rhapsodic smile as if in involuntary defiance—but on the whole he thought he was walking and breathing much better today than yesterday. A young female doctor walking past the three of them stopped and nodded to André. The gaze with which she followed André's movements expressed a little more than an expert's analytic curiosity. Theo glanced at Eduard; it was obvious that their relationship was not strictly a therapeutic one.

How do you like her? asked André, after she had gone on. Do you think I ought to marry her?

They had first met on the cold tiles of the radiation department, when in the light of the viewer she explained the bright spots on the photo. With his eyes fixed on the catastrophic results, his hands had searched for hers. It had been love at first X-ray.

Eduard was speechless. It was true that André's Don Giovannism had survived extreme situations before. But the fact that even the torture of chemotherapy wasn't enough to make him give up his vice, the fact that he was still chasing whatever skirt he could find even while virtually chained to his bed, even as the Stone Guest was struggling to pull him into the deep—this proved André the equal of his literary predecessor.

Marry? asked Eduard. And what about Esther?

Isn't there finally some citizens' initiative fighting for the right—of women as well as men—to go on marrying new partners while still keeping the old one? asked André.

It was true, answered Theo, such mores did exist, but still

only for men and in countries a little farther east; he quietly improvized the cry of a muezzin. André tuned into the gibberish with amazing virtuosity, he was capable of imitating twenty different languages without articulating a full word in any one.

In short sentences expanded by long pauses André explained how things had gone following the wedding.

After his parents had left, he had fallen into a state of complete debilitation, as if the main reason for the life-knot he had just tied had vanished with his parents, leaving him stuck with the knot but not the life. Esther wasn't faring much better. After her mother and Yuri had found an apartment, the newlyweds felt deserted in the freshly emptied rooms and had no idea where to begin with each other. On the day of his catastrophic X-ray result he had asked Esther for a divorce.

I've probably lost our bet, said André. For some time now it hasn't been a matter of whether or not I'll show up with my skis on the appointed day in Sils-Maria in the same old coupling but whether I'll be physically able to punch my own lift ticket once I'm there.

Talking had tired him out; his sentences were interrupted more and more often by the slow, sighing breath. He had to get out of here, he whispered, out of this city, out of this language, out of all these stories. There was only one man in the world who could save him, would Theo and Eduard be prepared to accompany him to Paris? Next week or, at the latest, the one after—he'd keep them posted about the date.

As André's bed was made ready for the night and the young doctor was measuring his fever and taking his pulse, Esther arrived. She greeted the friends without any embarrassment.

The doctor watched Esther as she stowed away the scores, books, notebooks, and clean laundry; when one book fell on the ground, she picked it up and helped Esther arrange the other items. Eduard watched the two women half in admiration, half in disbelief. Was it André's need that revoked all laws of competition, of possession, all rights of prior claim? André had always had a talent for making women his accomplices; he gained instant access to their generous nature by not hiding any of his weaknesses, and by giving himself as he was—a tender destroyer, a deeply wounded hero, who readily accepted guilt and was always prepared to confess that he had bitten off a little more than he could chew.

JUST BEFORE SHE HUNG UP, Jenny dropped the sentence that changed the world, casually, as if she had almost forgotten it: By the way, I'm pregnant. Then came a pause filled with Eduard's loud silence, and then: he didn't need to say anything now, he could take his time. And something else: she was happy and wanted the child, of course only if he did, too.

She hung up, he didn't have a chance to complain about her manner of telling him. He knew that voice, this tone straight out of a Western from other occasions, but it had never been as inappropriate as now—Jenny, the poker-faced cowboy. For God's sake, Jenny, sometimes it's all right to lose your composure! His initial joy gave way to his fear of the pain the news would inflict on Klara. Was it even possible? It can't be! I have it in writing!

He couldn't remember having ever relied upon his infertility. Just so he wouldn't be forced to admit his defect, he had always been careful to avoid the vestige of risk which Dr. Nastase had underscored. Always or almost always? Memories were not reliable judges, as a rule they took the side of whoever was remembering, they were not to be trusted. Besides, Jenny had warned him. Already he could hear her reply to his questions, see her sarcastic shrug of the shoulders: Well, that's the way it is when you get involved with such a super-fertile woman. I told you before, when I'm in love it's enough for a man to look at me twice in a certain way, and I'm not always joking when I say things like that.

He was amazed to register that all the debates raging inside his skull were stilled by a feeling of pride. So, some force had decided—all calculations to the contrary—that he would become a father. Heaven knows, there could be worse news than that. The more immediate circumstances of parenthood were, to be sure, startling, impossible to foresee with any reasonable accuracy, but hadn't nature itself—or to give it a more modern name, chance, the only god Eduard believed in—issued its decree?

For the first time his life was being changed by a completely unplanned event. Why not simply accept the umpire's ruling? After all, the idea that the solution to a given riddle was not always to be found where one was looking was a basic tenet of scientific research.

Objection! You're making it too easy for yourself! That's all a bunch of untenable excuses and self-justifications, parachutes of self-deception which won't open now that you've taken the leap. If you'd stayed true to Klara, this alleged accident of chance would never have happened. You and only you are the director responsible for staging the miracle before which you are now kneeling in feigned piety.

The mere question of how to inform Klara of his fatherhood was enough to spoil every thought about it. He could hear his own words coming back to haunt him, quoted with scorn: Relationships always break apart for internal reasons. No, there was no way he would allow the pregnancy to bring him to set up house with Jenny. Inwardly he was still a long way from detaching himself from Klara; nobody, including

Jenny, would benefit by his letting himself be forced blindly into precipitous decisions which would determine the course of his life for the next twenty years. Suddenly he had an overwhelming desire to gain some distance from both of them.

A nearly forgotten fantasy returned, an image of fatherhood that showed a clearer picture of the child than of the mother. Had he not from time immemorial dreamed of a life as a twosome instead of a threesome? Of course, this father-child idyll offered no insight into minor matters such as who would feed the baby, who would change the diapers, who would tend the infant when he was off at work.

At the same time he sensed that his urgent reluctance to be pressured in his emotional decisions, his insistence on following only his own, internal guides—all resulted from a basic impulse to flee. In the middle of the flood he was dreaming about a sealed room where, undisturbed by outside influences, he could determine his next step. In truth, however, he had locked the door behind him, and even if he still had to ratify his decision internally, he had made it long ago.

He asked himself how others acted in similar situations; after all, the conflict which was threatening him with internal breakdown was primarily characterized by its ordinariness. Wherever he looked he encountered signs that the two sexes' ability to live together was rapidly diminishing. Every person suffered the slings and arrows of this contemporary fortune as a private fate, but that didn't change the fact that the experience was always as irrevocable as an earthquake. More than half of all marriages, according to statisticians operating nationwide, ended in divorce. How did this majority accommodate to the relentless new law that limited the time two people were allotted to live together? Where did all these involuntary test subjects find the strength to dissolve shared accounts and households, to look for new apartments, to orchestrate moves, to divide furniture and children—and all this after work between 5 and 10 p.m.? He could only take his hat off to all these nameless heroes and heroines. When he considered the effort required to separate, the trials and tribulations of a lifelong partnership seemed downright enticing. The energy consumption of a constantly changing life was enormous; the state was entirely right to hinder this wasting of human resources.

He had arranged to meet Jenny in a café far from The Tent, where they were safe from witnesses. On his way there he again found a temporary equilibrium in the image of a single father traveling around the world, leading his child by the hand.

She's half a child herself, he thought when he saw Jenny. In her light dress she looked girlish; she had tied back her hair, which accentuated the Botticelli line of her neck and chin. He was moved by the idea that this scarcely grown woman was so ready to accept what nature had proposed and to share a life with someone she still didn't know completely, just like that, without any trial period, and the protective instinct which he had always considered a spiteful sister of desire aroused a new feeling inside him. Why not just go away with her, take off to some warm country, a cheap hotel, a bungalow on a beach, reading and writing letters until the child was born? In the global village of molecular biologists there were many people who knew his work, it wouldn't be that difficult for him to fulfill his duty as breadwinner.

Jenny didn't ask him for decisions, she only explained her own feelings and considerations. Maybe everything was too quick, maybe she was too unprepared, and as always you could say it was the wrong time, the wrong man, the wrong professional situation. But for what and for whom should she wait, for what right moment, what ideal father, what constellation? For the chance that she might fall in love again three years later? Her body and her feelings told her that she wanted the child despite the unripe circumstances, and she had seen too many people who, by waiting for the right moment, had missed their chance to make the best of the wrong one.

As she spoke his gaze fell upon her girlish hand reaching for the glass, and suddenly he saw his own hand on the tablecloth, as if through a magnifying glass. On the back of his hand, between his thumb and forefinger, he discovered the first markings of approaching age, rough patches of skin which refused to smooth out even when he stretched his fingers. The grown child who was talking about transience with such passion had noticeably more time than he to wait for some right moment.

He felt and said: I'm looking forward to the child, but hardly had he brought this simple sentence to his lips, this sentence he heard amplified by trumpets and full choirs, than he sensed a trapdoor swinging open beneath his feet. It wasn't the familiar hoary voice of doubt causing the dissonance, nor was it the *memento mori* of the avenging Commendatore. The voice now cursing him was a wonderfully clear soprano, and it sang in *recitativo secco*: "I lie, believing that Heaven will avenge me."

Isn't the strength of a new love measured by its capacity to destroy scruples, to annul unilaterally all rights of entitlement that once belonged to the old love? Only if the passion is stronger than the torment of conscience does it have a right to live.

You're going to become a father, Jenny told him over the phone two days later, whether you want to or not. For a moment he was relieved: the responsibility for what he would have to tell Klara was no longer his alone, and now that it was decided, he realized that all thoughts of resisting stemmed from his fear of hurting Klara. But as he rehearsed the lines he would use to communicate the decision, he again wanted to reach for the receiver and take everything back. Was it guilt or was it love which chained him so to Klara? Would he feel the same pangs of conscience if he no longer loved her? It was as if he were about to stick a dagger into the dearest person in the world.

On the street he couldn't help noticing a poster on a column. In huge letters the Protestant church was quoting Christ to advertise a peace seminar: LOVE THY NEIGHBOR AS THYSELF! And if I can't stand myself, Eduard asked the poster, what do you recommend, then? Evidently the Savior, presumably content with who He was, hadn't given much consideration to a case like Eduard's. What guidelines would he give to one of the guilty, to one of the perpetrators? Because that's all he was: a culprit hiding behind his scruples, a murderer with a sensitive soul. No matter how much he referred to the complete lack of premeditation, the moods of nature, the mistakes of science, the torments of his conscience—in the eyes of the international tribunal of love he was guilty. Expelled forever from the golden fields of great and beautiful feelings, closed to the sensations of despair and sadness, of love and pain, of righteous wrath and dignified revenge, to which all innocents have easy access. The entire loving world would enact a permanent sit-down strike, so as to block the door that led to his tiny, biologically determined bit of happiness.

Earlier he had found solace in literature, but now he put each book down after only a few pages; they burned his hand. In vain he searched contemporary authors for some advocate. Literature took up for the victims, it did not voice the sorrows of the perpetrators. Male heroes in particular, inasmuch as they owed their existence to male authors, were as a rule innocent. Abandoned, battered by belligerent women into a state of loneliness and left to their beautiful sorrow and pain. Was it really possible that the authors of these moving tales of suffering and woe had never been guilty of a comparable love crime? That they were always the betrayed, not the betrayers; always the beaten, never the beaters; always the sufferers, never those who caused the suffering? It seemed that a wrongdoer was literarily viable if the crimes he inflicted on others could be shown to result from a much larger wound he had suffered previously. But why was there no depiction of the lying, the meanness, the shortcomings, the false promises, the outbreaks of violence and brutality which he had to confess? Why did they all want to be so innocent, why did they wipe away the dirty traces of their passion, erase every clue that would show their guilt?

Eduard could claim no extenuating circumstances. Even if he had unwittingly become an offender, he was by no means a victim. Whatever he decided, he would still be guilty.

Scarcely had he allowed himself to think about the child and a future with Jenny when he found a letter in his mailbox sent from Milan with a clear message joyfully conveyed. He read Laura's letter twice, three times, a fourth time, but the main sentence never changed. Laura was pregnant. Her post-script preempted any reaction on his part: she was looking forward to the child and had decided to have it.

There was no chair which could have borne Eduard's weight. No, he cried into the empty rooms which in his mind's eye were filling up with nothing but changing tables and cribs, never in this life, it can't be, it wasn't me, it won't be me, I have it in writing! There's a mix-up, you've both made a mistake, I'm not the one you mean! I have the proof in my pocket, I'll make you copies, it's impossible for me to be the father of all these children.

And what if he were, nevertheless? Science knew no irrefutable truths, the only constant was the notorious underestimation of human error.

With Laura, he had to confess, prophylaxis had never been a subject of conversation; the dangers they had exposed themselves to had been immediate enough to suppress any thought of future risks. Accursed science! Insidious Dr. Nastase! I'll sue both him and the criminal laboratory for damages, for child support! Who was playing cat here to his mouse, which god had dubbed him a fool and punished him with the scornful ridicule of all third-party bystanders?

Over the phone, Nastase listened to Eduard's stream of invectives with astonishing patience and mailed him a photocopy of a publication which had aroused great interest among his colleagues. The article offered a plausible explanation for Eduard's case, which according to the previous state of the science should never have been possible. The new theory even had a name, albeit an unwieldy one: "semen competition hypothesis." The postulate held that men in a situation of sexual competition produce significantly more and more mobile sperm than men who lack such competition. The first sign of such a connection came from a study of apes. Zoologists had noticed that the testicles of chimpanzees, relative to body weight and size, were four times as big as those of gorillas. A British researcher had explained the phenomenon through the different position of the male in the respective clan. Groups of gorillas were always dominated by a single male, who chased away all potential rivals and had the females for himself. The unchallenged leader of the band could thus get by with a rather modest production of sperm. In the more democratic society of chimpanzees it was common practice for any and all males to copulate with any and all females in heat. As a result, male chimps found themselves in a fierce biological contest and needed to constantly produce sperm in order to have a chance at propagation. It was precisely this ever-present readiness, so the apologist presumed, which led to the development of over-sized testicles in the chimpanzee.

The British scientist had had the unusual idea of testing his hypothesis with the help of human subjects. He managed to find twenty-five willing couples and drew up a sexual profile for each. Next he divided them into "gorillas" and "chimps." All the couples had to do then was perform according to their own inclinations and aptitudes—either as gorillas or as chimpanzees. The data collected showed a "clear negative correlation" between the number of sperm produced by a man and the length of time he had been with his partner. "Among couples who had spent only a short time together, the sperm count per copulation was found to be six million, as opposed to one million among long-term partners." Not without pride the author noted this was the first experiment which used people in order to understand the behavior of apes.

So I am a chimpanzee, Eduard told himself. He had little desire to check this realization in the mirror, nor did the knowledge make him feel any wiser. Even if Dr. Nastase's handout did help identify the apish character of Eduard's drives, his feelings remained all the more puzzling. Or were they, too, directed by the ape within? Was it stress, sheer exhaustion, or an odd mutation which caused him to welcome Laura's happy news with less than the appropriate glee?

The feeling of doubt soon gave way to curiosity. He was moved and even—why deny it—proud. What was so bad about the news? The more exactly he recalled Laura's image, the less her being pregnant made him anxious. It was true that he seldom saw her, that he knew her only from a few encounters which were always as unpredictable as a hike inside the crater of Mt. Etna, but had he not experienced the happiest moments of his life with her? She had never forged any future plans with him, in fact she was militantly opposed to the idea, and now she accepted her pregnancy with the same fearlessness with which she abandoned herself to her whims of desire. Was it not cause for joy that this woman wanted to have a child by him? It would have black curls, it would sing, it would say papa to him with the accent on the last syllable. Besides, it would be inconsistent of him to accept one verdict of nature but not the other. No ape, neither chimpanzee nor gorilla, would do that!

To be sure, the annals of human folly contained few similar sentiments, but he could no longer count on role models, he had to dare think and pronounce the impossible. The truth was that he loved Laura, too, in a different way, but no less than he did Klara and Jenny. Fate had dealt him an unexpected solution to the puzzle which had jolted him out of his prone sleeping position and all his other securities. It wasn't true; he could love! He did love!—the only problem was that there were three women! He didn't suffer from an inability to love, he merely lacked the talent for exclusivity. The sole flaw of this tripartite love was that it was condoned only among apes.

Despite all his unmade decisions he did not feel overpowered by the additional task of accompanying André and Theo to Paris. For the first time he believed he understood how people managed in times of war. The amount of energy available for the mobilization or pacification of feelings such as anxiety, mortal terror, relief, hope, and horror was presumably no greater in war than in peace. The only way it could work was for this constant quantity to be distributed equally among many extreme threats at once. Otherwise it would be impossible to understand how people survive the loss of a house, the anxiety over finding the next piece of bread, and the death of a relative all in one single day. Strangely, he had the feeling that he could, with equal strength, take care of Klara, Jenny, Laura, and André.

In his borsalino, with his dark glasses and a long cashmere scarf wrapped around his neck, André looked like a dying mafioso. When Eduard spotted him sitting next to Theo in the airport lobby, for the first time he had the feeling that André had lost the battle with his enemy. The man could hardly keep himself erect; after half a sentence he raised his chin and inhaled deeply.

I'm looking forward to Paris, and to you playing host, André said with a weak smile at Eduard. Remember, you still have some gambling debts with me.

Eduard had wanted to wait for a better moment, but he couldn't help blurting out the new twists of his story.

Theo didn't even attempt to stifle his laughter. That was what Eduard loved about him, that Theo refused to be cowed by anything, and that he felt most at home in a labyrinth.

What's really so bad about it? Theo asked.

If I were in your shoes I'd want a child, said André.

Just don't ask which one, interjected Theo, when Eduard hesitated to answer.

He's all wound up, said André; he better stay here until his various paternity suits have been cleared up. We can't use someone in Paris whose head isn't screwed on right.

Eduard tried to argue, but André stopped him from saying another word.

Not until the flight to Paris had been announced for the second time did they notice that the gate had been changed to the opposite end of the airport. After a few steps André couldn't go any farther; he sat down on the luggage cart and let Theo and Eduard push him. They ran to the gate. When they had to hand over their luggage and leave the cart, Theo picked up André piggyback and carried him to passport control.

If it's a boy, a really nice name would be André, André called out to Eduard, his words punctuated by his coughing.

Theo would be even nicer, gasped Theo, barely able to breathe under André's weight.

Maybe he won't have to choose at all, André cackled, before he disappeared down the gateway with Theo. If they're both boys, then the whole problem's solved!

A few days later Theo called from Paris with encouraging news about the doctor to whom André had entrusted himself. He had the impression that Professor Mandelstam was a

complete believer in classical medicine, and that he had acquired his reputation as a miracle healer solely by his art of
adjusting the mixtures and doses of chemotherapy to each
individual patient. In his diagnosis, André's will to live would
be the most deciding factor.

André's vital spirits had also been lifted by the news from
Warsaw that the premiere of their *Don Giovanni Project* had
been planned for next spring, reported Theo. Each day they
spent a few hours working to fine-tune the libretto to the
music, and vice versa. André was again displaying bouts of
light-headedness, he was absolutely determined to go skiing
in Sils-Maria, they had just been discussing who should
shell out for a bet that no one had won. They had decided
it should be the one who had lost first—in other words,
Eduard.

When Eduard hesitated to answer Theo's question about
which child he had chosen, his friend got sharp with him.
He was now too far away and too concerned with André to
put Eduard's head straight, but he would write—no, not a
telegram, just regular mail.

As it turned out, Theo's letter, which arrived a week later,
contained no concrete advice; it just told a story about a
friend of Theo's who had disappeared without a trace.

The young film director X had two life companions about
the same age, who looked so much alike it was difficult to
tell who was who, a fact which X ridiculously refused to admit. They each bore him a child—almost on the same day.
In the first year of his double fatherhood, X was still able to
manage an amazingly entertaining TV film. The critics were
all beside themselves, they especially praised how he had portrayed a certain paradox: in the course of the film, a double
marriage which at first glance seemed very unconventional

proved to require an almost military logistical planning. The hero of the story followed an embarrassingly precise daily and weekly schedule, which enabled him to divide his powers most equally: three days with A, three days with B, one night taking care of A's child, one night B's—only on Sunday was he alone in his one-room apartment. Replacing the conventional family with a double family ultimately resulted in the doubling of constraints. The whole thing was interpreted as a cheeky satire on the sexual revolution in the capitalist West; only a few in the know recognized the confession of a desperate man.

After this highly praised debut X was quickly forgotten. His later screenplays, people said, lacked the agility of his earlier film; the irony had given way to a tendency toward sentimentality. People who knew him looked on with growing horror as the unhappy man persisted in living through all the mathematical variations of the triangle. The "great solution" he had so high-handedly attempted, and which had been actually modeled on a commune—X with two wives and their children in one apartment—ended in a fiasco. Both variants involving separation of bed and board followed in rapid succession: X plus A minus B, then X plus B minus A. After suffering through all possible combinations, the community broke up into its component parts, first X minus B, then X minus A minus B. Finally Theo had lost sight of X completely. After becoming so emaciated by his daily routine, the man had evidently dissolved into nothing.

It would be worth discussing the possibility of loving two or even three partners at once, wrote Theo, if you could divide all the inevitable consequences and side effects of love equally among the partners: desire, jealousy, protective instinct, the fear of loss, the need to show weakness and helplessness, the wish for a child, and so on. You yourself are proof that it's all a lot of drunken drivel. Your feelings sound like garbled sentences consisting only of infinitives; to yearn for, to hate, to be happy, to regret, to reconcile, to wish for a child—these are all passions without an object, and ultimately without a subject as well. Love triangles are never equilateral, the constellation is bound to create hierarchies.

So back into the old trap, you ask me, into the double drawer of marriage or a marriage-like existence? We seem to have succeeded only in discovering which arrangements between the sexes no longer function, but that's all we need to know. The rest depends on the courage and invention of every individual.

Eduard gradually found his way back to his own pangs of conscience. Since he had no luck reaching Laura by phone, he wrote her that he might have received her news more happily if it weren't for the fact that another woman was expecting a child by him, to whom he was going to fulfill his responsibility.

Lothar called and asked whether Eduard had come across the latest, very interesting news from Minneapolis about the twins project. Eduard told him he hadn't and got hold of the article.

The new report read as though its authors had intended to pronounce a Solomonian judgment in the ongoing dispute between Lothar and himself. The article contained a thorough discussion of the inheritability of the most diverse personal characteristics, from religiosity to reactivity. The result proclaimed neither him nor Lothar to be correct. To be sure, the study stressed that without exception all the traits under investigation did have a strong genetic base—which Lothar had always denied. From the data on identical twins, inherited factors accounted for 45 percent of a given individual's "traditionalism" (a high regard for morals and religion, a certain affinity for ideologies), 58 percent, for "constraint" (reserve, caution, dependence on the ideas of others). But where "achievement capability" was concerned, for example (stubbornness, perfectionism, ambition), hereditary factors accounted for only 39 percent. In the end, the sum of genetic influence converged toward 50 percent, strangely enough. The other 50 percent was explained by the environmental factors so highly acclaimed by Lothar. "The genes," the authors concluded, "sing a prehistoric song, and while we would do well to resist falling under its spell, we would be foolish to stop our ears to it completely."

25

SHE HAD DECIDED TO GET AN ABORTION, Laura wrote from Milan, and described a dream. She was hiding in an old, wood-paneled apothecary, inside a drawer. Someone came in, opened all the drawers, seemed to be looking for her. She jumped out of her hiding place, ran for the door and down the street. All of a sudden she was leading a child by the hand, she could no longer run quickly enough. Her pursuer caught up with them. She found a knife in her skirt and stabbed it in the neck of the man, who was now recognizable as Eduard. She remembered, wrote Laura, how good it felt sticking the knife into his soft neck, over and over.

Eduard was hardly relieved by Laura's decision. It also made it very clear that his power to decide things was severely limited. With the peculiar fearlessness often born of despair, he had inwardly prepared himself for a second fatherhood. Now that Laura had decided otherwise, all he felt, to his own astonishment, was sadness.

He had agreed to drop in on Klara after ten days. He had no intention of telling her about Jenny's pregnancy over the telephone. He would drive out there and expose himself to her anger and pain. But as it happened, when she phoned him, his overly calm voice betrayed him. What was going on with him, she could hardly recognize him, his voice was alienating, almost businesslike; why did he keep lying to her, who no longer expected anything from him. He should say what he was keeping from her, his presumptuous consideration kept her in a state of dependency she had already overcome.

The decision, the hesitation, finally the sentence for which there was no merciful formulation. The greater evil would be vagueness, he couldn't leave any opening for hope. He explained that Jenny was expecting a child and that he approved.

You can't tell me that kind of thing over the phone! Klara shouted. For two days I've been all by myself here, what am I supposed to do now!

They agreed to meet the very next day: he would fly down and she would drive up to meet him. Both trips would take about the same amount of time; the city where they would meet was not too far from his boyhood home.

That night before the trip he slept deeply and dreamlessly for the first time in ages. It was as if the creature in Jenny's womb had been waiting for him to confess before it really became alive. Evidently the conscience nagged only about imagined crimes; once they had been committed, it stayed quiet. There was no longer anything more to decide; he had passed from the feeling of guilt into the state of guilt.

He had only a few hours to prepare for the departure. He was almost relieved to realize that the decision entailed a certain bureaucratic effort, which seemed to strengthen it *ex post facto*. Letters had to be hurriedly written and mailed, appointments canceled, accounts balanced, pressing phone calls had to be made. He didn't know how long he'd be away. Just as he was trying to close his suitcase, Jenny walked in. He opened the lid to stuff in some woolen fringe that was sticking out. Jenny's gaze fell on the long winter scarf that was lying on top. She seemed to sense right away that it was a present from Klara. With a caustic smile she helped him cram the scarf into the suitcase. Together they walked to the entrance to the building. At the door she turned to him: Don't you have anything to say to me just now?

He saw how she had to use her entire weight to open the door. She walked off toward the bus stop without looking back.

The waiter was reading the morning paper, the attendants in the self-service diner were arranging sausage and cheese sandwiches wrapped in cellophane inside the display windows. He was the first guest in the airport restaurant. The book he had taken along was one he had read fifteen years before. At that time, possibly in the hope of a similarly moving fate, he had been able to identify with the suffering of the abandoned professor and with all his threatening letters, but the old feelings no longer surfaced; in vain Eduard searched for exonerating parallels.

As he was leafing through the book, someone walked up behind him. Klara had arrived hours before the appointed time, she must have started out just after their telephone conversation. Her features seemed glazed over, her lines dark, as if highlighted with liner, her mouth had more lipstick than usual, her entire face was so taut it threatened to pop at the slightest touch. When he stood up he read in her eyes the demand for distance, for avoiding any embrace. Tears were streaming down her face, unaccompanied by any other sound than the clinking of knives and forks: only now did he notice that the neighboring tables had filled up with customers who were devouring weisswurst and beer for breakfast. Klara's first sentence was: Until now there was only *one* worst piece of news imaginable—but this time you've outdone yourself.

They drove south in Klara's car. A strong wind chased the clouds toward them in dark, low-flying heaps, punctured by occasional rays of sunlight which fell on far-flung points of the landscape, causing a window, a car roof, a gutter to flare up like a quick straw fire and then glow back down. Isolated spinneys of trees rose along a jagged line that cut through the foothills of the gently climbing landscape—sharp and irregular as blotches of ink. On the horizon masses of cloud gathered into craggy, blackish-blue mountains, so that Eduard could no longer tell whether he was seeing the airy haze or the peaks of the Alps.

The clouds racing toward them seemed to double the speed of the Fiat. He avoided looking at Klara and concentrated solely on the view through the side window. The nearer objects were flying by like wild shadows; only the heavy, distant lines of the landscape stayed fixed.

Klara suggested they visit the nearby village where Eduard had spent his childhood. He didn't understand what drove her there. Did she hope to ride off with him into the past, since the way to a common future was blocked? But at that point he would have agreed to anything. As they sped along the winding country road, it seemed as if Klara was bent on making all his nightmares come true. She raced through narrow passageways, thundered over poorly surfaced bridges, and twisted around the steeply sloping cliffs in daring proximity to the edge of the road and at speeds guaranteed to provide a grand finale to a broken love. Involuntarily he pressed his feet against the floor, as if he could slow down the car. He asked whether she wasn't too tired, whether she wasn't in a condition which induced reckless driving, she ought to consider that she was not only endangering him but other drivers as well. Klara, however, had no intention of giving him the wheel—he could get out whenever he liked, hitchhike, take the train—she would drive at whatever speed she wished. He had the feeling she was looking for a way to travel backward in space and time. She didn't slow down until they drove into the narrow basin that enclosed the village of his boyhood.

He had always thought the valley looked like the bottom of a lake, whose cliffs climbed steeply to the unattainable peaks of the Alps. Looking at the two sister mountains in whose shadow he had grown up, the large and the small Waxenstein, he suddenly remembered the crazy man who, every summer, attempted to climb the smaller, still unconquered mountain, only to fail anew each time. They used to stand in the village square following the man's climb with binoculars, as he crept up the perpendicular wall like a dark insect bent on dying. Scarcely able to make out his tiny movements, they waited silently for the moment when this presumptuous man would part from the wall and float down in an incredibly slow motion, which at that distance almost seemed controlled. After the fall was complete, the people quickly dispersed; a few set out to rescue the hapless soul, who somehow always managed to survive. The rest of the year he spent having himself patched back together in order to try it all over again the following summer.

Eduard remembered a remote forest inn on a lake he had once crossed in a rowboat with his father and Lothar. Since that time the old wooden house had become a hotel, the large new wing cast a shadow that practically spanned the entire lake; only a few water lilies, bobbing on the sad, wrinkled water, reminded him of the lake of his childhood. From the boat, when the water was still, he had seen the stone mermaid at the bottom of the lake, the half-open mouth that breathed water instead of air; the arms which, moved by the refraction of light, had seemed to reach out, again and again. Now the only thing which glinted inside the muddy broth were goldfish: a slate shingle advertised home-grown trout.

Klara found the filleted fish with its half-open mouth and dead eye repulsive, she shoved the plate away in disgust. What did Jenny's pregnancy and his acceptance mean for him and Klara? She didn't look at him.

No wriggling out, don't leave any hope which he'd only have to shatter once again, he had to tell her more than he knew and more than he had promised Jenny.

He hadn't intended what happened, he wasn't even capable of intending it, but now that it had happened, he approved of it, and his common sense told him that the child would mean a final separation for him and Klara. There existed something like a decree of nature, and he was no longer young enough to resist it.

You of all people, who can't even tell a cherry tree from an apple tree, are suddenly calling on nature in your defense! Now all you're missing is the shepherd's crook and a pair of sandals so you can go forth and spread the good news!

Her anger caused her to forget all possible embarrassment. He wasn't going to get away with this so easily. She would talk to Jenny, convince her to have the necessary abortion, unmask him to André and Theo and all his other friends. He shouldn't expect a betrayal like that to remain unatoned, there was such a thing as justice. His professional career was over, it wouldn't do for a respected scientist like Professor Eduard Hoffmann to be such a bastard in private; she would expose him, disfigure him, puncture his eardrums, mangle his face.

He said he took all her threats seriously but would stand by what he had decided.

Then in a fit of disgust, exhaustion, and fatigue she stood up. Maybe she'd just emigrate to the U.S. or some other country; at any rate, she had no intention of living in the same city next to him and a child he had had with someone else.

A couple had sat down next to them in a cozy little nook. Judging by their age they could have been celebrating their silver anniversary, but their violent gestures, which neither age nor weight seemed to have mellowed, indicated a young lovers' quarrel. Eduard and Klara could only guess at what was being said from the couple's body language. The man absentmindedly took a few violets from the vase on the table and crumbled the flowers over the fingers of the lady. She looked at him as if expecting an apology, but the man just gave an embarrassed smile and wiped her hand off with a napkin, letting his own hand linger by her as if in appeasement. She brusquely rejected his offer, turned away, stood up, and marched off to the door. He, too, got up, patted the corners of his mouth with the napkin, then carelessly let it drop to the floor. When he followed the woman outside, he waved to the waitress as if to signal that this was not the best moment to settle accounts. Eduard noticed the man was dragging his right leg. Eduard then asked for his check; as the waitress wrote it up, she kept glancing down at the napkin on the floor. The table with the two half-emptied plates remained deserted.

Klara insisted on taking a walk through the village. He no longer knew his way around, his personal landmarks had all disappeared or become unrecognizable; the village of his childhood had become a popular resort. Only the church with its onion-shaped dome and the surrounding parish buildings and farmhouses matched the drawing in his memory.

All the houses had been freshly painted, generally in the style of the little pictures which children brought home from church on Sundays: even the farmhouses he thought he recognized looked brand-new. The doors and windows were framed with plump cherubs carrying rosy canopies; ornately scrolled rhymes painted on the walls attested to the piety of the inhabitants. Everything was scrubbed and clean, as if a master of the Bavarian Baroque had just laid down his paintbrush.

Back then the place had been inhabited by gnomes and ghosts, by dark, violent fairy tales which fueled a craziness that never quite erupted. The people were mistrustful, taciturn; the sounds they uttered were hard and tough like rocks tumbling down a mountainside, all their emotions were charged with an enigmatic hidden violence. Once a year the demons appeared on the streets, the spirits which otherwise stayed hidden in the mossy grottoes and dusty rafters. Then they would march through the village in bright, flapping garments and great wooden masks, with drums, rattles, and switches. You could feel them breathing down your neck and hear the wooden lips utter threatening sounds. Every now and then one would break out of the parade and chase down a panic-stricken, fleeing child who had ventured too close, catching him by the hair with its clawlike fingers. Then the demon would toss the child in the air with one hand, catch him, shake him, and thrash him with the switches.

Now at every corner a forest of wooden signposts gave the

hiking distance—in meters and minutes—to the various local attractions. Everywhere you could hear the trekkers
pounding the gravel paths with their hiking sticks, and see
them passing by in their loden jackets, their smoothly polished leather hiking shoes, their freshly creamed but wrinkled faces. The resort attracted primarily retirees—the
Reiners still among us, thought Eduard. He was certain that
among the walkers were veterans of the movement that had
burst forth a half century earlier to save the world. But now
all he could read in their eyes was a relentless will to recu-
perate, and if they were possessed of a mission, it meant
following a different set of orders: fresh air, fifteen kilometers
daily, stick to the diet.

He headed back to the car; he wanted to look at the village
from above. On the steep macadam road which led to a sce-
nic overlook, they again encountered the elderly couple. The
BMW was parked by the side of the road along a sloping
curve, the man was kneeling beside the rear wheel, the wind
was blowing through his sparse hair. The woman had her
back turned to him; she was holding a wreath of daisies and
quietly moving her lips as if in prayer. Eduard drove past with
his face turned away: he had no desire to help change a tire
just then.

He avoided every word about the scene. He was convinced
that Klara saw in the woman a fellow sufferer whose hopes
had been shattered by some incomprehensible sentence. The
woman was beautiful, still capable of arousing and requiting
desire—why was she fighting like a wounded animal for this
limping old man? Why was it she who was asking, crying,
begging? Why was he the one who was closing himself off,
defending himself embarrassedly, and turning away from
her—for the sake of some short-lived new happiness? Was

there no end to this tug of war, no age at which a person was safe?

But Klara read the scene entirely differently. In her eyes the man was the one paying court and the woman was either dismissing him entirely or making new conditions. Hadn't Eduard noticed in the hotel how the woman had constantly evaded the man's touch, how she had accepted his kisses with her face turned away, as if they were more a burden than anything else?

They climbed out and hiked up the footpath to the knoll. From there the hills flowed down toward the valley in bulging swells. He had told Klara of his childhood dream of pushing off and gliding over this sea of hills, his featherless body soaring straight out into the open, into the wonderful and frightening emptiness. This was where he had practiced flying as a child, this was where they had offered gifts and enacted magic rituals to prepare for the arrival of the archangel Michael, who would teach them to fly.

He wondered at her calm attention, it was as if she found in that other time a distance, perhaps even a strength. Klara was the only person with whom he shared his stories, the only one who shared her own stories with him; she made him feel that he was giving up something he could never replace, that he was surrendering a part of his life. Wasn't this knowledge the greatest power an abandoned lover could wield, the secrets he had captured and would carry forever? Whoever dissolved the old tie was tempted to erase whatever the previous years had written and step into the world with the lie that life was just now beginning.

They found a room for the night in a small pension behind the village church. It was completely furnished in untreated pine. As Klara stepped over the threshold, she cried out and grabbed him by the shoulder. Something had fallen from the door frame; something hard and round had hit her on the shoulder. The proprietress thought she was imagining things, but Eduard had also caught sight of something quick as lightning above her head and then had felt her body react. It had felt strange, as if an unseen hand were jabbing her with a finger or a stick, Klara explained. As they crawled around the floor in their room looking for a solution to the riddle, the proprietress herself picked up a small piece of wood in the corridor, no bigger than a five-mark coin. She had never seen anything like that, she swore. The knot from the wood had had so many years to spring out of the doorjamb, but had apparently decided to wait for Klara to cross the threshold.

Just a matter of chance, said Eduard. The proprietress shook her head. People in the village said that wood can think.

Klara insisted on visiting his mother's grave. The cemetery dropped down toward the valley in terraces and resembled a walled parish garden. Most of the gravestones bore the same three or four last names; for several centuries this final resting place had been reserved for the long-established families of the village. Eduard walked among the lower rows of graves; he believed he knew the exact place where his mother was buried beneath a modest wooden cross. But at the site he remembered there was a twelve-year-old gravestone with a strange name. He wanted to call off the search; Klara's strange insistence made him uncomfortable. He saw her walking back and forth among the gravestones high above him. A peasant woman, who was on her knees murmuring prayers beside the grave of a relative, looked suspiciously at the strangers who were crossing the cemetery with unquiet steps and disturbing its silence with their muffled shouting. Klara still wouldn't give up even after she had read all the inscriptions, none of which belonged to his mother. She suggested they look up the caretaker and ask him.

They were interrupting supper. The man was Eduard's age and answered in the melodic dialect he knew from his childhood and which he had never been able to acquire. A grave couldn't just up and disappear, the man said. However, he remembered that the grave in question had been handed over to a woman from the village who was now buried there. Considering the limited space of the cemetery it was necessary and common for the older dead people to make way for the younger folks, with the permission of the surviving family, of course. What would happen if everybody buried there insisted on keeping his place for all eternity. The dead had to show a little sympathy for the next generation, they had to squeeze a little closer together.

As the man spoke, Eduard began to match the name he had read on the gravestone with a person from his memory. Frau Kramer—that was the woman who had helped out with the housework after his mother had died. Father had evidently complied with her request and promised her the grave in the village cemetery.

Eduard suppressed the question of what happened with the previously buried remains in such cases. He was bothered by the idea that his mother's ashes were lying next to or underneath the mortal remains of the household help. Had Father thought about that? Why hadn't he refused? Was it his Protestant disregard for all things of the flesh? Or was it the ongoing vexation Lothar had described? His nearly boundless willingness to help?

Why hadn't either brother ever bothered to look after their mother's grave, asked Klara. Were they so caught up in their wars of succession and their conflicts of interpretation that they had overlooked such a simple thing as that?

Klara fell asleep immediately after they turned out the light. He listened to her breathing for a long time, while the nearby church bells tolled every quarter hour.

When he woke up late the next morning, he found the bed beside him empty and Klara's bag gone. A letter was lying underneath the door.

"I don't believe in this decree of nature, to which you are supposedly submitting. Even if it were chance circumstances which brought us together, circumstances beyond our control, we still have to try as hard as we can to subject them to our own determination.

"Maybe you're right that each person could live with thousands of possible partners instead of just one. Still, you have to acknowledge the one you've given your heart to, even if it was by 'chance'—that's how the human heart is made. You owe this decision to me and even more so to yourself. That's the difference between us. You see, I didn't just love you 'at times,' as I so often heard from you. My love was a constant, steady feeling, which of course left plenty of room for anger and disappointment, but not for any 'intermissions.'

"Maybe men are just made differently. It's going to take me a long time to detach myself from this relationship. And I can't imagine that you're going to go leaping into your new life without some period of mourning either. In my opinion you're being very careless in giving up the years we shared, and I hope for you that if you recognize your mistake, you'll find the courage to come back, even if I won't want you anymore by then."

He spent a few days in the village. Once he called Paris to talk to André. But André had just left.

⫯⫯⫯⫯⫯⫯⫯⫯⫯⫯⫯⫯ 26 ⫯⫯⫯⫯⫯⫯⫯⫯⫯⫯⫯⫯⫯

EDUARD DIDN'T SEE KLARA AGAIN for a long time. Sometimes, on the way home, he found himself heading toward his old street or writing his previous return address on a letter. Far more often he was amazed how quickly they had lost sight of each other. A few months before his daughter was born he moved into a four-room apartment with Jenny and resumed his work at the institute. Since that time he hardly left the house at night. The Tent had been sold, the new owner was a fan of nouvelle cuisine and offered half portions at twice the price. The former clientele had emigrated to the surrounding side streets; Eduard knew the new pubs of choice by name only. The tiny creature with a mighty voice who was now dominating his nightlife had first and foremost revolutionized his sleeping habits. By ten o'clock every night Jenny and he were overcome by an irresistible exhaustion.

Once he ran into Klara on the street, just by chance. They agreed to see each other soon, but the actual meeting didn't occur until months later, after two or three phone conversations. She still wasn't ready to go out when she let him in. Was he always so punctual nowadays, she hardly recognized him.

The question surprised him, he couldn't remember ever not being punctual. While she got dressed in the next room behind the half-opened door, he paced up and down in the hall. The walls had been freshly painted, the clothes hooks were full of objects he didn't recognize, everything seemed familiar and unfamiliar at once, he didn't know where he should go. When she saw him looking at her, she tried to close the door to her room with a casual move of her foot, then stopped. They were old friends.

He wondered at her free-and-easy tone. Klara treated him with the distanced familiarity used to greet former class-mates. Over the telephone he had been overwhelmed by the feeling of recognition; apparently his ear had filtered any-thing it didn't recognize out of her voice, out of certain key words and their intonation. Now that he was face to face with her, he noted several distinct deviations from his mental image. Did the senses have their own division of labor? Are the ears conservative, attuned to similarities, while only the eyes focus on difference?

She seemed younger, more self-assured, freer in her movements. Had she been dressed like that, so aware of her body, when they ran into each other three months ago? Her nailpolish revealed a new style, her hair was shorter, she was wearing a leather skirt—a little too short, Eduard thought.

You look tired, said Klara.

And you amazingly well rested, he replied.

You think so? I didn't get to bed until three in the morning.

How's that? he asked.

Judging from the rings underneath your eyes, that would be about the time you got up.

The child woke up.

Speaking of rings, said Klara, since when have you been wearing them on your fingers as well as under your eyes?

Klara didn't seem to expect an answer, she enjoyed putting him on the spot.

She threw on a light-colored coat with padded shoulders he had never seen before. Only the cashmere scarf which she wrapped twice around her neck fit the familiar image, the scarf and the pumps. Klara always had to worry about towering above her escort, thanks to her long legs. But when he looked again, even her heels seemed two centimeters higher than before. All in all, she was dressed a little too sexily, in any case too sexily for the guy standing behind her wearing a windbreaker. For a moment they were framed together in the mirror. Klara checked her lipstick and eyeshadow—signals in a competition in which Eduard could participate only from the sidelines.

You've put on weight, she said casually, and blew out her cheeks to show him the most noticeable place. Is it because you're drinking so much?

Not at all, I don't have any time to.

Klara laughed disinterestedly, as if where a flaw like that was concerned it didn't matter what the reason was, the fact that it was there was enough.

They drove along the canal to a restaurant in the northeast corner of the city, where they had often been before. Klara had never liked The Tent and for a good year had avoided it and all other places where she might run into Eduard and his friends. The waiter greeted them as effusively as always; his glances testified to the discretion of a witness who would never reveal the status of a relationship even if placed under torture. Before they sat down, Klara said hello to two girl friends at a table in back of the restaurant.

The first half hour they spent exchanging news, like married people after a long period of living apart. Klara told him about the advantages of splitting up. She felt freer with her work as well as with her friends of both sexes. What was more, she had discovered completely new strengths and passions in herself. Disgruntled, he wondered how he had prevented her from opening up and blossoming like that when they were still together. Earlier she had made the mistake of pushing him, of trying to force him to change his mind, Klara continued; she had been possessed by the idiotic idea that she couldn't live without him. Instead of relief, Eduard felt annoyed that she was explaining her addiction to him as an act of idiocy. Evidently her suffering caused him less distress than the thought that she could get along quite well without him.

Why wasn't he saying anything about himself? asked Klara. She had recently driven by as he was pushing the stroller. She noticed that he was pushing from the side, with only one hand—something she'd seen only fathers do. How was he coping with his new life, with the baby, with a young family?

Eduard had spent the wee hours tending the child, who had clutched his little finger with her tiny hand. The whole time he just stared into her face. She didn't remind him of anyone he knew, at most of an ancient Buddha, both tender and cruel, concerned only with herself, indifferent toward other people. He had watched the child with great curiosity and felt distinctly that something had now begun. The most amazing thing of all was her energetic, stubborn breath, which moved the little body from head to toe, it sounded like the breath of a grownup.

Why couldn't he bring himself to tell all this to Klara? Portraying the joys of fatherhood was obviously a more abstract task than listing his new hardships. With grownups you can postpone almost anything; cancel, if necessary call in sick. You can't use arguments like that on a baby. It's an earthquake, a wonderful one, but it's also devastating, it comes without warning and leaves no stone unturned. Even certain phrases have become unusable for me: "Sleep like a baby"—ridiculous, only people without children could say things like that. The rings under my eyes are proof, babies don't sleep gently at all, they wake up every couple of hours, and when they do sleep they turn around like a spinning top.

He was living with more routine than ever before, Eduard concluded his report, he hardly ever saw André and Theo. They would nod to him sympathetically when they parted around ten, and spare him the comments they undoubtedly made as soon as he was out of earshot. The baby had effected a change in him which no person and no duty had ever been able to do before—he was leading a thoroughly predictable life.

It's crazy, said Klara, you ought to see me. I go out almost every evening, I never look at the clock, I let people pay court to me, often I stay out all night. The only thing I miss every now and then is my earlier life.

She spoke about her lover with the greatest candor. She had met him the day Eduard called to tell her about the birth of his daughter. She had noticed the man before, but on that day she greeted him for the first time. He was shy, but very attentive, had nothing of the blustering charm Eduard so admired in Theo and so haplessly attempted to imitate. The ease of their meeting made it clear to her that she had done the right thing during the previous months. Maybe she had had to come to the very bottom of her despair in order to fall in love once more. Some connection with Eduard remained, perhaps it would be there for the rest of her life,

but after all, you have to make new rules, you have to re-
define who you are.

I'm never going to allow anyone else to suck me into such
an emotional whirlpool, said Klara. Not that I'm not afraid
of the protective mechanisms I'm slowly developing. It's an
ability, not a weakness, to lose yourself in passion. And that's
what I miss most, this dumb and generous feeling. They're
all so gentle, so cautious with their passion, these young
men; they never let themselves go.

Why the plural? Eduard wanted to know.

In Klara's eyes sarcasm struggled with embarrassment. She
had a second lover. The first never tired in bed and was so
inventive he should apply for patents, but he was a little lame
in the head, incapable of making quick decisions and con-
vincing others, even in small things; she had to take the lead
in every undertaking. The second was a bon vivant and a
highly entertaining connoisseur of art, he kept surprising her
with his detailed knowledge of the Italian Masters, their im-
itators and counterfeiters. Unfortunately, he had one habit
which was a little difficult to put up with. Whenever their
lovemaking reached the point of panting and gasping, a gap
in his teeth would start to whistle.

Eduard wasn't in the mood for laughing. The free manner
in which Klara reported the chaos of her love life, the way
she made him confidant and advisor, both engaged and enraged him. Klara was describing a lifestyle which lay in his
distant past. He had a sentence on the tip of his tongue
which seemed illuminating and witty, but all of a sudden he
could no longer resist the urge to yawn.

He should go home, said Klara, he belonged in bed.

Eduard didn't argue.

Klara didn't want to go home just yet. They parted with

great tenderness, promised to call each other. Klara stayed behind and sat down with her two friends. Once he was outside, he looked through the window at the three women sitting around the table. Klara was talking, the others were listening attentively.

THREE DAYS BEFORE THEIR OPENING he met André and Theo in the lobby of the Warsaw Opera. Although Eduard had only a vague idea of the circumstances surrounding the repeated postponement of the premiere, he had the curiosity of someone directly involved.

No sooner had André left the Parisian clinic than he and Theo renewed their fight over the final version of the text. The two friends couldn't agree on how their contemporary *Don Giovanni* should end. They both felt that it would be a cop-out to resort to an avenging Commendatore, a feeble quoting of the original. The social consensus that would have lent authority to such an appearance no longer existed. But should they allow their *criminel de coeur* to get off scot-free? Theo considered the question of guilt superfluous, he felt that the real worth of Don Giovanni's excesses lay in the matéreal itself and that value judgments were boring. André was allergic to the very idea of "matéreal" and smelled one of Theo's attempts to critique "bourgeois morality" by taking it *ad absurdum*.

André wanted to condemn the libertine to the ultimate confines of his library, a struggling writer laboring over his life confessions, an old man in failing health, ending his days under the thumb of a tyrannical housekeeper. The two didn't settle their dispute until some dramaturges from the Bureau of Censorship in Warsaw intervened. These hard-liners suddenly discovered that the libretto smacked of "late bourgeois decadence"—one even spoke of "thinly veiled attacks on socialist morality" and suggested putting an end to the production. The pressure of the censors brought André and Theo back together. By threatening to move the premiere to Vienna, André finally succeeded in fixing a final date.

It was the first time in ages the three had seen each other. Next to Eduard and Theo, who were still in their travel clothes, André looked like a traveling prince in the company of two royal guards. Maybe he wanted to reward his body for not forsaking him, thought Eduard. He kept his bare head covered with his Italian borsalino, which he lifted briefly to show Theo and Eduard the fuzz where new hair was beginning to sprout. He had on a cashmere coat that reached down to his ankles, a long olive-green scarf was draped around his neck, his shoes glowed with the luster of a carefully restored piece of furniture.

How do I look? he asked with his Chopin smile. His worried expression made it clear that he wasn't expecting a polite answer.

You must have a fan up there in heaven, said Eduard.

You're still a long way from being beautiful. But now at least people can say you're looking good with a straight face, said Theo. Eduard, on the other hand, looks like he has just been released from intensive care.

Ever since he became a father he's seemed a bit worn out, said André.

And what about love?

Their answers sounded noncommittal. The age of reckless frivolity seemed to have come to an end. Eduard described the amazing changes a three-month-old baby can wreak in the lives of its parents. Where sleeplessness reigns, desire is silent. Theo confessed that he was continuing on his own the ascetic life he had practiced with Pauline. It was true he kept meeting new women, he even took some of them home, but once there all he did was read them his poems. Only André was in his usual high spirits; he reported not without some bravado that he was making wedding arrangements with the doctor from the X-ray room. They intended to take their honeymoon right after the opening.

And why are you carrying that stick around? asked Theo.

He pointed to the cane inlaid with mother-of-pearl André was holding in his left hand. Eduard had noticed it as well, but had immediately suppressed the observation—he suspected the metastases might have moved to André's joints. André lifted the cane like a foil and fenced with the air.

A slight fall from grace, and the ensuing prompt punishment.

During the first rehearsal he had climbed onstage to show the bumbling tenor how one embraces a woman. Someone in the darkened house applauded, and André saw a female figure he didn't recognize sitting in the third row. In the light that was spilling from the prompter's booth she seemed the embodiment of all his dreams, the one and only woman chosen for him by his chaotic patron in heaven. In order to get a better look, he took a step in her direction. Just when their eyes met, he lost his balance and fell crashing into the orchestra pit.

And then what? asked Theo.

With a shrug of his shoulders André confessed he had arranged to meet Alina that night at the Hotel Victoria.

Theo took them into a bar he knew from before near the Gdańsk train station. It was a little dingy and gloomy, but the general mood was good; the people sitting at the tables and at the counter seemed in good cheer. Theo ordered vodka in Russian. The bartender, a slight man with stubbly hair, looked at him with bright, attentive eyes and shook his head.

No more vodka, he said in English, as if he didn't care to recognize Theo's Russian. With his hand he gestured to the ceiling, as if he wanted to show where the desired object had disappeared.

In that case a beer, said Theo in German. But the bartender didn't know or didn't want to know the language of the Western neighbors either.

Have you tea? asked Theo, this time in English.

Sorry, no more tea.

What do you have, then? Theo wanted to know.

Nothing, the bartender said, smiling, stretching out both arms and holding his empty hands up as if he wanted to embrace the entire vast extent of "nothing." A few patrons made the same gesture and repeated the word in comic despair. Only now did Eduard notice that they were all sitting in front of empty beer, wine, and tea glasses.

Absolutely nothing, said the bartender, as he took an empty bottle of vodka from the display and poured three full glasses.

And what does nothing cost? asked Theo.

Nothing, said the bartender.

The patrons were enthusiastic: Nothing! they kept calling out, and invited the three newcomers to sit down with them. Sooner or later someone would show up with something, but no one knew when or what that might be. They put their heads together, whispered among themselves, and nodded encouragingly to the three. How would they manage with this boundless nothing?

André looked at the clock. He suddenly remembered he was supposed to be meeting Alina at the Hotel Victoria. They went out, stood on the curb, and André waved his cane into the headlights of the oncoming cars.

No more taxis, said Theo in English. When he claimed to know the way to the Victoria, André looked at him doubtfully.

Would you for once in your life admit that you don't know something? André asked. I'm not up to a lot of walking.

At that hour, long before midnight, the city looked like a subterranean copy of the original which Eduard had seen by day. They walked through the empty streets, to the echo of their own footsteps, and saw the unknown dark city stretching before them like a cave lit by flashlights. Eduard recalled how he, André, and Theo had once talked about setting off just like that, without a goal and without a compass, on a trip during which time would not be measured in minutes and seconds but in experience, and where every adventure was possible.

Suddenly André stopped. He couldn't go on, he didn't want to anymore, he could hardly walk, much less dance with Alina. Would Eduard and Theo be interested in representing him?

Theo and Eduard waved him off. No, they were not interested and would accompany André only in order to protect Alina from him.

What's wrong with us? asked André.

Maybe we're all a little more mature, said Eduard; older, corrected André; lazier, suggested Theo.

Victory Square, the plaza in front of the Hotel Victoria, seemed like a lavishly illumined landing strip belonging to some deserted civilization. As they came nearer, they saw Alina waving to them through the tinted glass windows of the lobby. In her glittery dress she looked like the daughter of a pop star from the fifties, trying on her mother's clothes. Her face was made up in a way which would be considered garish on the other side of the Wall; on this side it only seemed a sign of protest against the omnipresent gray.

André suddenly behaved as if he had caught sight of a miracle healer. He dragged his injured leg across the rest of the plaza so quickly that he was the first to arrive at the entrance. When he reached the lobby he immediately took Alina aside and talked to her as if to demonstrate his right of prior acquaintance and his claim as the one who had taken such a plunge out of love for her. He stared at Eduard and Theo as if he was impatient for them to leave.

Alina didn't seem to mind the idea of spending the evening with three men. While Eduard was making common cause with Theo, she kept smiling at them in such a way that neither was sure which one she meant. Eduard no longer felt tired. Theo recalled his unquenched thirst from the Nothing Bar. When Alina finally asked André whether he didn't want to bring his friends along, he acted as if he had never dreamed of doing anything else.

The liveried doorman shook his head when Eduard and

Theo tried to buy a ticket to get in. Alina translated: No entry without jacket and tie. They had left their suits in the opera's guest house; the only one who passed the dress code was André with his Armani jacket. The attempt to use an extra bill to convince the cashier to change his mind failed.

Alina had the idea of sharing the jacket—three men and a jacket. She would go in with the first man wearing the jacket, send him out a half hour later, then wait for the second jacket wearer, spend the next half hour with him, and so on. André drew the longest straw.

I don't know why I should be so happy about all this; after all, it's my jacket.

Do you have enough money? asked Theo.

Alina confirmed Theo's suspicion that the dance bar would accept only Western currency. Since André was carrying nothing but zlotys, Eduard and Theo pooled their cash and stuffed the bills into André's breast pocket.

Woe unto you if you run out the back door with her, Theo called after the two of them.

They sat down in the plush armchairs of the hotel lobby. The square stretched out before them like a frozen lake; the cars that were pulling up to the hotel all looked alike except for the different stripes caused by the bars of light coming from the lobby. Only once did they see a pedestrian, a bearded man wearing a silk parka, who pressed his nose against the pane and then rapidly disappeared.

Don't we ever get wiser? asked Eduard. Does it never stop, this competition, this push to prove ourselves? Is there no age when you can withdraw with dignity?

He hoped for Eduard's sake that Eduard never reached the age he was evidently dreaming about, answered Theo. You should turn the question around: even if it did all amount to nothing more than a craving for approval and recognition—which Theo doubted—how could anyone come up with the absurd idea that he might someday outgrow that need? Where do all your dignified gentlemen obtain their laughable certainty that they no longer need to prove themselves? Anyone who bows out of the game of the sexes, anyone who no longer wants to know whether someone in the world finds him pleasing is either a megalomaniac or a coward.

When André came back he was a little tipsy. For weeks he hadn't drunk any alcohol and now he and Alina had rushed to down an entire bottle of champagne. Cursing, he took off his jacket and passed it to Theo. The idea of leaving Alina in Theo's crude hands bothered him. She had a delicate disposition and had recently had her heart broken. He was afraid, even convinced, that Theo wouldn't find the right tone and would spoil everything.

And what was it that you so daintily whispered in her ear? asked Theo.

I described my tragic fate in love, replied André. That for a year I've been pining over a woman who fled from me. That practically every day I've been sending her love telegrams, which have nearly devoured my entire honorarium for the libretto. That Alina is the first woman who has aroused any feeling in me at all since Pauline left. And that's why I've just written her a poem, which, if she wants to come up to my room, I will be delighted to read to her.

Theo swore revenge. How was such a deception even possible, since Alina had seen André on the stage of the opera?

She works in the cloakroom, André replied, how is she to know the composer from the librettist?

Eduard wanted to know how the story of the abandoned poet had stood the test.

It would probably only work in my delivery, he said. Alina is made for me as Theo. Incidentally, my private recital is scheduled to start precisely one hour from now.

Theo checked his appearance in the window. The jacket fit him in the sleeves but pinched his shoulders when he bent his back. The waist, on the other hand, was far too wide. Cursing André's proportions, Theo climbed the stairs.

Which one of us are you going to be, André called after him, me or Eduard?

I'll think about it on the stairs. They're both ungrateful roles.

The cashier didn't make the slightest grimace when Theo paid him the entrance fee.

Eduard and André passed the time speculating about Theo's performance for Alina.

I know, said André, he's going to pass himself off as a slightly goofy scientific genius. What good would the Nobel Prize do me, he'll say, when I have been deprived of the most simple, the most important thing in the world: Love! Can you imagine a man who doesn't have the faintest idea what love is? This very day, right here in Warsaw, a Bulgarian soothsayer prophesied that I would meet the woman who would save me. When I look at you, Alina, I begin to believe in chiromancy.

No, he's going to look her in the eye with this existential horror and confess that he has just arisen from his death-bed—

Nonsense, he has cancer of the lungs and only weeks left to live, André corrected.

—and he doesn't even know whether he'll survive the opening of his opera, Eduard continued, and has decided to spend his last 43,200 seconds with her, Alina.

Eduard looked at the clock when Theo climbed up the stairs. He had exceeded his allotted time by twenty minutes. Shaking his head and laughing, Theo took off the jacket which he had draped loosely over his shoulders and passed it on to Eduard, but made no effort to explain himself.

Well? asked Eduard and André.

Well what? said Theo. I just took up where you left off.

Where's that? asked André.

Theo shrugged his shoulders.

What do you mean shy, he said finally, sly is more like it, your angelic Alina is really a devil in disguise, and a pretty daring one at that. You've been bamboozled. She's not a coat-check girl at all but a student of literature. And I didn't notice any great gaping love wound either.

There's just the question of which of us has been bammed and which one boozled, said André.

Why not both of you? asked Eduard.

Well, whatever happens, I'm afraid your recital will have to wait for another day, Theo said to André.

You aren't by chance planning to give her a private concert, are you; perhaps the overture to *Don Giovanni* on moonlight piano? asked André.

When Eduard asked which one of them he had pretended to be, Theo told him he'd just have to find out for himself.

The sleeves of the jacket didn't reach much further than Eduard's elbows, the bottom button dangled somewhere near his solar plexus.

You look irresistible, said André.

The walls of the dance bar were papered in red velvet; the clusters of spotlights affixed to the walls spread the intimate atmosphere of an operating room. As soon as he was downstairs, Eduard wished he had a pair of sunglasses like all the musicians were wearing—they were singing American hits with Hungarian accents on an absurdly high stage, while three generations were spinning and twirling on the dance floor below. All the women, regardless of age, were heavily made up and dressed in a decidedly feminine style—décolleté and high-heeled. The men wore dark evening suits, a few sported the uniforms of the Polish Army. Only the shoes of the disco delegation stuck out as ungainly: they didn't suit the winged, often virtuoso dancing.

Alina was in the process of teaching a Polish officer how to dance a samba. In the middle of a turn she waved to Eduard, who waited at the bar until the musicians put down their instruments. The officer accompanied Alina to her bar stool and parted from her with a kiss on the hand. The bottle of champagne in front of her stool was empty.

Another bottle of Russian champagne? she asked.

Eduard nodded and discreetly felt the breast pocket of André's jacket. There was still money inside, but it was impossible to guess how much. As she was sitting down, Alina lost her balance and grabbed Eduard, then laughed out loud.

The third man, the third bottle, she said, and placed the arm she had used to grab Eduard around his neck. I don't know what I'm doing anymore, I'm completely messed up, I think I'm in love.

Let me guess. With Theo? asked Eduard.

Alina laughed and squirted a mouthful of champagne in his face.

You mean the tubercular man with his poems? You can keep him as far as I'm concerned.

So then Eduard? asked Eduard.

Alina's laugh turned into a hiccup. The belated father with the weasel eyes who composes on the changing table? she asked. I practically threw up when he told me about his experiments on mice. Who are you, anyway?

Eduard hesitated. I honestly don't know.

Alina looked at him curiously, as if waiting for him to convey some crucial information, but then all of a sudden she stood up.

You know what? I have an idea. Give me the jacket.

Eduard was too surprised to refuse. As far as he was concerned, the jacket suited Alina best of all. She pulled it on and then went to the door. He didn't understand her brainstorm until he saw her coming back with André wearing the jacket, who strode in holding his arms up like a boxing champ. But he had to cede his title immediately when Alina once more asked for the jacket. Again she walked out of the bar. When she came back with a jacketed Theo in tow, Eduard and André applauded.

What may I bring you? asked the bartender, in polite confusion at seeing all three men together.

The same as before.

To Alina!

She's really brilliant, what's keeping her anyway?

She was right here a second ago!

When the bartender presented them with the bill, each of the three men followed his reflex and reached for his breast pocket. With all the dressing and undressing no one had found it odd that Alina had taken the jacket from Theo, who had been the last to come in. She was still wearing it when she walked over to the stairs.

The three men waited in their shirts until dawn. Neither Alina nor the jacket with the money ever came back.